Homestead

Applause for L.L. Raand's Midnight Hunters Series

The Midnight Hunt
RWA 2012 VCRW Laurel Wreath winner *Blood Hunt*
Night Hunt
The Lone Hunt

"Raand has built a complex world inhabited by werewolves, vampires, and other paranormal beings…Raand has given her readers a complex plot filled with wonderful characters as well as insight into the hierarchy of Sylvan's pack and vampire clans. There are many plot twists and turns, as well as erotic sex scenes in this riveting novel that keep the pages flying until its satisfying conclusion."—*Just About Write*

"Once again, I am amazed at the storytelling ability of L.L. Raand aka Radclyffe. In *Blood Hunt*, she mixes high levels of sheer eroticism that will leave you squirming in your seat with an impeccable multi-character storyline all streaming together to form one great read." —*Queer Magazine Online*

"*The Midnight Hunt* has a gripping story to tell, and while there are also some truly erotic sex scenes, the story always takes precedence. This is a great read which is not easily put down nor easily forgotten."—*Just About Write*

"Are you sick of the same old hetero vampire/werewolf story plastered in every bookstore and at every movie theater? Well, I've got the cure to your werewolf fever. *The Midnight Hunt* is first in, what I hope is, a long-running series of fantasy erotica for L.L. Raand (aka Radclyffe)."—*Queer Magazine Online*

"Any reader familiar with Radclyffe's writing will recognize the author's style within *The Midnight Hunt*, yet at the same time it is most definitely a new direction. The author delivers an excellent story here, one that is engrossing from the very beginning. Raand has pieced together an intricate world, and provided just enough details for the reader to become enmeshed in the new world. The action moves quickly throughout the book and it's hard to put down."—*Three Dollar Bill Reviews*

Acclaim for Radclyffe's Fiction

In **2012 RWA/FTHRW Lories and RWA HODRW Aspen Gold award winner *Firestorm*** "Radclyffe brings another hot lesbian romance for her readers."—*The Lesbrary*

Foreword Review Book of the Year finalist and IPPY silver medalist *Trauma Alert* "is hard to put down and it will sizzle in the reader's hands. The characters are hot, the sex scenes explicit and explosive, and the book is moved along by an interesting plot with well drawn secondary characters. The real star of this show is the attraction between the two characters, both of whom resist and then fall head over heels." —*Lambda Literary Reviews*

Lambda Literary Finalist ***Best Lesbian Romance 2010*** features "stories [that] are diverse in tone, style, and subject, making for more variety than in many, similar anthologies… well written, each containing a satisfying, surprising twist. Best Lesbian Romance series editor Radclyffe has assembled a respectable crop of 17 authors for this year's offering." —*Curve Magazine*

2010 Prism award winner and ForeWord Review Book of the Year Award finalist *Secrets in the Stone* is "so powerfully [written] that the worlds of these three women shimmer between reality and dreams…A strong, must read novel that will linger in the minds of readers long after the last page is turned."—*Just About Write*

In **Benjamin Franklin Award finalist *Desire by Starlight*** "Radclyffe writes romance with such heart and her down-to-earth characters not only come to life but leap off the page until you feel like you know them. What Jenna and Gard feel for each other is not only a spark but an inferno and, as a reader, you will be washed away in this tumultuous romance until you can do nothing but succumb to it."—*Queer Magazine Online*

Lambda Literary Award winner *Stolen Moments* "is a collection of steamy stories about women who just couldn't wait. It's sex when desire overrides reason, and it's incredibly hot!"—*On Our Backs*

Lambda Literary Award winner *Distant Shores, Silent Thunder* "weaves an intricate tapestry about passion and commitment between lovers. The story explores the fragile nature of trust and the sanctuary provided by loving relationships."—*Sapphic Reader*

Lambda Literary Award Finalist *Justice Served* delivers a "crisply written, fast-paced story with twists and turns and keeps us guessing until the final explosive ending." —*Independent Gay Writer*

Lambda Literary Award finalist *Turn Back Time* "is filled with wonderful love scenes, which are both tender and hot." —*MegaScene*

By Radclyffe

Romances

Innocent Hearts
Promising Hearts
Love's Melody Lost
Love's Tender Warriors
Tomorrow's Promise
Love's Masquerade
shadowland
Passion's Bright Fury
Fated Love
Turn Back Time
When Dreams Tremble
The Lonely Hearts Club
Night Call
Secrets in the Stone
Desire by Starlight
Crossroads
Homestead

Honor Series

Above All, Honor
Honor Bound
Love & Honor
Honor Guards
Honor Reclaimed
Honor Under Siege
Word of Honor
Code of Honor

Justice Series

A Matter of Trust (prequel)
Shield of Justice
In Pursuit of Justice
Justice in the Shadows
Justice Served
Justice for All

The Provincetown Tales

Safe Harbor
Beyond the Breakwater
Distant Shores, Silent Thunder
Storms of Change
Winds of Fortune
Returning Tides
Sheltering Dunes

First Responders Novels

Trauma Alert

Firestorm

Oath of Honor

Short Fiction

Collected Stories by Radclyffe

Erotic Interludes: *Change Of Pace*

Radical Encounters

Edited by Radclyffe:

Best Lesbian Romance 2009–2012

Stacia Seaman and Radclyffe, eds.:

Erotic Interludes 2: *Stolen Moments*

Erotic Interludes 3: *Lessons in Love*

Erotic Interludes 4: *Extreme Passions*

Erotic Interludes 5: *Road Games*

Romantic Interludes 1: *Discovery*

Romantic Interludes 2: *Secrets*

Breathless: *Tales of Celebration*

Women of the Dark Streets: Lesbian Paranormal

Amor and More: Love Everafter

By L.L. Raand

Midnight Hunters

The Midnight Hunt

Blood Hunt

Night Hunt

The Lone Hunt

HOMESTEAD

by

RADCLYfFE

2013

HOMESTEAD

ISBN 13: 978-1-60282-956-5

This Trade Paperback Original Is Published By
Bold Strokes Books, Inc.
P.O. Box 249
Valley Falls, NY 12185

First Edition: November 2013

THIS IS A WORK OF FICTION. NAMES, CHARACTERS, PLACES, AND INCIDENTS ARE THE PRODUCT OF THE AUTHOR'S IMAGINATION OR ARE USED FICTITIOUSLY. ANY RESEMBLANCE TO ACTUAL PERSONS, LIVING OR DEAD, BUSINESS ESTABLISHMENTS, EVENTS, OR LOCALES IS ENTIRELY COINCIDENTAL.

Credits
Editors: Ruth Sternglantz and Stacia Seaman
Production Design: Stacia Seaman
Cover Design by Sheri (graphicartist2020@hotmail.com)

Acknowledgments

When I first moved back "home" or about thirty miles from where I was born and raised, I felt as if a giant circle had been closed. I'd left in part to follow a dream, in part to find myself. I'd done both on my journey through college and medical school, through love and loss and discovery—and here I was, back in the country. I wrote *When Dreams Tremble* that year, thinking about the time I had spent working at "the Lake" the summer I graduated from high school. That book is still one of my favorites, and when I decided to write another book "close to home" it felt natural to connect the two stories. Circles never close in life, they just overlap and expand.

Homestead is not a sequel, but a few old friends do show up—and the themes of returning home—a little world-weary but maybe a little wiser—play through both stories, as does the hopeful theme of second chances. As I said when writing *Code of Honor* (speaking metaphorically then) when we return to a favorite place we feel a sense of comfort and belonging, and a part of us comes home. In writing these stories, I have literally come home (our farm is featured on the cover of the book) and parts of me wander the landscape. I hope you enjoy visiting the characters who emerged to keep me company.

Thanks go to Sandy Lowe, whose hard work makes mine easier; to Ruth Sternglantz for knowing my writing better than I do; to Stacia Seaman for always finding ways to make me better; and to my first readers Connie, Eva, and Paula for reading the early drafts and urging me on.

Sheri, many thanks for always finding the heart of the story.

And to Lee—*Amo te.*

Radclyffe, 2013

For Lee, for sharing the vision

CHAPTER ONE

Tess balanced a fifty-pound bag of sweet feed on her right shoulder and wended her way through the aisle of the Agway toward the checkout counter. The burlap scratched the side of her neck with each step, as irritating as a bit of straw trapped under the waistband of her jeans. A trickle of sweat, sticky and hot, ran down the center of her back. The strands of strawberry-blond hair that had escaped her John Deere gimme cap clung to her cheek, resisting her efforts to swipe them away with the sleeve of her red-and-blue-checked cotton shirt.

Too damn hot already and not enough rain on top of that. Early June felt like mid-August—a sultry heat sat heavy on the cracked dry surface of fields where corn and soybean seedlings withered under cloudless skies. Heat waves rose from the steaming earth and clouded the horizon with shimmering curtains of haze. The milk cows lay down in what shade they could find, too dulled by the scorching sun to graze on the little pasture grass that would grow. Her feed bills were soaring in an effort to keep their weight up and their milk flowing. If the weather didn't break soon, her projected profits in corn and milk were going to suffer. And she had precious little room for loss, not this year. Her goal was to grow all the silage and haylage her herd would need year-round, and she was close to reaching her goal—or she would be if the heat ever let up. She'd invested so much in her crops, if she had to supplement with store-bought feed she would have almost no profit to carry over into the next year's budget.

"Help you there, Tess?" Jimmy Larsen asked as he rounded the corner with a length of hose in his hand. The skinny twenty-year-old wasn't much taller than Tess's five-seven and probably only had twenty pounds on her hundred and thirty. When he wasn't working at the feed shop, he worked around the farm doing odd jobs and giving her and her foreman a hand.

"No, I've got it, Jimmy, thanks." Tess smiled and moved on before he could strike up a conversation. He was well-meaning and harmless, but he'd had a crush on her since she'd babysat for him when he was ten, and she'd run out of ways to politely deflect his awkward advances. Fortunately, whenever he was at the farm, they were both too busy to do more than mutter a passing hello.

She joined the line at the makeshift checkout counter behind two brawny men in sweat-stained cotton shirts that looked pretty much like hers—dusty and pocked with bits of hay—as they discussed the main topics of conversation for farmers everywhere: the weather, the economy, and the price of feed. When they'd moved off, she balanced the bag against the front of the long board counter and pulled out the thin stack of folded twenties she'd pushed into the front pocket of her jeans when she'd left the house. Earl Bundy, barrel-chested with cheeks as flushed as his curly red hair, manned the counter. The county was littered with Bundys, one of the original founding families along with the Whitesides and Pearsons, and Earl had run the local Ag store as long as she could remember. He glanced at her absently, and then his pale blue eyes sharpened as he focused on her.

"Well there, Tess," Earl said, his rough voice sounding like gravel crunching under the tires of her truck, "I was right sorry to hear about Ray. I woulda been there for the service but the wife was off at her mother's and I had to drive out there to get her. She won't fly, you know."

"Thanks, Earl. That's fine." Tess believed the sincerity of his words, even though she knew her stepfather hadn't been very popular with most of the locals. Ray Phelps hadn't been born in Washington County; he hadn't been a farmer by birth, but rather by marriage; and he'd never been of the land the way she and her mother were, despite two decades of working it. Earl's sympathies were for her more than Ray, and she appreciated it.

"So," he said, drawing out the word thoughtfully, "you still planning on going organic? Big change, especially running things all by yourself."

Tess felt the hairs on her arms stand up and imagined if she'd been her long-departed coonhound Molly, the fur along her spine would be standing on end too. Never mind that farmers' wives and daughters had worked the land same as the men and boys for centuries—driving plow teams and tractors, baling hay, and trucking produce to market—the idea of a woman in charge was still an oddity. Just as she'd understood his genuine sympathy for her loss, she also understood that beneath his question lay sincere concern as well, so she stifled the growl that wanted to climb out of her throat and nodded. Laying two twenties on the counter, she said, "Yep. Another six months and the whole herd will be certified."

She didn't add if the soil tests, the milk tests, the water tests and Lord-knew-how-many other tests all came back free of pesticides, metal contaminants, hormones, and a list of about two hundred other chemical derivatives. She couldn't think about that right now or the little kernel of panic that festered in the pit of her stomach would blossom into all-out terror.

He cleared his throat and rang up the sale. "Well, if you need any help, I can always send Earl Junior around to give you a hand."

"I appreciate that." Tess pushed the change from the second twenty into her pocket. She wasn't above accepting help when she needed it, but Earl Junior was the last person she wanted to show up offering a hand. He'd been offering a hand and a lot more than that ever since eighth grade, and despite the number of times and ways she'd said no, he didn't seem to be getting the message. Even the wedding ring he now sported hadn't deterred his efforts. Being a single woman in a small community was a bit like being male in an old folks' home—a sought-after minority—and though she'd never made it a secret she wasn't interested in male company, some people chose to ignore that message too. "Things are under control. But thanks."

She reached down to hoist the feed again.

"Although," Earl went on, "seeing as how they'll probably be drilling soon, you might not have to worry about working the farm for all that much longer. You might be able to make a killing and retire." He laughed and closed the cash drawer with a thump. "I know quite a few folks are hoping to do that."

Icicles rained down Tess's spine and she straightened, leaving the bag where it leaned against the counter. "What do you mean?"

"I heard over at the Grange last night that the planning board was set to repeal the moratorium on drilling that was voted in a number of years ago, especially since Rensselaer has gone ahead and done it already. They say the state's gonna put a stop to all that anyhow before long—too much money in gas to leave it under the ground."

"That doesn't have anything…" Tess decided the less said the better. She'd learned a long time ago that silence and secrets were often far safer than misplaced trust. Too often, those who you thought were in your corner turned out not to be. "When is the vote supposed to come down?"

He scratched beneath his collar, his expression contemplative. "They're saying sometime in the next month or so, but they're already moving rigs into Johnsonville. I hear they're about to start drilling out at the Hansen place."

Her farm lay adjacent to the county line dividing Washington and Rensselaer, and the Hansen place was only a thin strip of forest away from her pastureland. She didn't know nearly enough about what Earl was talking about, but she would very soon. She grabbed the sack and swung it onto her shoulder, barely noticing the weight pressing her down. "I guess we'll have to wait and see after the vote then, won't we?"

"Well, there's some folks that are talking about some kind of petition, trying to stop things before they get started. I don't know. There's a lot of money tied up in those drilling rights. Farm your size, who knows what it could be worth?"

The chill moved deeper, threatening to freeze her in place. She couldn't let her worry show—she couldn't afford to appear vulnerable. Earl wasn't the kind of man for whom subtlety came naturally, and she doubted he was probing for information. All the same, if word got around she didn't have firm control over her operation, she'd have trouble. She'd had offers for the place before Ray was in the ground, and some of them had come in the form of veiled threats. Nothing she could call anyone on, but she'd heard what hadn't been said. Sell now while the price was good—wait until her crazy plans turned sour and be at the mercy of whoever would bail her out.

"Thanks again, Earl," Tess said, her chin up and her voice steady. "You stay cool now."

As she shouldered her way out the door and across the gravel parking lot to her red Ford F-450 pickup, she imagined Earl's gaze following her. She didn't like feeling like a deer in the gunsights. Time for that to change.

❖

Clay stretched under the warm water, working the kinks out of her shoulders as the shower spray beat against her skin like a thousand sharp needles. She hadn't really registered how rigorous a workout she was getting from the enthusiastic sex the night before, but she was feeling it now in places where she usually didn't. Although come to think of it, the recreational part of recreational sex had gotten to be sort of routine in the last…well, longer than she wanted to consider, so maybe she was out of practice. Last night had been a surprising and satisfying exception—the backs of her thighs were pleasingly tight, and her neck burned when she leaned her head back to wash her hair. Recalling a particularly passionate response from her bedmate, she wondered if that little interlude had left a mark, not that she cared. The mild discomfort was well worth the reward, and she was long past the time and place where signs of her recent activities were an embarrassment.

Smiling, she fingered the side of her throat. Charlotte from Charlotte had been adventurous, surprisingly talented in more ways than one, and damn good company. A PhD in biophysics, Charlotte hadn't been able to find a job in her chosen field and, taking her sister's advice, had signed on at American Airlines as a flight attendant. Somewhere between the bouts of mind-blistering sex, they'd had several interesting conversations about movies, books, and the economy. The only thing Clay hadn't been willing to discuss had been the family business. No doubt Charlotte would've appreciated what she did for NorthAm Fuel, but as her job pretty much dictated every other part of her life, she didn't want it coming into bed with her.

The phone rang outside the shower, and she cursed under her breath. She hadn't checked in with the office last night and no one should have this number except her assistant Ella, and Ella would have tried her cell. At six a.m. she doubted the hotel staff were calling, which hopefully meant a wrong number. Before she could decide whether or not to answer, the ringing stopped.

Clay rinsed, toweled off her hair—grateful she kept it short enough not to require anything more than that—and slung a dry towel around her torso. Padding barefoot over the cool marble tile of the hotel bathroom, she stepped quietly into the bedroom, wondering if Charlotte would still be there. She was.

Sitting up in bed, thick black curls straggling down over her milky shoulders and the wrinkled white sheet folded neatly below her full breasts, Charlotte smiled and held out the phone. "Millicent would like to speak to you."

Clay winced inwardly. Of course Millie would track her down. Millie had been tracking her down and meting out discipline as only Millie could for twenty-five of Clay's thirty-three years on earth. Millie was the conscience Clay's status would have silenced.

"Should I go?" Charlotte mouthed silently. Her full curves that had fit so well against Clay's more angular, taller body looked very inviting outlined beneath the sheet.

"No. Stay," Clay said in a normal voice. She would have liked to keep some things about her personal life private, but she'd long ago given up that pipe dream. Nothing about her life had been private since the day she was born. Being the sole heir to a dynasty tended to place her more into the category of commodity than person, even to those closest to her. She took the phone and sat down on the side of the bed next to Charlotte. "Good morning, Millie."

"I'm glad I caught you," her father's executive assistant said without the slightest hint of sarcasm or criticism. Despite her willingness to take Clay to task for her peccadillos, Millie had been one of the few people who had unflinchingly supported Clay through rumor, accusation, and scandal. Her father had not so much supported her as *handled the problem*, and she wasn't sure to this day if he'd cared about her side of things or not. She wasn't even sure he'd believed her explanation.

Clay shook off the past with an irritated shrug. The past was the past, and none of that mattered any longer. "What's the emergency?"

"I'm afraid your travel plans have been changed."

"What this time?" Clay tucked the phone between her ear and her shoulder and slid her hand under the sheet onto Charlotte's smooth thigh. Charlotte wasn't due to fly out until the afternoon and neither was she. Her morning plans had been no more complicated than room service, breakfast in bed, and more of Charlotte. She eased her fingertips over the firm curve of Charlotte's thigh onto the creamy, soft skin high up on the inside of her leg. Charlotte made a humming sound of pleasure and pressed her hand over Clay's through the sheet.

Charlotte's hand was smooth and feminine, with tapering fingers and manicured nails painted a pale pink. Clay pictured her own hands, as much like her father's as her thick dark-brown hair, chestnut-brown eyes, and muscular build—strong broad fingers, slightly calloused at the tips, moving now over Charlotte's tender flesh. The image made Clay want to earn her reputation as a ruthless corporate pirate and plunderer. She grinned at Charlotte. "One minute."

Charlotte regarded her from beneath half-lowered lids, her dark eyes smoky with invitation. "Hurry."

Clay's clit tightened. "I'm kind of busy right now, Millie. I'll call you when I get to—"

"You're not going to Kansas City. We need you in the Hudson Valley."

Clay stiffened. She understood the *we* to mean her father, since it wasn't unusual for him to decide he needed to pull her from one job to another at a moment's notice. She wasn't just the vice president for operations of her father's many enterprises, she was his general all-around troubleshooter. If a job was going bad, he sent her to find out why and to fix it. If that meant cutting political deals to find ways around problematic zoning regulations or strong-arming subcontractors to keep on deadline, she did it. She was used to the nomadic lifestyle and no longer fought the reality that her life was never really her own. She'd never been bothered by being unpopular. She'd never really wanted friends—not the ones she'd grown up with, who were more impressed by status than substance.

Usually her destination barely registered—one hotel, one drilling field, was pretty much like every other. The corporate jet would take her wherever she needed to go. But the one place she did not want to go was the Hudson Valley. "Where's Ali? The Johnsonville project is his baby."

"Alejandro is in Switzerland, overseeing the shipping deal. And this isn't really his thing anyhow. Robert wants to break ground. We're already moving in the crews."

"Then send—"

"Roberta," Millie said, one of the only people who ever called her by her given name—her father's namesake—and only then when

Millie was making an unassailable point. "Your father wants you in the Hudson Valley. There's been a change in the county regs, and the window of time may be small for us to establish our presence."

"So he wants me to get the rigs in and make it more expensive to get rid of us than to—"

"I don't believe a discussion of business strategy is warranted given the circumstances," Millie said coolly, as if she had X-ray vision to go along with her nerves of steel.

Of course, maybe she really *could* see where Clay's hand had wandered.

"Fine," Clay said, biting off the word and restraining herself from taking out her anger on Millie, a messenger she did not want to kill no matter how unpleasant her missive. "When?"

Millie laughed softly. "Now that's a silly question. The jet's fueling now and Ella is overseeing the arrangements. How about an hour and a half?"

"Ninety minutes? That's a little—"

Charlotte moved Clay's hand higher and pressed it to the V between her thighs. She was warm and wet, and a muscle in Clay's belly twitched.

"Tell them two hours." Clay disconnected and tossed the phone onto a nearby chair. She drew the sheet down, dropped the towel on the floor, and stretched out on top of Charlotte. Her five-ten frame covered Charlotte's completely. Charlotte's breasts were full and firm against hers. The muscles in her chest, honed from working in the field whenever she could, tensed as she gripped Charlotte's wrists, pinning her lightly to the bed.

Charlotte licked water droplets from her neck. "You're still wet."

Clay kissed her and settled her hips between Charlotte's thighs. "I was about to say—"

"If you've only got two hours, don't say anything." Charlotte wrapped her legs around Clay's hips and nibbled on her lip. "Just fuck me."

Clay rarely took orders, but when a beautiful woman in bed gave instructions, she didn't argue. Charlotte didn't seem to notice when her mind drifted to the upcoming trip and a place she'd hoped never to see again.

CHAPTER TWO

Hands tucked into the front pockets of her jeans, Tess stood in the shade of the main cow barn as the last of the milk was pumped from her holding tanks into the transport tanker that idled in front of the wide-open double doors. Just after six, the last major chore of the day was finished. The heat was unrelenting, she'd been up since four, and she was tired of worrying and feeling helpless. Shaking off the fatigue, she waited patiently while the driver disconnected his hoses, checked gauges to measure the volume of milk he'd added to that already on board, and closed the ports on the refrigerated truck's body. He finished his tabulations, including the milk temperature, spot bacteria count, and overall milk quality, and handed her the form to review. After she initialed the tube of milk he'd taken from her lot to be tested later and handed it to him, she took the clipboard from him, scanned what he had entered, and signed off on the delivery receipt. He gave her a copy, tucked the clipboard under his arm, and glanced out over the pastures. The grass was grazed down to almost nothing. "Sure could stand a little rain, huh?"

"Sure couldn't hurt," Tess said, amazed how an understatement could become the mantra of an entire region. The milk yield had been down for the last few days. When the cows didn't graze, they didn't make as much milk. Things weren't serious yet, but they would be if they went much longer without rain. Unlike some of her neighboring dairy farms who weren't organic, she couldn't supplement her feed with anything hormonal or chemical to bolster milk production even if the substance was technically approved, not if she wanted to maintain her organic dairy certification. And she needed that to close the deal with Empire Yogurt—the next stage in her plan to make her farm into a solid, profitable operation for the long term.

Greek yogurt was the key to her success. The demand for organic Greek yogurt was skyrocketing, and the consumption of milk in the production of the higher-milk-content yogurt was enormous. Yogurt plants needed more milk than local dairies could supply, and Rolling Hills Farm—*her* farm—would be one of the few organic dairy farms in the state. She was in the right place at the right time to build a long-term relationship with the specialty yogurt producers. She was almost at the end of the first year of her five-year plan. In just a few more months, she would meet the state requirements for organic certification, and as soon as she had that, the deal with Empire Yogurt was waiting to be inked. She just had to hang on until then.

"It's the un-perfect storm, huh?" Tess said. "Mild winter, warm spring, and not enough rain. Water table's about tapped out."

"Well," the driver said, "this drought can't go on forever." He tipped his cap. "See you tomorrow."

"I'll be here," Tess said and watched him drive away.

She would be here, rain or no rain. She had always known this was her place. Sure, she'd entertained leaving when she was thirteen or fourteen and was tired of the quiet life on the farm and the lack of excitement in the local scene. There hadn't been much for a teenage girl to do except hang at the Tastee-Freez or spend time at the 4-H club. The nearest movie theaters were half an hour's drive away, and her mother didn't want her riding with the older boys and girls, so she was pretty much stuck with the same kids she'd been in school with all her life. For a time, she'd imagined going to New York or Boston or some faraway city to go to college, maybe study to be a veterinarian or a fashion designer. Then when she was seventeen, she'd gotten a job at the lake and left home for the first time and everything changed. She'd discovered why she'd always been best friends with the boys but hadn't taken to dating them the way most of her girlfriends had. With the city kids who came with their parents from New York City and Montreal to vacation at the lake, she'd discovered there was far more to life than she'd realized. And then she'd fallen in love, lost her virginity, and gotten her heart broken all in one long, unforgettable summer.

She'd survived, although the distant echo of pain and disillusionment still rang in the silence of a sleepless night, and she'd learned valuable lessons—that people were not always who or what they seemed, and the big wide world was no different than the small community in which she'd been raised, except maybe, on the whole, a little less honest.

The sound of a water bucket being kicked over caught her attention, and sighing, she strode into the barn. She walked down the double row of stalls, checking that the cows were safely bedded down. She left them chewing the feed her foreman, Tomas, had forked out for them and, satisfied that all was in order, turned the classical music on low and the lights out. The strains of Bach followed her across the fields for the quarter-mile hike back to the house. Maybe the soothing music didn't calm the cows and help them make more milk the way some scientific studies suggested, but they seemed to like it, and so did she.

Once inside, she put the kettle on the stove for tea and sat down at the long, scarred oak table and powered up her laptop. For once, the satellite Internet connection was strong. She searched for *gas fracturing in New York* and scanned a dozen articles. Finally she found a name—NorthAm Fuels. A few more searches and she pulled up the corporate home page. She got up, made tea, and sat back down with the remains of the sandwich she'd picked up at the café in the village earlier. She nibbled and sipped and clicked through pages.

Suddenly a name jumped out at her, and she set her mug down with a thud that vibrated through the tabletop. Vice President of Operations, NorthAm Fuels: R. Clayton Sutter.

Tess stared at the name, a knot of dread sitting heavy beneath her breast. Clay. She'd wondered—tried not to—where she was, who she had become. She laughed to herself, the pain as bright and fresh as it had been a lifetime ago, before she ruthlessly quelled the memories. What did it matter who Clay had become, she had never even known who Clay was.

She forced herself to keep scanning through the public pages, recognizing most of the information for the slick marketing ploy it was. But she found what she needed on a multicolored map of the US, highlighting various deep-underground gas and oil deposits. Red stars marked drilling sites. NorthAm's New York operation was about to get under way, and her farm was right in the middle of it all.

Rising swiftly, she sorted through the cabinets in the mudroom for the regional telephone book. She wasn't sure exactly what she would say after all these years even if she found her, but she needed advice, and she didn't want to confide in anyone local. In this tight-knit community, nothing was ever a secret, and for this, she needed privacy.

❖

Clay didn't know how nearly fifteen years could vanish without leaving a trace of something—anything—that truly mattered, as if those years and all she'd accomplished amounted to nothing, but as the jet circled the Albany airport, she felt like she was eighteen again, on her way to her last summer of freedom before starting down the path her father had designed for her. She hadn't flown to upstate New York that summer, though. She'd gotten a new Land Rover Defender soft top for graduation and insisted on driving up from the Hamptons with her motorcycle in a trailer on the back. She'd also had a bodyguard in the front seat next to her, the one point her father had not been willing to concede. She could spend the summer at the family vacation home on Lake George, but she wasn't going to go unprotected. He seemed to think kidnappers lurked around every corner, and she knew she could only push him so far. Besides, she'd figured she could lose Manny at will, and she'd been right. Her father hadn't wanted her to have a female guard after she'd had a not-so-private tryst with one of his aides the night of her high school graduation, and that had been a strategic error of the kind her father rarely made. Manny couldn't follow her into the bathroom—and bathrooms always had windows. After the first few times she'd left Manny stranded, he'd given up and decided to enjoy the vacation. And so had she.

Those few weeks had been a beautiful lie, a summer idyll when she'd let herself believe she could be anyone she'd wanted.

Clay squinted against the slanting rays of the sun sifting through the clouds and looked north out the window as the jet banked, as if she might see the sprawling thirty-six-mile lake nestled in the heart of the Adirondacks, but she couldn't pierce the distance any more than she could rewrite the past. She hadn't been back to the lake since that summer, but she hadn't forgotten the place, or the people. Sometimes when she thought of it, and she tried hard to keep busy enough not to look back, she thought perhaps that had been the last honest time in her life—even though she'd spun a web of deception with everyone that mattered. In her heart, at least, she had been honest.

The intercom hissed and the voice of Ron Arnold, the pilot, filled the cabin. "We'll be on the ground in just a few minutes, Ms. Sutter. Local time is three twenty. Sunny and eighty-nine degrees."

Clay pressed the intercom button on her seat arm, said, "Thank you," and buckled her seat belt.

Across the aisle from her, Ella Sorenson, a tall, leggy blonde who might have been a postcard model of the voluptuous Swede, buckled hers and said, "A car is waiting. We'll be ready to leave as soon as the luggage is off-loaded."

A former Secret Service agent, Ella was a vast improvement over Manny in terms of security, although much harder to ditch, and she was also the best assistant Clay had ever had. Ella should have been running a division at Sutter Industries, and Clay had told her father that a dozen times in the last five years, but Ella chose to stay on as Clay's right hand. Ella was the closest thing she had to a friend, other than Millie. They'd never slept together. Ella had a strict rule about not sleeping with colleagues, and Clay had never pushed. Ella was just about the perfect assistant and bodyguard, other than her annoying habit of insisting that Clay keep her phone on at all times. GPS tracking. At least it didn't have video.

"I'll need field clothes," Clay said. "Can you have—"

"Doris is sending up another suitcase and your gear today. Should arrive in the morning."

"Your efficiency is scary."

Ella smiled. "I should think by now you'd be immune to my greatness."

"Nope. Still impressed."

Ella laughed softly and Clay turned to the view out the window. The rolling hills of eastern New York, an artist's palette of green splashed across a canvas of brilliant blue sky and rich dark fields, rose to the distant mountains of Vermont. From the air, not much appeared to have changed. Albany crouched along the Hudson across the river from Rensselaer and Troy, its capital complex towering over older neighborhoods of brownstones. Tracts of urban sprawl—developments divided into one- to two-acre lots with McMansions squatting beside unnaturally blue swimming pools and serpentine drives—ringed the city. A few miles farther out, the countryside emerged relatively unscathed. Clusters of small villages that hadn't changed much in two hundred fifty years lay scattered amidst acres of farmland.

Gazing over some of the richest soil in the Northeast with her engineer's second sight, Clay imagined the layers of shale and compressed rock deep beneath the surface, containing the pockets of natural gas that waited to be liberated by her drills. Nearly five hundred trillion cubic feet of natural fuel waiting to be harvested—enough to meet the nation's gas needs for three thousand years at the current rate. Fuel, an essential commodity for an industrialized nation, was as powerful as military might in redistributing the international balance of power. That wasn't a fact that carried much weight with the people who were opposed to the concept of fracking, or who just wanted to keep industrialization from infringing on the rural landscape, but Clay didn't plan on making some vague political arguments as to why the locals should welcome NorthAm and her drills. Creating independence from foreign fuel sources would bolster not only the national economy but the local one as well. The influx of money and new jobs was something most people could get behind.

Her father's goal had always been power and money, and fuel was both. She couldn't pretend her work wasn't part of that quest for dominance in the industrial realm, but her company created hundreds if not thousands of jobs and revitalized local economies in areas of the country where poverty had been a way of life for decades. The men and women who poured in to maintain a drilling operation needed housing, food, entertainment, and medical services. Villages that had been little more than ghost towns were suddenly booming. She was proud of that.

The wheels touched down with barely a whisper and the jet slowed to a stop. Clay unbuckled, rose, and stretched. The cockpit door opened and the first officer, Gloria, a tight-bodied short-haired redhead in a well-tailored navy-blue uniform, stepped through. Gloria smiled at Clay. "Enjoy the flight?"

"I did, yes."

"Plans for dinner?"

Across the aisle Ella closed her iPad, stood, and took her briefcase out of an overhead compartment. She murmured, "Seven a.m. site review."

"Uh-huh," Clay said, contemplating inviting Gloria for dinner and perhaps some after-dinner recreation, when Ron exited the cockpit and pushed open the cabin door. A sultry breeze blew in, carrying a wave of nostalgia that catapulted Clay back in time. The pine scent of the forest mixed with the crystalline clarity of the wind off the lake flooded over her, filling her with a longing so intense she reached out to grip the seat beside her to steady herself.

"Everything all right?" Gloria asked with a quizzical look.

"Fine," Clay said abruptly. The question in Gloria's eyes changed to surprise and a little bit of hurt, and Clay added quickly, "Sorry. Long day—short night. I'm a little tired. Rain check?"

"Of course." Gloria's expression softened. "We'll be at the Airport Marriott overnight if you change your mind."

"Thanks." Gloria and Ron disappeared back into the cockpit to complete their post-flight check, and Clay turned to Ella, who had her cell to her ear. "What's the plan?"

"The car is coming around now. We'll get your luggage loaded and—"

"You know what?" Clay said, suddenly unable to face one more hour scheduled by someone else. "You take my things to—where are we going?"

Ella flipped open her iPad, although Clay doubted she actually needed to refer to it. "It looks like Millie has us in a B and B somewhere near the job—the Rice Mansion in...Cambridge? That's about forty—"

"I know where Cambridge is," Clay said. What was Millie thinking? "I'll be there later."

"Do you want me to arrange for another car—"

"Yes. Wait, no." Clay grabbed her briefcase and handed it to Ella. "Put this with my luggage, will you." She took off her suit jacket and handed that over also. "Take this too."

"All right, but—"

"Don't worry," Clay muttered. "I'll make the meeting."

"Keep your phone on," Ella called as Clay brushed by her and took the steps two at a time down the airstairs that had been pushed up against the body of the jet. Ignoring the black company SUV, she hurried the other way into the terminal and over to the information counter.

A matronly woman in her sixties looked up with an open smile and twinkling blue eyes. “Welcome to Albany. Can I help you?”

“You can,” Clay said, leaning on the counter. “Where’s the closest motorcycle dealer?”

CHAPTER THREE

Tess listened to the phone ring, unsurprised when the answering machine clicked on. Finding someone home seemed to be a rare occasion these days. She listened to the message, on the verge of hanging up, when the beep to record came on and she suddenly felt like a coward—like history was repeating itself—something she swore she'd never let happen. She took a breath, willed her voice to be steady. "Leslie, I know this is going to seem like a strange request, and you probably don't even remember me, but this is Tess Rogers and I—"

"Tess!" Leslie sounded out of breath. "Sorry, I was down at the dock when I heard the phone ring. That hill seems to be getting bigger and bigger all the time." She laughed, sounding the way she had when she was seventeen—full of energy and joy.

Tess's chest tightened, remembering the last time she'd seen Leslie Harris.

"Hey, Les!" Tess set down the square blue plastic cleaning caddy filled with solutions and paraphernalia and waited while Leslie climbed the narrow dirt path up the hill from the boathouse at the edge of the lake.

"Oh my God, it's so hot! You want to go swimming?" Leslie pushed blond hair out of her eyes, her smooth, even complexion tanned from a summer spent on the water, or in it. She wore a navy-blue halter top that showed off her lean belly above denim shorts and long tanned legs. She wasn't even conscious of how attractive she was, and Tess liked her for that. It seemed that all the girls, or most of them, who came to the lake for the summer were beautiful, or wealthy, or, most often, both. Sometimes, Tess felt like the ugly duckling surrounded by swans, even though she knew there was nothing wrong with her. It was just hard not to feel less when she was so different. Leslie never made her feel that way, even though Leslie was the boss's daughter.

"Sure," Tess said. "Anything I can do to help you get ready for the party?"

"I think just about everything is all set." Leslie looked around, probably checking for her parents, and said in a stage whisper, "Except the beer. Mike is taking care of that."

Leslie reached for one of the mop buckets Tess was about to carry up to the shed in back of the main lodge, and Tess protested. "You don't have to—"

"I've got it." Leslie grinned at her. "Come on. You're done for the day, right? I have to get in the water."

"Just a sec." Tess took her work list out of the back pocket of her khaki shorts and double-checked her room assignments. She'd done all the single rooms in the lodge first thing in the morning, and the lakeside cabins in the afternoon. Once she'd changed the sheets and towels, washed whatever dishes had been left in the sink, vacuumed, dusted, and cleaned the bathrooms, she'd checked off each room as having been completed. After two months, she was fast and efficient and hardly thought of her job as work.

Being a chambermaid was a piece of cake compared to farm chores. She shared a little apartment in the basement of the main lodge with another girl, got cheap board and minimum wage. Best of all, she got to live at the lake, away from home, away from the farm and the farm kids, and she got to meet exciting girls like Clay. She blushed and put her head down. She knew all the other girls talked together all the time about their boyfriends—who was the best kisser, who tried to go too far, and who was worth going too far with—but she never joined in. She didn't mind being on the outside for once because her secret was so special. Just like Clay.

"Earth to Tess..."

"Tess?"

Tess blinked, and the sun-kissed memory disappeared behind familiar clouds.

"I'm so sorry," Tess said. "For a second there, just hearing you, I was back at the lake."

"Well, I *am* back at the lake." Leslie laughed, the sound so much a part of her past Tess's heart ached. "Would you believe it?" Leslie paused. "Where are you?"

"At the farm—where I've always been."

The line went silent for a moment, and Tess realized that more than just a span of years separated them. Remembered how she'd left, and what she'd left unsaid. "I'm sorry I disappeared—I wanted to call, wanted to tell you, but I—"

"Tess," Leslie said softly. "Don't apologize. You left a note. You said you had to go. Family emergency, you said. I missed you, but I understood."

"It's a long story," Tess said. "An old story now. But how are you? I'm sorry…I should have asked already. It's just so…good to talk to you."

"I'm wonderful. Like I said, I'm living back at the lake with Dev."

Tess mentally sorted through the boys who had always flocked around Leslie, trying to come up with a face to fit the name, and then she did. Dev. Devon Weber. The girl on the motorcycle, the one who sometimes showed up at the lodge with Clay. The *girl*. "Oh my God. Dev Weber."

"Uh-huh."

"I remember her." She hadn't really known Dev all that well—she remembered a dark-haired, silent girl, a little tough in her dusty black boots, black jeans, and white T-shirts, a little wild and dangerous like Clay. They'd looked a bit alike, but Clay had been different—Dev had been withdrawn and brooding, Clay had been a charmer. She told funny stories and flirted and made Tess feel special. Leslie and Dev—how had that happened? "I didn't know you—"

"No one knew," Leslie said, and her regret echoed through the line. "God, I didn't even know…wouldn't let myself *really* know…for the longest time. But I know now, and I'm making up for it."

"Congratulations, then." Tess thought about the irony of the situation. Leslie had been in love with a girl too and hadn't told anyone, just like her. They'd been friends and never shared their secrets. For the briefest moment she allowed herself to wonder what might've happened if they had, but she pushed the thought away. She wasn't Leslie, she never had been. And her story couldn't have ended any differently than it had, no matter what she had done or said. Clay had walked away.

"So, what's going on?" Leslie said. "It's great to hear from you, but—"

"This sounds awful but I don't know any other way to say it—I need legal advice about something personal. When I thought of who I could trust, I remembered reading about you graduating from law school. Your parents put it in the local papers—"

"Oh God, they put everything in the paper. So embarrassing."

Tess laughed. "They're just proud of you. But anyhow, your name just came into my head and I took a chance. Your mom gave me your number. I hope that's all right."

"Of course it is. I have to tell you, though, my work is kind of specialized—I do a lot of industrial legal consultation and—"

"Then I guess I got lucky," Tess said, "because I think that's exactly the kind of advice I might need."

"Well, tell me what's going on, and if I can't help, I can probably refer you to someone who can."

"If it's all right with you," Tess said, "I'll make an appointment and come and see you. I want to do this properly—I want to pay—"

"Let's find out what you need first," Leslie said. "When I moved back to the lake permanently, I opened an office in Albany. Let me check my calendar."

"Thanks, I appreciate it."

"Don't be silly. I'm so glad you called. Hold on…"

Tess walked to the window and looked out over the back pasture while she waited. The herd of deer that lived in the woods separating her property from neighboring farms were grazing in the hay field behind her house. She counted thirteen tonight. Her horses ambled indolently in the summer pasture across from the big barn, nibbling on grass. One of the cats chased a toad on the rough stone patio outside the kitchen. She'd loved the lake, waking in the morning with the windows open and the crisp, fresh breeze blowing in from the water, and the pine needles crunching under her sneaks as she walked to the farthest cabin to begin her day, and the clean woodsy scent that filled the air. The farm had its own beauty, its own earthy scents, its incredible mystical silences. She loved both places, but the lake held only sadness for her now.

"I was supposed to be in court tomorrow afternoon," Leslie said, "but there's been a continuance, so I'm open. Why don't you meet me at noon and we'll have a working lunch?"

"That would be great—if you're sure?"

"I can't wait to see you. Here's my office address."

"Got it," Tess said, jotting it down. "I'll be there."

"Good. See you tomorrow, then."

"Bye, Les." Tess hung up and wandered around the kitchen, uncharacteristically restless. Usually by this time of night she was ready to read for an hour or two and go to sleep. Tonight, her memories plagued her. Finally, she sat down in the corner of the big kitchen at her mother's old pine desk, her desk now, to pay a few bills. On the rare occasions when loneliness or memories haunted her, she worked. And as she'd learned that summer on the lake, nothing lasts forever.

❖

Straddling her Harley, dressed in the bike gear she'd bought along with the motorcycle and her business clothes folded into a saddlebag, Clay headed north from Albany to Route 67 and followed it east across the Hudson River into Washington County. At seven thirty, traffic was sparse. As soon as she cleared a few small towns just past the outskirts of the city, she was in farm country and roaring over twisting single-lane roads bordered on both sides by fields of corn, hay, and pastures where cows, horses, and the occasional alpaca grazed. The Hudson wended through the hills to her right, coming into view for a few seconds as she tore over a rise. Hugging the turns, she caught glimpses of the setting sun glinting off the water and was pierced by remembrance. She'd ridden these roads before, yesterday it seemed, faster than she should have, feeling free and invincible and in command of her destiny.

The same roads, the same feeling of freedom, and she was headed to the same place. She knew she shouldn't but couldn't seem to take a different path—then or now. The job site—that's where she was going. She'd left Albany telling herself she might as well see the base camp now as first thing in the morning, get a sense of the place before she had to hit the ground running and start making decisions that couldn't be unmade. Once the drill bit into the earth, they were committed. Men and machinery were in until NorthAm got what it wanted, for as long as it took—months, years maybe, to reach the buried reservoirs of gas, to sink the drill casings, to inject the millions of gallons of water and sand and chemicals that would force the fuel to the surface. Tonight, before she made the call to break ground, she wanted to see the land untouched.

She knew where the camp was—she'd seen the geological surveys when she'd sat in on the plans to open a dozen new sites in the most likely areas for high-yield drilling. If she stayed on 67, she'd be there in ten minutes, but without a second thought, she cut left and followed the river farther north toward Route 40 and Cambridge and Tess's farm.

Not a thing had changed, other than everything. The same centuries-old farmhouses still commanded views of the river across acres of green, cows still clambered over slopes pockmarked with berry bushes and studded with apple trees, and the air still smelled like freedom. She flipped up the visor on her helmet and let the night air whip across her face, taking with it, for just a few precious moments, all her regrets.

She slowed when she reached the small cluster of white frame houses that marked the road leading past Tess's farm, her hand so tight on the throttle her fingers cramped. She forced herself to relax, telling herself she was just driving past on her way to somewhere else, but she slowed even more as she came over the rise and looked down at the sprawling yellow farmhouse nestled a quarter mile back from the road, a few lights on already, beacons of welcome that weren't meant for her. She eased back on the throttle, taking in the fresh red paint on the big cow barn farther up the road that used to be yellow, the dry fields and the struggling corn, the fence lines so like Tess herself—neat, precise, careful. She glided around a curve and there was the packed-dirt driveway, the black metal mailbox exactly where she remembered it, and there was Tess, envelopes in one hand and the other shading her face, looking in Clay's direction.

She could have ridden past, pretended she hadn't recognized her, hadn't seen her, but that was a lie she couldn't bring herself to tell. Tess's gaze held steady on her as Clay braked and put a leg down, bringing her Harley to a stop on the road a few feet from Tess.

Clay pulled off her helmet, struck by the red highlights in Tess's blond hair and the way her features were even more beautiful than they had been when she was younger. "Hello, Tess."

"Clay," Tess said quietly.

"You look the same," Clay murmured.

"I'm not," Tess said.

CHAPTER FOUR

Clay was the last person Tess expected to see, and for a heartbeat, her head spun and a jumble of thoughts, all of them absurd, raced through her mind. Clay sounded just the same, her voice as smooth and rich as the dark chocolate of her eyes. Her chestnut hair, curling over the collar of her rough-grained black leather jacket, was an inch longer than it had been and still windblown and wild. Of all the things Tess might have recalled, she thought of Clay's hair and how she'd always liked the way it looked, as if Clay had just climbed off her motorcycle—ruffled and untamed. Just the way Clay had always seemed to her.

Tess folded her arms across her chest. She hadn't been taken in by appearances in a long time, so she let herself look. Clay stood, her legs sheathed in black leather, straddling the gleaming black bike, her dusty black boots planted firmly on the earth of Tess's driveway. She still looked like she owned everything around her. Probably assumed she did. Or would. Maybe that's why Tess had been so taken with her—her utter confidence was magnetic.

Tess pushed aside the tug of appreciation along with something even deeper, something more visceral she couldn't control but didn't have to accept—not any longer. That summer she'd been barely seventeen, just off the farm, and she'd never met anyone like Clay before. Handsome and outgoing and so, so charming. She'd been too blinded by Clay's image to see. If she'd known what a Land Rover was, she would have wondered how a girl had a seventy-thousand-dollar SUV. She'd never realized Clay's hair hadn't been cut in the front parlor of a homegrown hairdresser's roadside rancher the way hers had been, but styled in some expensive salon. She'd never seen Clay's house. Hadn't questioned much of anything. When they'd talked—and it seemed they'd talked all the time when they were together—Clay asked about her, made her feel special, and she'd gloried in the attention. Clay's rough and careless exterior had camouflaged her wealth and privilege to the naïve farm girl who hadn't known any better. But she knew better now. She'd been taken in then, but she wasn't innocent now.

"I heard you were coming to town," Tess said and felt the frost in her tone.

"Did you?" Clay said. "I didn't know myself until this morning."

"Well, I guess I should say your company's reputation precedes you," Tess said. "NorthAm Fuels, right?"

Clay nodded, her gaze appraising.

"I didn't know it would be you."

"Hoped it wouldn't be?" Clay said.

"Your words, not mine."

"Tess." Clay glanced away, drove her hand through her hair. "I don't know what to say—"

"There's nothing to say." Tess turned away, carefully placed the envelopes into the mailbox. She'd forgotten how Clay always made her name sound as if it were a sigh, as if just saying the word was as satisfying as a kiss. And for a second just now, Clay had looked genuinely disturbed. As if the past haunted her too. "No."

"What?"

Clay's whisper came to her on the wind the way her image used to come to Tess as she lay awake watching the clouds blow in over the lake, listening to the distant sound of thunder and imagining a motorcycle engine growing louder. Never again. Tess wanted to scream at her to get out of her driveway, out of her mind, out of the places deep inside that still remembered. Taking a breath, stepping out of the past with determination, Tess quietly closed the lid on the mailbox and flipped up the red flag to signal the postman to stop for a pickup in the morning. She pivoted toward the house, glancing at Clay over one shoulder as she walked away. "The time to say something would've been years ago. When it mattered."

Clay gritted her teeth. The anger in Tess's voice, the disdain in her face, cut deep. She couldn't give Tess the answers she wanted now, any more than she could have the day she'd left. Too many people's secrets would be revealed, and for what? She'd brought about the situation herself, and she couldn't undo the hurt she'd caused. Feeling helpless, she reacted instinctively and totally out of character, calling after her, "Did you ever leave the farm?"

Tess stopped, turned. "No. I never thought of it, not after I gave up the idea of running away with you."

"Jesus, Tess." Clay jammed the kickstand down with her heel, vaulted off the bike, and strode to Tess, kicking up small puffs of dirt and stones beneath her boots. "We were practically kids. Dreaming."

"Oh, I know," Tess said softly, her eyes like winter. "I know that now. Believe me."

"So, can we—"

"No," Tess said. The last thing she wanted was the old memories resurfacing. She knew they'd been young, knew she'd been foolish, and she was as angry at herself as she was with Clay. She'd believed without question, trusted with foolish innocence, and culpability in her pain was what she'd carried forward over the years. She would never go blindly into a relationship again, and though the lesson had been excruciating, it'd been an important one. Maybe she had more to thank Clay for than she'd ever realized. "We're not friends, Clay."

"I don't expect that," Clay said, surprised at how much she wanted Tess to feel differently. She was used to facing distrust and even dislike when she showed up in a new place to push through NorthAm's agenda, but she'd always believed Tess had seen the real her. Wanted, needed to believe that. She'd obviously been wrong. "I just thought we could talk."

Tess shook her head. "Why? We're strangers, and if what I'm hearing is true, we don't have anything in common anymore."

Clay frowned. "What are you talking about? What are you hearing?"

"You're here to start drilling on the Hansen property, aren't you?"

Clay rifled through her mental file folder of topographical survey maps, calling up the coordinates of the planned drill sites in eastern New York, superimposing the broken lines denoting property parcels. "Seventy-five acres a quarter mile off 74, mostly fallow fields, second-growth trees on the elevations, a tongue of the Marcellus Shale twenty-five hundred feet down. Is that the one?"

"You make it sound like it's on the moon."

"What?"

"Impersonal."

Clay frowned. "I'm not following."

Tess waved an impatient hand. "You know, Clay, this land is more than lines on a map and geological surveys. There are people on this land, families who've been here for hundreds of years. People, Clay, who are as much a part of the land as what runs through it."

"I know that." Clay tried to rein in her frustration. She was playing catch-up on this project, still had paperwork to review—something else that was atypical for her. She always made it a point to be on top of any situation before negotiations began, and she'd planned to spend the night going over all the data regarding local ordinances, community preparedness, and rights agreements. None of that would matter to Tess. "I can't say for sure exactly where we'll start, but that might be right. The Hansen place."

"Well, that happens to be right over that ridge." Tess pointed to a hill, backlit by the setting sun, behind her house. A dozen deer were silhouetted on the ridge. "And I can't say that's something I want to happen."

"Look, Tess," Clay said, "this isn't the way we usually do business. Once I get a look at the site, I'll be visiting the neighboring farms, explaining what we'll be doing and why it won't be a problem."

Tess smiled thinly. Clay was so adamant, so direct, her gaze never wavering. She would be so easy to believe. The thought was terrifying. Tess wouldn't be trapped again by the intensity in Clay's eyes. Couldn't afford to be, on so many levels. "You mean you'll be selling the company line?"

"No, I'll be giving the facts. Something you might want to hear before you form an opinion."

Tess jammed her hands on her hips. "The facts? Is that anything like the truth, Clay?"

"You don't know me, Tess—if you'd—"

"You're right, Clay. Finally we agree. I don't know you. I never did." A flush colored Tess's cheeks and she spun away, striding off down the drive.

"Damn it, Tess!" Clay stalked after her, her longer strides overtaking Tess's quickly. She grabbed Tess's arm and Tess whirled around, one hand raised. Clay stared, expecting the blow, feeling as if she'd been expecting it for a long time and not really minding. Maybe she'd feel better if Tess did strike her. She deserved some penance, after all.

Tess backed up a step, an expression of horror draining the color from her face. "I'm sorry." She looked down at Clay's hand grasping her wrist. "Please let me go."

Clay dropped her hand. "Is there any way we can start again?"

"None at all." Tess's gaze was shuttered, her voice curiously flat. "If there's something you need to discuss, please call me first. Don't drop by."

Clay looked out over the farm. So much she wanted to ask. To know. "I won't. I'm sorry."

"Yes," Tess said softly. "So am I. About so many things."

"I'll call," Clay said, knowing it had always been too late.

"Good-bye, Clay."

Clay didn't move, willing Tess to turn back, willing her to see beyond the shadows to the bright sunlit summer they'd shared. But Tess kept walking, rounded a bend, and disappeared behind a trio of tall pines.

"Idiot," Clay muttered, heading back to her bike. What had she expected, showing up out of nowhere after all these years—a kiss and, and… She stopped beside the bike, seeing nothing—nothing other than Tess's face, the heat in her eyes. Once that heat had been desire—Tess had always been so glad to see her, so open, so welcoming. Pulling her in for a kiss, a caress of fingers through her hair. She, not Tess, was supposed to have been the experienced one—she hadn't been a virgin after all. Not really, not technically. That day in the solarium while everyone celebrated on the patio, Vicky had taken her hand, guided it under her dress, beneath the silk panties, placed it just so. Clay had been drunk on the feel of her, high on the soft gasps of pleasure, too caught up to hear footsteps on the marble tiles as Vicky bit her neck and climaxed in her hand. Nothing about Vicky compared to Tess—to the unself-conscious, unfettered joy Tess had taken in their mutual pleasure. There had been no one like her since. Maybe after the first time, there never could be again. "Idiot."

Clay jammed on her helmet, threw a leg over the Harley, and stomped on the starter. The engine growled, roared to life, and Clay tore away, throttling too fast, her back wheel skidding on the tight curve in front of Tess's cow barn. She nearly dropped the bike right there and, heart racing, throttled back and fought the shuddering, bucking machine back into line. Killing herself or someone else was not going to change the way Tess felt about her. She deserved every bit of Tess's recriminations and should have expected worse. She'd done nothing to change what had happened, hadn't known how to stand up for herself or for Tess and maybe, somewhere deep in her heart, she hadn't wanted to. Maybe she'd known all along that those few idyllic months at the lake were pure fantasy, and she'd selfishly allowed them to go on. All because Tess had looked at her as if she could do anything, and when she was with Tess, she'd believed that she could. Tess had had such faith in her, she'd let herself dream—about freedom, happiness, love. Tess had set her free, and she had not cared who might pay the price for that freedom.

And when it all came crashing down, she wasn't a hero anymore. She'd fallen into line the way she always had, acquiescing to her father's demands, accepting his rationalization—that her leaving was the only way to protect Tess, that a public scandal would ruin her as well as Clay.

"We can weather anything," her father said, "but this girl—can she? In a town like that, where the rumors, the speculation, will never end? If you care about her, Clayton…"

If you care about her, he'd said. And Clay had lied, yet again. Under her father's calculating gaze, she'd said, "It wasn't anything serious. Whatever you heard is an exaggeration."

Her father nodded, as if hearing what he'd expected to hear. "Very well. The situation is being handled. Manny will take care of retrieving your belongings and the Defender. You won't be needing the motorcycle at Stanford. Arrangements have been made for you to arrive early in California. You should see to packing."

Three weeks early. He wanted her out of the house, out of the state. She'd wanted to drive north again. To see Tess. To explain. As always, he'd read her mind and preempted her desires.

"You understand," her father said with cool finality, "you cannot see this girl again. For her own good."

You cannot see this girl again.

Clay took the corner onto Route 74 at forty miles an hour, overshooting the lane and swerving over the centerline. The headlights of an oncoming vehicle momentarily blinded her, and she yanked the bike back by instinct as a cement truck blasted by, horn blaring.

For her own good. Her father had given her the perfect excuse for walking away.

Chapter Five

Clay stared at the high painted-tin ceiling in her big room on the second floor of the B&B. She hadn't slept much. She didn't usually, often working late into the night, sleeping a few hours, then getting up to work again. She'd learned to sleep on the jet when she needed to, in trucks, in trailers on the job site, or most any other place. She was basically a nomad and had gotten used to being rootless.

The night before, she hadn't even gotten her few hours of routine sleep, too keyed up from her meeting with Tess. Too stirred up in ways she hadn't been in so long she'd forgotten she even could be. She didn't live a boring life—business challenged her, fieldwork satisfied her, and sex took her mind off what might be missing from her life in the few hours when she wasn't working. Most of the time she was content, but seeing Tess had reminded her that once there had been something more. After losing something, it was easier to pretend you'd never had it and didn't need it, and Tess had just made that a lot more difficult.

Tired of the ceiling and her own dark thoughts, Clay abandoned bed at four thirty, showered, and dressed in field clothes—forest-green khaki work pants, brown cotton shirt, construction boots—and went out to look around the village. Cambridge was a quiet little town in the midst of rolling hills and farmland, too far from the big cities to be within easy commuting distance, and populated mostly by families who'd been there for centuries. For a span of four blocks in the village proper, the main street, aptly named Main Street as it was in almost every small New England town, was lined on both sides with small businesses—an IGA market for essential food shopping, a gas station/convenience store, two antique stores, a diner, a bar, a pizza shop, a Chinese-takeout storefront restaurant, the post office, and the ACE hardware store, the biggest building in town.

Most of the places hadn't changed since the last time she'd ridden through with Tess behind her on the motorcycle. They'd come down from the lake together a time or two, once when she'd told Tess she wanted to see where she lived, once when Tess had asked her for a ride back to the farm. She remembered meeting Tess's stepfather when he'd been on his way out to the fields, recalling the hard glint in his eyes as he'd surveyed her, the way he'd asked her name and how she knew Tess. He hadn't been belligerent, but her gut told her he was dangerous. In hindsight, she'd been right. Ray Phelps. Tess rarely spoke of him except to say she'd been eight when her mother had married him and fourteen when her mother had died in a car accident on an icy winter road. Phelps had died not that long ago—Clay's father had sent her an e-mail with the news. She'd been surprised at the time, wondering why her father had kept tabs on the man. Whatever the reasons, he was out of the picture, and the farm was Tess's now. Tess looked as if the life suited her.

Clay walked to the end of the tiny business district where the residential houses began, crossed the street, and headed back to the diner. Ford, Dodge, and Chevy pickup trucks crowded both sides of the street in front of the diner. Inside, the few tables and most of the stools at the long counter were filled with men and women in work clothes like hers, sitting silently with newspapers in front of them or talking quietly over coffee. She threaded her way down the long, narrow aisle to a stool at the far end of the counter, aware of everyone watching her, some with blatant curiosity, others with casual interest.

A young woman, maybe twenty, with light-brown hair pulled back in a ponytail and a sky-blue scoop-neck T-shirt that said *Susie's Café* in white letters, headed her way with a coffeepot in her hand. She filled the white porcelain mug in front of Clay and said, "Need a menu?"

"No, I'm good," Clay said, nodding at the coffee. "How did you know?"

The girl smiled. "Nobody comes in here before five who doesn't want coffee."

"True enough." Clay poured some milk into the coffee, sipped it, and raised her eyebrows. "This isn't Maxwell House."

"Sure isn't. Green Mountain French Roast, ground fresh for every pot."

"Things are getting gentrified around here."

The girl snorted. "Not hardly, but there's no reason we can't have good coffee. So what will you have?"

Clay scanned the whiteboard on the wall across from her where daily specials were written in black script. "I'll have that farmer's omelet. Whole-wheat toast. Thanks."

"Sure enough."

Clay drank the very good coffee and ate the equally good cheese, ham, mushroom, spinach, sausage, and potato omelet while organizing her day in her mind. Around her, the low murmur of voices gave her a comforting sense of community, something she never really noticed in big-city restaurants, where no matter how many people were congregated, everyone seemed to occupy separate islands in a vast ocean. Disconnected, alone. Another thing she'd gotten used to.

Meal done, she was reaching for the bill when a strain of conversation rose above all the others, catching her attention.

"Heard they're going to start drilling pretty soon," a husky male voice said from somewhere down the counter.

Clay let the bill lie where it was and motioned for another cup of coffee. As she worked on her refill, she listened.

"I hear Pete Townsend's trying to put a stop to all that," a second man said. "Doesn't want them contaminating his land."

"Pete doesn't want anything to change, that's his deal. Me," yet another person chimed in, "I think it's a good idea. These gas people—they bring money, lots of it. Not just for the ones who sell them the rights, either, but for everybody. They got to truck it all out, don't they? They gotta build roads for them big trucks, they gotta have houses for the people who're working there. They gotta eat, right? I've read about these things. Everybody ends up making money."

"Yeah," a woman piped up, "unless you happen to be one of the ones whose water gets contaminated by all the stuff they flush up along with the gas. The Whiteside Creek runs right through where they're supposed to be drilling, and most of our land gets water from there. If that water gets tainted, our crops and our livestock are going to get sick. Maybe us too."

Clay shot a glance down the counter at the woman. Fortysomething, blond hair held back with a simple gold clip, elegant features, and diamond-hard blue eyes. Pretty and pissed.

"I'm with Pete," the woman went on, "and so are a lot of us. We don't need these people coming up from wherever they're coming from to take what they want and then leave us with the mess. This land is farmland, that's what it's meant for, and that's what we ought to be paying attention to."

The hubbub of voices grew louder as people tossed out opinions, talking over each other, dissecting the issues. Clay had heard it all before and often came up against prejudices fostered by the lack of facts. People only knew what they'd read or heard, usually not from the fracking companies. The media always liked a good story, and good stories were often one-sided. In most situations, an advance team from NorthAm came into an area to deal with community relations well before site work began, but this time she'd been tossed into the fire and she'd have to deal with resistance on her own. But not in the diner at five in the morning—she wanted to do it face-to-face, family by family, for starters.

Just as she was making a mental note to have Ella set up a town meeting once she had a sense of where most of the community was going to fall out, Ella walked in. All conversation stopped. Clay might have gotten a few curious looks, but Ella, even in casual clothes—which for her meant tailored black pants, a form-fitting white tee, and a light blazer to cover her weapon—drew outright stares. She strode over to Clay as if oblivious to the attention, but Clay knew she could recite exactly where everyone was seated and what they looked like.

"Morning," Clay said.

"Couldn't sleep?" Ella nodded to the counter girl who set down a full mug of coffee by her right hand. "Thanks."

"Just can't wait to get started," Clay said.

Ella laughed. "I'll bet. I'm guessing we'll need a town meeting before this is done."

"You guessed right." Clay thought of the conversations she'd just heard, thought of Tess's automatic distrust of her and the company. She really needed to talk to the farmers, including Tess.

That idea was the best thing about the morning so far.

❖

Tess walked her best milker into the milking stall and tethered her with a loose lead rope to the ring mounted on the wall. After dipping each udder into a container of Betadine, she attached the suction tubes to each one and started the automatic milking machine. Immediately, thick white fluid streamed into the collection tubes. Tess ran her hand down the cow's flank as the milk ran into the sterile lines that carried the milk to the storage tanks. On a good day, this cow—Buttercup—would give her over a hundred gallons of milk. And Buttercup'd eat the same amount of food—at least a hundred pounds of corn, hay, and grain—and drink fifty gallons of water. Multiplied by eighty, the herd consumed an incredible amount of feed. She relied on her fields for the corn and alfalfa to sustain her herd, and if she didn't get it this year, she'd be dipping into her bank account to supplement before long.

The door at the far end of the barn creaked open, letting in a shaft of early-morning sun, and her foreman, Tomas, a suntanned fifty-year-old whose hair was still as coal black as it had been when he was twenty, strode toward her. Tomas had been on the farm as long as she could remember, starting as a young man working the fields. He'd grown with the needs of the business, taking courses in animal husbandry at night at the community college where Tess had eventually gotten her degree. He'd never wanted to leave and buy his own farm, saying he could never find a place as beautiful to work or people as friendly to work with.

"How are things looking?" Tess asked.

Without Tomas, Tess doubted she'd be able to handle everything that needed to be done on the farm. Even with plenty of help, farming was a seventeen-hour-a-day job. Most dairy farms in the country were family-owned businesses because it took a family of one kind or another to run a farm—tending the cows, rotating them out to feeding stations or the fields and into the barn for milking twice a day, ensuring they had the right feed mixture and timely veterinary care and a clean, healthy living environment. Add to that the stress of calving, feeding and caring for the young, not to mention documenting their entire lives from birth until they were culled from the herd or died from other causes. The state regulated everything about dairy farming from the health of the herd to the soil composition to how the milk was stored and transported. When she wasn't directly overseeing the milking, the care of the stock, or the state of the fields, she was doing paperwork. When she returned to the house at night she always had one form or another to complete or update. On most farms, the extended family—spouses, children, multiple generations of family members—divided up the chores. With her mother gone and now her stepfather, Tomas was a critical member of her farm family.

"The yield is down a little," Tomas said. "The heat."

"I was afraid of that." Tess sighed, took the clipboard he handed her, and ran her eye down the totals for the morning milking. Off about 10 percent. "How's the silage holding up? I think we might be able to get another cutting from the back fields next week, but it won't be ready for feed for a while."

"We'll be all right for a bit." He slipped a stick of spearmint gum from the ever-present pack he carried in his front pocket and offered her one.

"Thanks, no," Tess said as she always did. She'd given up telling him she detested spearmint gum when she was ten.

"Calves are all looking good. Growing fine. Vet's due tomorrow," Tomas said as he folded a piece into his mouth.

"Right." Tomorrow was Saturday already. Ordinarily she never forgot appointments, but she'd been a little distracted, what with the news about the drilling…and Clay. Tess grimaced, shook her head. "Eight o'clock, right?"

"Yep. I can take care of it if you want."

"Thanks, but I'll need to be there." Tess switched off the milking machine as the amount coming down from the near-flaccid milk bag slowed to a trickle, removed the suction tubes from the udders, and wiped them down again with Betadine. "You'll have enough to do with the milking. Transport will be coming around right about then too."

"Okay. I was thinking to have Jimmy move some of the chop over for the heifers—the pasture's looking a little thin."

"Good, thanks. I have to be out this afternoon. Call me if anything comes up."

"Will do." Tomas released the ties on the cow to take her back to her stall. "You plan on being at the town meeting tomorrow night?"

"That's tomorrow too?" Tess rubbed her eyes, nodded. She tried to make the town meetings whenever she could, but this was one she couldn't afford to miss. The issue of drilling would undoubtedly be on the agenda. "I'll be there."

Satisfied that everything was under control for the moment, Tess started back for the house and her second cup of coffee. A black pickup truck turned into the drive just as she reached her porch. She stopped and waited, recognizing the driver as he drew near. Pete Townsend owned a big farm south of hers. Whenever she ran into him at Grange meetings, he was always friendly, but she wouldn't say she knew him well. She had a feeling she knew what this visit was about, though.

"Hi, Pete," she called as he stepped out of his truck. He was a big clean-shaven man, still fit with just a bit of softness around the middle. As usual, he wore a khaki work shirt, pants, and heavy boots, his close-cropped salt-and-pepper hair covered by a black Yankees cap.

"Tess," he said, walking up the stone path toward her. "Got a minute? Sorry to drop in so early. You've probably got milking—"

"No problem. Milking's done." Tess came down the stairs, trying not to let her annoyance show at his veiled suggestion that she wouldn't have the morning's work well in hand by seven a.m. "Come on in. I was just about to have another cup of coffee myself. I've got some blueberry muffins from Caroline's. If you're of a mind."

"I'm always of a mind," he said, ruefully patting his stomach as she led him around the back to the kitchen.

She brought coffee, plates, and butter and set the muffins in front of him. She sipped her coffee and waited while Pete broke a muffin in half and generously buttered it. "I suppose you're here about the drilling."

He took a bite, chewed, sipped his coffee, and swallowed. "I am. Things are moving pretty fast, faster than we expected, and I don't think we're ready for this slick outfit they sent in here. They've already got trailers and people up to the Hansen place and big machinery coming in every hour. If we don't do something, they'll be drilling by the end of next week."

"It seems to me that horse has already left the barn," Tess said. "Hansen and quite a few others signed over their gas rights years ago, didn't they? And now the state seems pretty determined that the drilling goes on."

"All that's true, but other townships have been able to block the drilling, and we might be able to slow them for a while—make them prove they're not going to compromise our farms."

Tess agreed with him, which was exactly the reason she planned on talking to Leslie that afternoon, but that was her business. "I don't imagine that will be easy."

"It might be if we all stand together. You're closer to Hansen's place than I am, you've got to be worried." Pete paused with the last remnants of muffin in his hand. "I know Ray was talking to them back a ways."

A cold hand skimmed down Tess's spine. She hadn't known that. And she wasn't about to confess that to Pete. "Anything that affects my farm concerns me."

"I'm hearing they're sending in some kind of big shot to run this project—like we'll be impressed or too intimidated to stand up to him."

The big shot was Clay. Tess thought about what Clay had said the night before, that she would be speaking to the farmers about the drilling and how it might affect them. She'd have a tough sell with Pete and his ilk, but that wasn't Tess's worry. She didn't want secondhand information from anyone, including Clay. "Well, I'm certainly interested in the facts, and you can be sure I'm going to be looking out for the interests of my land and my animals."

He studied her silently and she held his gaze. If he was taking her measure, she didn't mind. She was used to it.

"I know quite a few people have talked to you already about selling," Pete said casually. "And I understand this is your family home. But you've got five hundred acres of land that needs tending. That's a lot of work for one wo—person. Might be we could strike a deal where you can keep the house and a little bit of land, sell me the fields and the stock—"

"No," Tess said, keeping her tone friendly. "I'm not interested in selling. You might pass that word along because the message just doesn't seem to be sticking."

He smiled. "Thought I'd give it a try." He stood, picked up the cap he'd set on the table. "I'm hoping you'll see things my way, Tess. The more people that oppose the fuel company, the better chance we'll have at keeping them out. And believe me, that's what we want to do."

"Thanks for stopping by, Pete."

Tess walked him to the door and watched him drive away. She wasn't surprised he'd made an offer for her farm and briefly wondered what else motivated his opposition to the drilling. Pete struck her as the kind of man who always had a contingency plan. Clay would handle him, although Tess didn't know why she believed that. She knew nothing of the woman Clay had become. And she didn't want to.

She really didn't want to think about Clay at all, even though she'd done almost nothing except exactly that since Clay had appeared out of nowhere, as if she'd never been gone.

Chapter Six

Clay held the door for Ella as they left the diner.

"You really should let me know when you're going out," Ella said.

"I hardly think I need protection around here." Clay gestured to the mostly empty streets on the short walk back to the small lot behind the B&B where Ella had parked the SUV.

"I know you can take care of yourself, but you underestimate your own importance. And if you're not worried about yourself, just consider what happened to Doug in London last year."

"I know, I know," Clay said. Doug Hedley, NorthAm's UK division head, had been mugged and his briefcase stolen along with some important merger papers. The theft had seriously compromised the final deal. They'd never been able to determine if the attack was specifically targeted or random, but industrial espionage and blatant strong-arm tactics were becoming commonplace in the highly competitive world of international fuel acquisition. Add to that her father's high profile and substantial wealth, and Clay was a potential target for kidnapping or attack. She didn't like the lack of privacy that went along with personal security, but she wasn't consciously trying to make Ella's job harder. "I was going to call you at a decent hour."

"I was awake." Ella unlocked the SUV with the remote.

"Well, you obviously knew where I was."

"Knowing where you are isn't good enough. I need to be with you." Ella paused, regarded the Harley next to the SUV, then eyed Clay. "Is that by any chance—"

Clay gave her the smile that usually got her one in return—with most women. "Guilty."

Ella shook her head. "Just be careful—and stay in touch with me. The diner felt decidedly cool this morning."

Clay sighed. "I have some work to do."

"Well, you've had practice. You're good at putting things into perspective for people."

"Thanks."

"I still want you to keep a low profile for a while."

"I'll try to behave," Clay said.

Ella nodded, looking skeptical. "That should be interesting."

Laughing, Clay settled into the passenger seat and opened the briefcase Ella had brought along, content to let Ella drive. Ella was a good driver and Clay needed the time to review the specs on the job. When her cell phone rang, she checked the readout and answered. "Hello, Dad."

"How's the weather?" Her father's deep baritone resonated even with a sketchy connection. He'd always been able to command a room with just a look and a word.

"Hot."

"So I hear." He said something in a low murmur to someone else and then came back briskly. "You've got some loose ends up there that need immediate attention. Millie will email you with the details on the acquisitions still in the works. You'll want to sew those up as quickly as you can."

"What do you mean, acquisitions? I thought Ali had that all taken care of."

"We didn't expect to green-light this project so quickly, and Ali hadn't pressed to close the deals. We need to have unrestricted access to all drill sites to determine the optimal locations. Let's move this along before someone in the legislature changes his mind again. Once we're drilling, forward momentum will make it impossible to stop us."

"What kind of budget—"

"Whatever you need. Take a look at what we negotiated originally and work from there. You ought to be able to handle negotiations with a bunch of farmers."

Clay bit back a retort. Arguing with her father had always been an exercise in futility. Thinking of Tess's opposition and the resistance she'd heard that morning, she suggested, "Maybe we should back off a bit and do a little more advance work. There's a fair amount of opposition—"

"And that's exactly why we need to move faster. We've got a toehold—now I need you to expand it. I'm confident you will."

"Right. I'll look over Ali's paperwork as soon as I can. Then I'll set up meetings with the landowners."

"I trust you won't complicate issues with old history."

Clay squeezed the phone hard enough to make her knuckles ache. "The past has nothing to do with what's going on here now."

"Good. I'm glad to hear that. I'll expect a report tomorrow."

"All right, I'll do what I ca—"

"And don't forget Annabelle's birthday celebration. You're expected."

"On my calendar." Clay's stepmother number two was a younger version of stepmother number one and, while pleasant enough, was essentially a stranger. "Wouldn't miss it." She disconnected and slid the phone into the front pocket of her pants. She looked out the window, the blaze of her temper blocking out the scenery.

"Problem?" Ella asked quietly.

"Nothing more than usual." Clay clenched her fist on her knee. Her father still assumed he could direct her private life as well as her professional one, maybe because she let him.

"Can I help?"

"No," Clay said softly. "This one's on me."

❖

Tess reached Albany with ten minutes to spare and parked on Lark Street around the corner from the address Leslie had given her. Climbing the wide stone stairs to the three-story brownstone, she was reminded of how it felt being the girl who came to work at the resort rather than one of the girls spending the summer there vacationing. But Leslie hadn't really been one of those privileged girls, either. She'd been the daughter of the resort owner, and there had been plenty of days when she and Tess had worked side by side when things got busy. By the time Tess pressed the brass doorbell next to the wide walnut doors, she'd forgotten past insecurities. She wasn't that girl anymore and hadn't been for a long time.

A female voice came over the intercom. "Yes?"

"Hi, I have an appointment with Leslie Harris today." Tess automatically glanced up at the camera tucked into the corner of the alcove and smiled.

"Of course. Come right in."

The lock buzzed, and the ornate brass doorknob turned in her hand. The foyer was as elegant as some living rooms she'd been in—old slate squares on the floor, dark walnut wainscoting, and above that, wallpaper in a muted floral print Tess guessed was original. She followed the winding mahogany staircase upward to the second floor where a discreet plaque announced *Leslie Harris Attorney-at-Law*. She entered a waiting room with a thick Oriental carpet and dark wood trim where a woman in a pale-green linen dress that complemented her auburn hair and moss-green eyes sat behind an old-fashioned cherry desk.

"Tess?" the woman said.

"Yes."

"Estelle Clinton, Leslie's paralegal. She's just finishing up a phone conference and will be with you in a minute."

"Thanks."

"Do you need anything while you're waiting? Sparkling water? Coffee? Tea?"

"No, I'm fine, thanks," Tess said again and sat in one of the casual chairs arranged in a small seating area in front of the windows. Watching people walking by, she tried to remember the last time she'd been in the city. Two years? Three? In the last few years, more and more of the farm work had fallen to her, which provided a convenient excuse for her progressively hermitlike life. She hadn't dated anyone after a few casual relationships during college that were more friendly than passionate, and though she detected some interest in a few women she bumped into regularly in the village and at Grange meetings, she always managed to sidestep any possibility of intimacy. She was tired of disappointing the ones who hoped for something more—something she seemed unable to give and had forgotten how to feel. She told herself she was too busy for a relationship, and that was partly true. The other part she didn't want to look at too closely.

A door opened behind her and she turned, grateful for the sound of footsteps dispelling her self-analysis. Leslie looked exactly the same, a more sophisticated version of the girl Tess remembered. About Tess's height, Les was blond and willowy, with ocean-blue eyes, a classic heart-shaped face, and arching cheekbones. Dressed in charcoal pinstriped pants with low black heels and a crisp open-collared blue shirt, she managed to look totally professional and incredibly attractive at the same time.

Tess stood and held out her hand, refusing to think about how she appeared in her yellow cotton shirt, brown pants, and loafers. "Leslie, I—"

"Tess!" Leslie folded her into a hug and squeezed. "It's great to see you."

Leslie smelled like almonds and vanilla, just like always, and her slightly husky voice was as warm and friendly as Tess remembered. A lump formed in Tess's throat, and for a second she had trouble getting the words out. "You smell the same."

"And you look terrific."

"I'm so sorry I waited so long," Tess whispered.

Leslie held on to her shoulders and leaned back, her eyes glowing. "That doesn't matter. You're here now and I'm so glad. Are you hungry?"

"I'm starved," Tess said, laughing.

Leslie looped her arm through Tess's and tugged her toward the door. "Come on, then. Me too. Estelle, I'll be back in a couple of hours."

"All's quiet here." Estelle waved a hand. "Have a good time."

Leslie took her to a small, unassuming bistro around the corner where they were seated right away at a round table for two near the front window.

"It's not fancy," Leslie said, "but they bake their own bread and their sandwiches are great. Salads are good too, if you'd prefer."

"I'll follow your lead," Tess said.

While they waited for the food Leslie ordered, Leslie said, "Before we get too far into things, let me explain a little bit about what I do. You might want to talk to someone else."

"When I said I wanted to consult you," Tess said, "I don't actually know if I need legal representation. Mostly I need an informed opinion, and I wanted one from someone who I could trust to give me straight answers. And confidential ones."

"Good enough," Leslie said. "My practice mostly deals with corporate development issues, particularly when environmental regulations and questions of compliance come up."

Tess nodded. "So how much do you know about fracking?"

"A lot more than you might think." Leslie waited while the waitress placed enormous sandwiches in front of them. "Dev is a researcher for the state Environmental Conservation Department, and her specialty, more or less, is water. Well, water and everything that's in it, especially fish." Leslie smiled as if thinking of some secret joke. "Believe me, that's made for some interesting conversations around our house."

Tess laughed. "I can imagine."

"Dev has testified at a number of state hearings concerning the impact of deep hydraulic drilling and has compiled reports on the impact of fracking on the water table, aquatic life, and a lot of other things." Leslie stopped, shook her head. "In fact, you probably should be talking to her and not me."

"I might want to," Tess agreed. "But they're about to start drilling close to my farm, and I'm worried. I'm not the only one. Quite a few farmers in the area are opposed to the drilling, and I'm not sure anyone really has enough information to make an informed decision."

"What did the representatives from the gas company say? They can generally project how deep they have to go, the proximity to the aquifer in your area, the composition of the propellant they'll be infusing—and how all that could potentially affect surrounding terrain."

"Clay just got into town yesterday," Tess said, "and we haven't really heard anything yet."

Leslie tilted her head. "Clay. Not the Clay from the lake?"

"Yes," Tess said.

"Wow. Talk about coincidences."

Tess felt her face warm and looked down at her plate. "A surprise to me too."

"So what do you want to do?"

That was the question Tess had been turning over in her mind since she'd learned about NorthAm. She took a breath. "Is there a way to at least delay them until those of us who might be affected can get a clear picture of what's going to happen?"

"Probably. An emergency injunction could be obtained fairly quickly. It wouldn't stop things indefinitely, but it would buy some time and give everyone the opportunity to discuss the issues. Perhaps there are alternatives to where they plan to drill or some information they can provide to help allay concerns."

Tess nodded. "How would we go about that?"

"You need an attorney to represent you—or a number of landowners, if possible." Leslie explained while they finished their meal. "Now, I'm simplifying some here, but a case can be made that the drilling presents possible harm to humans through water or other environmental hazards, and on that basis we could request a prohibitive injunction."

"Doesn't that require some kind of evidence?"

"Not necessarily," Leslie said. "That's the power of this kind of argument."

"It all sounds so complicated," Tess said.

"It's possible that none of it will be necessary, and a few conversations will help put everyone's mind at ease." Leslie leaned back with a sigh. "That's generally the best outcome—legal action can be long and costly and is often not necessary."

"I hope you're right."

"So," Leslie said, sipping the espresso she'd ordered, "tell me about Clay. You haven't seen her since that summer at the lake?"

"No," Tess said softly. "We…lost touch."

"But back then, you were…?" Leslie's brows rose questioningly.

"Yes, for a while," Tess said. "You know, summer fling."

"Sometimes those flings are the beginning of something a lot more serious," Leslie murmured.

"You and Dev," Tess said. "I knew you went to school together, but I didn't realize you were involved."

Leslie smiled. "For the longest time I didn't know what was happening between us. I only knew I wanted to be with her more than anyone else. And then when I did finally understand, everything got so complicated, and…" She sighed. "Well, we both made some mistakes. But we figured it out."

"You were lucky," Tess said quietly. Second chances made good stories, but there was no way to turn back time. Once love was lost, it stayed lost.

CHAPTER SEVEN

A knock sounded on the metal door of the trailer, and a second later Ella stepped inside.

"Hey," she said. "You've been locked up in here almost all day. You want something to eat?"

Clay pushed back from the workbench bolted to the long wall of the thirty-foot trailer where she'd spread out the survey maps of the surrounding counties. A big satellite dish sat on the roof, providing Internet access for the laptop she'd set up to review documents related to the job. If the wind didn't blow too much, she had a pretty decent signal.

"What time is it?" Clay asked. Someone in marketing had labeled the current job the *Adirondack Pilot Project*. The specs called for forty drill sites within a hundred square miles of where she sat. From the air, the rolling hills would resemble a porcupine of tower-quills.

"Almost four."

Clay rubbed her face and sipped some of the cold coffee from the thermos Ella had left for her early in the day. The thermos was about as empty as her stomach, and her stomach was sending out distress signals. "Did you eat?"

"Some of the guys got pizza a while ago—I saved you some."

"Thanks. Sorry, the day kind of got away from me."

Ella leaned a hip against the counter. "It's a pretty place. I found a spot in the shade." She indicated the iPad mini she carried everywhere with her, outlined in her jacket pocket. "I'm used to waiting. Problems?"

"I'm starting to think so." Clay grimaced. "I haven't had a chance to review all Ali's filings yet, but we've got more than a few uncrossed t's. Acquisitions have been scattershot. Whole tracts of land right in the middle of our projected drill fields are under active use, and we don't have clear right-of-way. Getting permits could be a problem."

"Have those owners been approached?"

Ella was more than just Clay's guard and assistant. She was smart and quick and had been around long enough to have learned a lot about the business. Oftentimes when it was just the two of them traveling from one project to the next, Clay talked things over with her. Ella's insights, unmotivated by personal gain and uninfluenced by corporate politics, often gave Clay valuable perspective. This time, she was going to need it.

"That's the big question." Clay tapped the survey map. "If we don't secure rights from a couple of places, we could be in trouble. From the looks of the geological analysis, we're going to be drilling under them if not through them."

"Well, the underground drilling rights will be easy to get, don't you think? If we're not putting derricks on the property, the acceptance will be higher."

"Ordinarily, I'd say yes, but the farming industry up here is a little different than what we're used to in Texas or even the Midwest. These aren't big corporate farms with thousands of heads of beef cattle being bred for market. In this area especially, we're looking at dairy farms. Not only that"—she tapped the map again, her pen bouncing on the words *Rolling Hills Farm*—"organic ones to boot."

"Well, that throws a spanner in the works," Ella muttered. "Operations like that tend to be paranoid about anything that even smells of chemicals."

"Tell me about it." Clay rolled back the desk chair, stood, and stretched the tight muscles in her lower back. She squinted out through the slatted windows of the trailer into the yard, a hundred square feet of packed earth that had once been a pasture. Men and women were off-loading eighteen-wheelers filled with machinery—front-loaders, bulldozers, drills, and derrick parts. Flatbeds carried prefab walls and roofs for temporary housing. Swarms of construction workers had already erected a cluster of barracks with sleeping quarters for eight, and rudimentary bathrooms with chem toilets and stall showers near the bordering woods. Tanker trucks pumped in water, time-rationed with automatic cutoffs, encouraging fast showers. The spectacle was so common she barely noticed it most of the time. NorthAm built mini-villages like this on every job site—mobile communities that could be erected or struck at a moment's notice. To the locals, NorthAm probably looked like a marauding raider laying waste to the countryside. And this was only the beginning of the siege.

In the next few weeks, the cranes and drill towers would arrive, and once that happened, the project would gain a momentum of its own, impossible to redirect. Before then, Clay had to assuage the community's concerns and secure the rights NorthAm needed to tap the underground fuel in the quickest, most cost-effective way. Without endangering the land or the water.

"So what's your next move?" Ella said.

"Time to go a-visiting," Clay said with equal parts uncertainty and anticipation. She'd been hoping for an excuse to see Tess again, but Tess wasn't going to be happy about what she had to say.

❖

Tess turned into the driveway a little after four. She and Leslie had talked long after lunch ended, catching up as they ambled through Washington Park past people sprawled in the grass with backpacks and laptops scattered around them, or walking dogs, or pushing strollers with children sleeping in the late-afternoon heat. Finally Tess couldn't put off the inevitable.

"I have to head back—afternoon chores."

"I guess I should go back to the office and wrap up too," Leslie had said, "but I really don't want to."

Leslie had dropped onto a bench overlooking one of the small ponds that marked the heart of the large park. A flagstone walkway, shaded by trees and shrubs, circled it.

Tess sank down beside her. "It's been great seeing you."

Leslie turned on the bench, one arm stretched out along the top, and smiled. "It has. I don't want to lose touch again."

"Neither do I," Tess said softly. "I'd love to see Dev again too."

"Then we have to get together soon." Leslie had smiled that smile she got whenever she seemed to be thinking about Dev. As if some secret pleasure had been brought to mind that eclipsed everything else.

Tess had wondered then what that would be like, to love someone whose mere presence was more important than anything else, and to be loved by them in return.

She'd still been thinking about it all the way home. Turning into the long dirt drive to the house, she shook off the musings and pulled her truck around the side of the barn and under the lean-to. She'd promised Leslie she would get together with her and Dev at their house on the lake, but she wasn't sure now she ever would.

The thought of visiting the lake sent a twinge of pain flaring around her heart. Silly. She couldn't avoid a place just because once upon a time she'd thought it was a fairyland filled with endless possibility and limitless promise. Just because she'd thought she'd found the future there and learned she had been wrong. She'd been taken with the fantasies of youth and hadn't realized until now she hadn't quite been able to let them go. She really should thank Clay for showing up and forcing her to face her own foolishness.

Feeling a little more settled, she stopped in the barn to check the mother cat who'd wandered in from the fields during a rainstorm and promptly deposited five newborn kittens in a bed of straw she'd carefully built on a wide, deep windowsill. Tess had been feeding the mother ever since, and every day the mother let her get a little closer to the sanctuary before hissing to warn her off. Tess made it to within three feet of the litter today and counted that all five kittens were still there and growing well. Two orange ones like their mama, a tortoise, a gray striped, and a black with a white blaze on its chest. She knelt down and held out her hand, and the mother cat ambled over to allow Tess to scratch behind her ears. Tess hadn't tried to pick her up and doubted the cat would like it, being as she was the independent sort. But no matter how independent she might be, she liked the attention.

"You're going to have to let me pick them up, you know," Tess murmured, stroking the cat's soft fur. "Otherwise, we're going to have a pack of wild kittens running around, and before long we'll have an entire country of them right here on the farm." The mother arched her back and looked unperturbed by the notion of a new generation of felines on her adopted territory. "But we've got time, don't we?"

The mother cat didn't answer, just purred to announce that she would consider Tess's concerns and let her know how she felt about trusting her kittens to a human.

Tess laughed and walked out to the barnyard. She stopped before she'd gone ten feet. A black SUV was parked by her front porch. She didn't know the vehicle, a shiny, new oversized monster designed more for carting people around than goods and equipment. Not a farmer's car. A corporate car. Her spine stiffened. She could only think of one person who might be driving a car like that around here, and she'd made it clear that person did not have an open invitation to drop in. She strode forward, her jaws clenched tight, formulating her verbal assault, just as the driver's door opened and a gorgeous blonde stepped out.

Tess slowed, surveyed the woman. She looked…Nordic, somehow. Her blond hair was so pure gold it almost seemed white. Even from twenty feet, the woman's deep-blue eyes, as crystal clear as a high mountain lake, were captivating. Tess had a hard time looking away as the stranger walked to the front of the car and stopped, waiting, her gaze holding Tess's. Another door opened and her passenger stepped out. Clay.

Tess didn't need to look to know. The heat-laden air shimmered, as if a pulse of energy coursed through it. Her skin tingled. Imagination, of course. Who else would it be? Tess steeled herself and pulled away from the blonde's hypnotic aura.

"I don't remember making an appointment," Tess said.

Clay smiled, the lopsided half-rueful, half-apologetic grin that once had Tess's heart melting a little. But it would take more than a smile to melt the ice that encased her heart now. She waited.

"Tess, sorry to barge in, and I promise not to make a habit of it," Clay said, the grin disappearing. "But I called and didn't get an answer, so I thought I'd take a chance you'd be out working somewhere." Clay gestured to the blonde. "This is Ella Sorenson, my assistant."

Assistant. Tess tried to square the memory of the rebellious teenager on the big black motorcycle with the present businesswoman who looked polished even in casual clothes, accompanied by an equally polished *assistant*. She couldn't.

"Hello," Tess said, trying to sound at least a little bit civil. She didn't know the blonde, after all, and her relationship to Clay really didn't matter. Shouldn't matter, anyhow.

"Please to meet you, Ms. Rogers," Ella said in a mellifluous alto that sounded cultured and confident and sexy. All the things Tess was not feeling right now.

Tess folded her arms across her chest and focused on remembering all the reasons she did not want to talk to Clay. "What do you want?"

"Can we talk?"

Tess stared off into the distance. Why, all of a sudden, had Clay appeared wanting to talk? How Tess longed to say no. She'd waited day after day after day for exactly this—for Clay to appear around some bend in the road, calling out that she needed to talk. Needed Tess. And night after night, she'd gone to sleep confused and hurt, her waiting for nothing. She sighed and cut her gaze back to Clay. Their eyes met and Tess's heart gave a little jolt.

She'd always loved Clay's eyes, so intense and penetrating, as if Clay were reading her mind without the need for words. Sometimes when she'd been cold, Clay would slip her jacket around her shoulders without being asked. When she was tired, Clay would ease an arm around her shoulders and guide her head down to her chest, never saying a word. She'd imagined Clay had known her, been able to intuit what mattered to her. Clay had touched her all the way through.

"Fine. But I don't have long. I need to bring the cows in soon."

"Thank you," Clay said.

"I'll wait for you outside, Ms. Sutter," Ella said, turning back to the SUV.

"You can't wait in the car," Tess called, feeling grouchy for no reason at all. "It's too hot out here. You'll roast."

Ella smiled over her shoulder, looking even more beautiful, if that was possible. "I'll turn the air-conditioning on, but thank you—"

"Don't be silly," Tess said. "Sit on the porch—it's shady. I'll bring you something to drink. Lemonade? Seltzer?"

Ella canted a hip, a whimsical expression passing over her face that Tess would swear was completely genuine.

"You know, I would absolutely love a lemonade."

Tess laughed, charmed in spite of herself. "Well then, go ahead and sit down. I'll bring you out a glass in a minute." She looked at Clay. "Let's go back to the kitchen."

"Thanks," Clay said, hurrying to catch up as Tess strode off without waiting for her. She swore she could hear Ella laughing behind her.

CHAPTER EIGHT

Sit anywhere," Tess said, not looking at Clay. She needed another minute to collect herself. Clay and the past had been too much on her mind all day, distracting her, destabilizing the order of the world she had built for herself. She couldn't let that go on any longer. At the refrigerator, she took out the pitcher of lemonade she'd made earlier that morning and rummaged on the second shelf for a can of soda. She paused before closing the door and half turned to face Clay. "Do you still drink Coke?"

Clay sat at the big oak table exactly where Pete Townsend had been a few hours before. She shook her head. "Gave it up. If there's enough lemonade, I'll have that. If not, water's fine."

Tess put the soda back in the refrigerator and poured three glasses of lemonade. She put two on the table and stood regarding Clay, resolving to forget, as Clay apparently had, the secrets they'd once shared. "We should start over—as if we'd just met. We really are strangers."

The words dropped like splinters of ice, plunging Clay into the cold. She turned in her chair and looked up, uncertain where Tess was going with her pronouncement, not sure if her comment indicated progress or something a great deal more final. "Can you do that? Just erase the past?"

Tess regarded her for a long moment, her expression unreadable. "Why not? It's not like the past has anything to do with what's happening now."

Clay wasn't so sure. Since she'd arrived in New York—since she'd seen Tess standing in the late-day sun by the mailbox at the side of the road—she'd felt as if doors were opening on memories she had buried and now wanted to reclaim. She liked the hum of excitement, of being alive, pulsing inside her. Feelings she'd lost and not known she'd missed until now. But she had a job to do, a mission to complete, and if Tess needed to forget they'd ever known one another in order for them to talk, she would have to try.

Her father's warning to guard against past entanglements came back to her, and she winced inwardly. He had been right, again. He'd known her history with Tess might be a roadblock to negotiations, but she wasn't going to let that happen. She wasn't going to let personal feelings affect her business judgment. "All right. We'll start fresh."

"Good," Tess said, although she didn't look any happier.

Clay smiled. "Will that make you less suspicious of me?"

"Afraid not. I'll be back in a minute." Tess took the glass of lemonade and left.

Actually, she was gone more like five minutes. Clay wasn't consciously counting, but her gaze kept straying to the big clock on the wall with its Roman numerals to mark the hour and broad, fat hands sweeping around its face. She hadn't been immune to the chemistry that had sparked between Ella and Tess outside in the yard. Ella's beauty was irresistible—even after all this time, Clay wasn't used to it. And Tess—Tess was radiant, as fresh and wondrous as spring blossoms opening after a rainstorm. Why wouldn't the two of them appreciate each other? She'd never seen Ella really notice a woman before, but Ella had clearly noticed Tess.

The tightness in her chest didn't ease until she heard Tess returning. She forced her shoulders to relax and sipped the lemonade. Tart and tangy, with just the slightest bit of sweetness lingering on her tongue after the initial burst of flavor. Tess's taste had been just the opposite, all light and honey until an unexpected explosion of heat raced through her mouth, scorching her to the core. The first time they'd made out, under a moonlit sky on the deck of a sailboat moored next to the boathouse where Tess worked, she'd planned to go slow, to be gentle, knowing Tess was inexperienced. Only Tess hadn't given her a chance to be either of those things. The first kiss had rocketed from tentative to tempestuous in a few breathless seconds, Tess's teeth raking her lip, her hands grasping Clay's shirt, palms grazing over her breasts until her nipples stood up like windswept stones in a storm.

"Something wrong with the lemonade?" Tess asked.

Clay jumped. "No. It's great. Thanks."

Tess's chair scraped out and she sat down, bringing with her a hint of honeysuckle and loam. "What do you want?"

Swallowing the sand in her throat, Clay said, "What makes you think I want anything?"

"I don't have time to play games," Tess said wearily. "You're here for a reason, and it can only have to do with the drilling. There's nothing else to bring you here."

Clay sat back in the chair, stretched her legs out underneath the table. She couldn't avoid the conversation, as much as she wanted to. She'd managed plenty of hard sells before, but this was more than a business transaction. This was…this was personal, and she couldn't let it be. "Do you think you can listen to me without prejudice? For just a minute or two?"

Tess studied the woman across from her. Clay Sutter was a woman you would notice—strikingly attractive, polished, assertive. Tess hadn't been lying when she'd told Clay they should start over from here. She didn't know this Clay Sutter. The Clay she'd known had been ready to take on the world, filled with passion and unbridled confidence. The woman at her kitchen table, despite her commanding presence, struggled with some kind of burden that showed in her eyes, in the rigid set of her shoulders, in the fatigue that burrowed through her voice. As strong as she had to be to do what she had come to do, she labored to carry the weight.

Despite the stirrings of sympathy, Tess was wary. Clay was a threat—the company she represented was potentially dangerous. Like most farmers, Tess didn't trust big business. She wasn't much of a fan of the government, either. When it didn't rain, when nor'easters blew the topsoil away, when floods rotted the seeds in the ground, no one came to bail them out. Oh, sure, there were government subsidies to be had, but most of that money went to the large corporate farms, owned by the wealthy few with the kind of influence to buy friends in the government. The average small farmer saw almost nothing from the millions of dollars set aside to presumably support them in times of market declines or natural disaster. No, in the end, the small farmer had only family, neighbors, and luck to count on. NorthAm was not her friend, and Clay was NorthAm. Tess would be foolish to trust her, even if they'd never met before.

But still, the shadows in Clay's eyes pulled at her heart.

"I'm listening," Tess said quietly, and she vowed to try.

"The Marcellus Shale extends from Ohio through Pennsylvania and southern New York. There are other drill sites already operational in Pennsylvania and Ohio, some in New York, but the deposits in the eastern part of the state have never been tapped. We—my company, NorthAm—are interested in a thirty-square-mile area of land locally that's directly over what we believe are the largest deposits of fuel in the entire shale. There could be enough natural fuel to increase the national yield by twenty-five or thirty percent. That would have a profound influence on fuel economics here and around the world."

"I suppose it would be unpatriotic if I said I don't care," Tess said, not entirely serious, but she still wasn't about to sacrifice her livelihood and the land she loved for some political game only politicians would benefit from.

Clay nodded. "I understand, and you're not the first farmer I've heard say that. I know you have to get up every morning before the sun rises and work until after the sun goes down to keep this farm going. What happens in the next state doesn't matter as much as what happens down the road, and what happens across the ocean maybe not at all. I just want you to know there's more at stake here than whether NorthAm makes a profit."

"All right, you've made your point. You're not quite robber barons."

Clay laughed softly. "Not quite, no."

Tess stood abruptly. She didn't want to be swayed by anything other than the facts, and Clay so close, her laugh so damn familiar, distracted her. "Why can't you find somewhere to drill that doesn't expose our farms to contamination? You can drill horizontally underground a long ways, right?"

"You've been doing your homework."

"Did you think I wouldn't? That I'd just let you walk in and…" Tess shook her head. "Sorry. This is personal to me—to you it's just business."

"No," Clay said softly, "it's not."

Tess stepped back before the tenderness in Clay's voice could wrap around her the way Clay's jacket had when she'd been cold—comforting and safe. Clay wasn't safe. "The question?"

"We do drill horizontally, have to in order to open the channels in the shale," Clay admitted. "But the more shallow the well, the less it costs, and the closer we can get to where we believe the largest deposits to be, the less water and sand and chemicals we have to pump into the ground to get it out again. Generally, the most direct route is the best all around."

"And the most direct route is somewhere on the Hansen tract?"

Clay blew out a breath. "Actually, the ideal location in this area is in a very localized area about a mile square. That's where we'd like to start."

Tess frowned. "Where?"

Clay walked to the kitchen window and pointed to the ridge behind Tess's house. "Right about on top of that ridge—at the junction where your land, the Townsend property, and Hansen's land meet."

Tess stared out the window at the view she'd seen a hundred thousand times. "My land. You want to drill on my land."

"On a little bit of it, yes."

"No." Tess gathered up the empty glasses and carried them to the sink. "I don't want you any closer to my farm than you have to be, and certainly not on it."

"Tess," Clay said quietly, softly, as if she was very, very tired. "Ray Phelps already negotiated for that tract of land up there. We have a signed letter of intent."

Tess spun around. Clay was just a silhouette backlit by the slanting rays of the sun as it dropped behind the mountains, her face in shadow. "I don't believe you."

"I have a copy of the paperwork for you. I'll leave it—"

"Ray isn't here," Tess said, hating the tremor in her voice. "He never said anything about it to me."

"Maybe he was waiting until we were ready to drill."

"It's my land now, and I certainly won't agree to let you drill."

Clay's shadow shifted and sunlight illuminated her profile, the bold lines of her face appearing as sharp and hard as a Roman conqueror's, carved from stone. "If we go to court it will be expensive. Tess, consider—"

"No," Tess said more softly.

"We might be able to keep the tower off your land," Clay said, moving closer, "but we're going underneath you, Tess, one way or the other."

"Not if there's any way I can stop you."

Clay held out a hand as if to touch her, then drew it back. "Let me survey on your property. I'll bring my team in and look at what's down there, map the aquifer, and chart the water runoff. If I could tell you with reasonable certainty that we won't have a problem with backflow into your land or your water, would you consider it?"

"I have to think about it."

"Tess," Clay murmured, aching to run her thumb over the shadows beneath Tess's eyes, to erase the pain and worry. "Just let me look. I can promise with what we would pay you for those rights, your farm would be secure forever. You could do anything you wanted to with it."

"Not if there's even a chance of contamination." Tess stepped back. The softness in Clay's voice, the tenderness in her eyes, the heat radiating from her body was too much. Tess felt herself bending toward her like a willow in the wind, called against her will, and she refused to be drawn in. "We don't have anything else to discuss."

"Take some time. We'll talk again." Clay wanted to tell her she wouldn't hurt her, but Tess had no reason to believe her. Tess pulled farther away, taking the heat and the sunshine with her, as if a cloud passed between Clay and the sun. She had nothing else to offer. "Thanks for seeing me."

Tess nodded wordlessly.

Clay let herself out through the white screen door onto the stone path that led from the kitchen to the barnyard. Ella came down the steps from the broad front porch to meet her.

"How did it go?" Ella asked.

"First volley." Clay noticed the empty lemonade glass on a small table next to the white wood rocking chair where Ella had been seated. "It's going to be a long war."

"Are you sure there'll be a fight?" Ella walked ahead and opened Clay's door before continuing around to the driver's side. She slid in and started the engine.

Clay climbed in and buckled her seat belt. "Tess isn't too happy, and Townsend is already stirring up the opposition."

Ella backed the SUV around and headed down the drive. “Tess doesn’t seem as unreasonable as some.”

“Did one glass of lemonade convince you of that?”

Ella smiled and stared straight ahead. “It didn’t hurt.”

Clay detected something more than passing interest in Ella’s voice. She didn’t like it, but she had nothing to say about it. She liked that even less.

CHAPTER NINE

The crackle of gravel crunching under the tires of Clay's SUV quickly faded away, leaving Tess alone in the silent house. She stared at the plain manila folder Clay had left on her kitchen table without touching it. If she didn't touch it, didn't read it, perhaps it wouldn't be real. Even as she avoided it, she knew she was only fooling herself. Trouble didn't disappear just because she closed her eyes, any more than the rain fell or the crops came in strong when she whispered a prayer to make it so. If what Clay had said was true, she had a whole lot of trouble coming her way, and she preferred to meet it head-on. Whatever had to be done, she would find a way to do it. She wasn't helpless, she wasn't without choices or friends. And she knew how to fight.

Squaring her shoulders, she walked into the mudroom, pulled on her chore boots, and headed out to help with the milking. Three hours later, the day was almost gone and heavy twilight blanketed the fields, the heat still lingering close to the ground, enveloping Tess in air so thick she could almost hold it in her hand as she trudged back to the house. Inside, shadows cooled the corners of the big kitchen, and Tess worked in the near dark, brewing a cup of tea and assembling a sandwich out of the previous day's roast chicken. When she was done with the preparations, she switched on the old chandelier that hung over her big oak table and sat down. The folder hadn't moved, still sitting squarely in front of her plate like a coiled snake ready to strike. *Rolling Hills Farm* was written on the tab in neat black letters. She wondered idly if Clay had written that. Probably not. More likely someone in an office far away who had no idea what the name stood for, no clue of the land and the life that went with it.

She slid the dozen neatly typed and stapled pages from the folder and started to read what Ray had done. By the time she'd digested the words, her tea was cold and her sandwich uneaten. She tried to find excuses for him, some explanation as to why he had made these decisions without telling her. She'd always thought they had a decent relationship—she couldn't say she loved him the way she had loved her mother, but he had been a part of her life for a long time, and though they shared little that was personal, she'd thought they had shared a love of the land. She couldn't square that belief with his signature at the bottom of a lengthy contract agreeing to allow NorthAm access to his land—her land—for money. A lot of money. She didn't know if he'd been paid, but she'd have to find out. If he hadn't been, if things hadn't gone that far, it might be easier to somehow undo the contract. Because one way or another, she had to. She wasn't going to let NorthAm violate her land, no matter how much money they offered her or how persuasive Clay might be.

❖

Clay closed her laptop, her eyes aching, and surveyed the lovingly restored room at the inn. Any other time she might have admired the authentic tin ceiling tiles and gleaming hardwood floors, but tonight the beauty was lost on her. The dull pain in her chest had nothing to do with the hours she'd spent poring through files or her missed supper. Thoughts of Tess plagued her, undercutting her concentration, tugging at her conscience—and her heart.

She needed some perspective, but first she needed a diversion.

Briefly she considered asking Ella if she'd eaten and decided against it. She didn't really want company. She wasn't feeling sociable. Less than sociable—more like she wanted a fight and hoped one found her. She grabbed a denim jacket from the clothes Doris had sent up and went out to see the town.

Choices were limited. The sign in the diner window said they closed at nine, and she'd just missed that. The convenience store on the corner of the one and only major intersection in town sold ice cream, hot dogs, and microwave burritos, none of which appealed to her, although each of them had been dinner on more than one occasion. Drawn by the murmur of voices, she continued across the street to a tavern where a few people congregated outside on the steps, smoking, watching the traffic, talking. They parted to let her in, questions in their eyes.

Inside, the one big room was divided into a dining section with a half dozen tables in one half and a long bar in the other. Men and women, drinks in hand, squeezed in between the bar stools, all of which were occupied. Clay had her choice of tables and sat down at one in front of the big plate-glass window and scanned the single page of a laminated menu. The TV over the bar showed a baseball game, the sound lost in the layers of conversation that flowed over the room. A few minutes later a waitress in jeans and a yellow T-shirt ambled over.

"How you doing?" the thirtysomething brunette asked.

"Not bad," Clay said, giving the friendly lie.

"Something to drink?"

"Whatever beer you have on tap would be fine."

"Know what you're having?"

"A burger sounds good—medium, with the works."

"You got it." The waitress smiled and left without writing anything down. Sometime later she returned with a tall mug of ice-cold beer.

Clay nodded thanks and sipped. Good beer. She slowly drank, letting thoughts of yield projections, ROIs, and budgets slowly drift away. Eventually, her mind was quiet for a minute or two before the conversation at Tess's hijacked her mind. She didn't hear the words—all she could see was the unhappiness in Tess's eyes, the pain she'd helped put there. Again.

The last person she ever wanted to hurt was the one she kept making unhappy. She might have been only the messenger this time, but Tess wouldn't see it that way. Tess hadn't known about Ray Phelps's arrangement with NorthAm. The shocked betrayal in her face was clear. Tess had worked the farm for him, put her heart into it, and he hadn't even bothered to tell her what he was doing. Even though Tess's stepfather had been the cause of Tess's pain, Clay had been the one to bring the reality of what Phelps had done into Tess's world. Tess probably blamed her as much as she blamed Phelps right now. Clay couldn't argue—she was guilty by association.

Clay tapped her fork on the tabletop, frustrated and more than a little angry. Tess's unhappiness wasn't her concern, couldn't be her concern—her responsibility was to secure the drilling rights they needed so the project could go forward as quickly as possible. She wasn't doing anything illegal, nothing she hadn't done a hundred times before. This time, though, what had always been routine had become personal, and she couldn't let it be. She rubbed her forehead as if to purge the self-recriminations, muttering her thanks when the waitress slid an enormous burger with fries in front of her. The place was filling up, and the noise level rose—a typical Friday night after a long workweek, everyone wanting to unwind. Clay couldn't unwind the steel spring ratcheted tightly in her chest, but she managed to fill her head with the cacophony of voices so she didn't have to think about what she had done or might need to do.

When she heard Tess's unmistakable rich, faintly throaty voice, she thought she was imagining it again—reliving the conversation in the kitchen—until she glanced up and realized her mistake. Tess stood at the bar, her back to Clay, talking to a big man in work clothes. He gripped her arm loosely, looming over her, their heads close together. Tess didn't look happy.

A surge of possessiveness Clay hadn't experienced in years pushed its way into her throat, reverberating there like a growl waiting to erupt. She swallowed down the ire, pushed the remains of her burger aside, and drained her beer. She needed the support of these people, and Tess was not hers to claim. Neither rationalization helped counter the acid eating at her insides. Tess was hurting and Clay was helpless.

"Ready for another beer?" the waitress asked.

"Yes, thanks," Clay said, not taking her eyes off Tess. While she watched, Tess glanced toward the door and smiled. Her face lost some of the worry lines that had been etched across her forehead and the corners of her mouth, and Clay automatically searched out who had put that look on her face.

Ella wended her way through the crowd and up to Tess, who said something to the man she was with and turned to face Ella fully, her fingers lightly grazing Ella's forearm. Clay wanted to look away but couldn't. Even seeing Tess with another woman was better than not seeing her at all. Ella laughed, nodded, and bent her head to murmur something into Tess's ear. Tess smiled at whatever Ella had said and looked younger and more carefree than Clay had seen her all week. She wanted to be the one making Tess laugh, bringing pleasure to her face, and knew she'd lost that chance a long time ago. Abruptly, she stood, yanked her wallet from her back pocket, pulled out bills, and left a handful on the table. Unfortunately, she had to walk past Ella and Tess to get to the door.

With her uncanny sixth sense, Ella looked in Clay's direction before Clay had gotten halfway across the room. Tess followed her gaze and the laughter left her eyes.

"Good evening, Ms. Sutter," Ella said smoothly as Clay stepped up to them. "I was just saying to Ms. Rogers that this seems to be the place where all the important work is being done, and apparently that's true."

"I've got a few things to do yet tonight," Clay said, practically shivering from the chill in Tess's gaze. "Unfortunately, I'm going to have to do them back at the inn."

"Of course. I'll walk back with you." Ella nodded to Tess. "I hope I'll see you again soon."

"Yes," Tess said, carefully not looking at Clay. "I hope so too."

"No need to leave, Ella," Clay said. "You're off the clock now."

Ella smiled. "Thanks, but I wasn't planning on staying."

Clay knew Ella had come looking for her, but she wouldn't say that in front of anyone else. "Why don't you get something to eat first. I'll wait while you order."

"If you wouldn't mind," Ella said. "I'll get takeout."

"Sure," Clay said.

Ella slipped off in search of the waitress, leaving Clay and Tess staring at one another.

"She seems pretty extraordinary for just being your assistant," Tess said, gesturing to the far end of the bar where Ella talked with the waitress. Soon the waitress was smiling and laughing as well.

"She is...extraordinary," Clay said. "She's also an exceptional assistant."

"And what else?" Tess asked, annoyance prickling under her skin even as she spoke. She wasn't certain what prompted the spurt of jealousy—that Ella was with Clay instead of her, or that Clay was with Ella. Ella was charming, and being around her for just a few minutes had sparked feelings Tess hadn't experienced in a long time. Ella's easy flirtations made her feel attractive and sexy, something she hadn't realized she missed. Something she liked. But as soon as Clay appeared, Ella's attentions had shifted. Clay had become her focus.

"She's also security," Clay said quietly.

"Security? You mean like a bodyguard?"

Clay shifted, looking a little uncomfortable and a little embarrassed. Tess couldn't ever remember Clay being either.

Clay nodded. "Yes."

"Why?"

"Company policy. All the upper-management people travel with security."

"Are you in danger?" Tess asked, her earlier anger at Clay dissolving into concern.

"No," Clay said dismissively. "Like I said, company policy. And besides, Ella really is my assistant, and she's very good at it."

"Oh," Tess said, "I don't doubt it. She seems very…capable."

"Is that what you were thinking?" Clay asked. "That Ella is capable?"

"What else?" Tess blushed. She wasn't about to discuss Ella with Clay, especially when she wasn't even sure what she was feeling. "Well. I should be going."

"Tess," Clay said, reaching for her hand. "I know you probably haven't had much chance to think about what we were discussing earlier, but if we could—"

The man Tess had been speaking with at the bar crowded in next to them, his hard gaze fixed on Clay. "Everything all right, Tess?"

"Yes," Tess said quickly. "Everything's fine."

"You the person in charge from NorthAm?" the big man said to Clay.

Clay straightened. "That's right. And you are?"

"The name is Pete Townsend."

"Mr. Townsend," Clay said, extending her hand. "Good to meet you. I've been looking forward to talking with you—"

"I'm not sure we have much to discuss," Townsend said. "Unless you're about to tell me you're planning to pick up and move somewhere else."

Clay let her hand fall. "I'm afraid that wasn't my plan, no. Maybe I can drop by tomorrow—say eight a.m.?"

"It's your time." Townsend turned to Tess. "You'll let me know about that other thing."

"I will. Good night, Pete." Tess waited until he was out of earshot. "He's not a fan of yours."

"I gathered," Clay said.

"Tempers are running a little hot right now," Tess said quietly. "Be careful."

"I've been through this before, Tess, but thanks. I appreciate you worrying about me."

"I'm not worried about you," Tess said. "I just don't want to see the community turned upside down by this."

"Right, I should've known that."

Ella joined them, a takeout bag in her hand. "Ready to go, Ms. Sutter?"

Clay looked at Tess as if waiting for her before answering. Tess cut her gaze from Clay to Ella and said, "If you really are interested in a tour of the farm, come by tomorrow morning."

"I am," Ella said warmly, "and I will if I'm free."

"Good," Tess said, ignoring the flare of heat in Clay's eyes. She liked Ella Sorensen and she had every right to her feelings. The idea of spending time with an attractive woman who seemed interested in her made her feel good. For the first time in a long time, she was going to do something for no other reason than it gave her pleasure.

Chapter Ten

They walked half a block in silence before Clay said, "I didn't know you were interested in farming."

Ella shot her a glance, her stride never faltering. "Since we'll be up here for a while, I thought it would be useful to get a sense of the local community. And Tess's farm is right in the middle of things."

Fighting off an irrational urge to challenge Ella's reasons, Clay slid her hands into her pockets where her fingers curled into fists all on their own. She'd been itching for someone to pound on, metaphorically at least, ever since she'd read Ali's reports and realized she was going to have to go after Tess's land. Seeing Tess in the tavern with Ella and being pretty much dismissed by Tess hadn't helped. Her hackles were up and she wouldn't need much of an excuse to growl. Except Ella wasn't the enemy. "Are you trying to tell me you're doing a little covert industrial investigation?"

Ella laughed. "I'm no spy. Besides, you don't need that kind of help. If there's something you need to know, you know how to find it out."

Clay stopped and leaned against an old-fashioned iron light pole with an actual working incandescent bulb shining from behind a frosted oval globe. The lamp cast a pale yellow circle on the sidewalk that slid over the curb and into the street. Clay's shadow cleaved it in half. "Personal interest?"

The laughter faded from Ella's face as she studied Clay with a speculative gaze. "I didn't realize there was an issue here."

"There's no issue."

"History?"

"Not for so long it's not even this lifetime," Clay murmured more to herself than to Ella. After the day she'd lied to her father and said her relationship with Tess was nothing serious, she hadn't disclosed a single minute of what they'd shared with anyone. Tess's past was hers to tell, if she wanted.

"Listen, Clay," Ella said evenly, "all kidding aside. I like her—there's something about her that's fresh and uncomplicated. Not to mention strong-willed and lovely to look at. She's different than most of the women I've—"

"I know," Clay said, the heat leaching from her blood as a heavy weight settled in her chest. She didn't need anyone to tell her Tess was special. She'd known that the first second she'd seen her. "I know she's all those things. And I don't have any business questioning you about your motives or your intentions."

"I don't mind."

"You should." Clay pushed away from the post and started walking again. Her shadow knifed along beside her, eventually fragmenting and disappearing into the dark. Ella caught up to her easily.

"Clay, slow down. You and I—our relationship is unusual. We're not the typical kind of friends, but we're more than colleagues. I'm here to do a job, just like you. I'm not immune to the attractions of a beautiful, exciting woman, but it's not something I need to pursue."

"No," Clay said, angry for what she'd already said and what she needed to say now. "Tess is not mine. I've got no hold on her, and no designs on her. If you want to see her on a friendly basis or something more than that, go ahead."

"I don't want problems between us."

"There won't be." Clay halted at the foot of the walkway leading up to the B&B, suddenly too agitated to face the thought of an empty bed and a silent room. "Go inside and have your dinner. I want to take a walk. I'm meeting Townsend at eight tomorrow. I'll see you in the morning."

"It's getting late." Ella glanced at her watch and then back the way they had come. "The tavern is about the only thing open, and that will close in a few minutes. You shouldn't be—"

"Ella." Clay laughed. "I'm a big girl. I've been out after dark before. Hell, I've even been out all night before."

"I know that." Ella frowned. "And I know this looks like a quiet little town, but all the same, it's my job—"

"Get your ass inside and eat your burger before it gets cold." Clay put on a smile. "I just need a little time to unwind—too many hours reading over paperwork. I promise I'll look both ways when I cross the street."

"All right, but keep your phone on and text me when you get back in."

"Maybe we should just get married," Clay muttered.

Ella gave her a long look. "Let me know when you're serious, and I'll consider it."

Clay's heart gave a little trip before she laughed. "Ella, you're way too much woman for me."

"Maybe," Ella said lightly, "but from what I've seen, you're a fast learner."

"Sometimes. Good night, Ella."

"I'll see you at seven," Ella said.

Clay sketched a wave and turned back the way they'd come. She wasn't planning on returning to the tavern, she just wanted to walk, and if Tess happened to appear somewhere up ahead, well, that would just be coincidence.

She passed the tavern, but the steps in front were empty now. She was alone on the streets, her footsteps falling in a hypnotic cadence on the sidewalk. Occasionally a pickup truck rattled by, and once, in the distance, a motorcycle engine roared as the rider accelerated through the outskirts of town. Striding past the small business district, she hoped the exercise would tire her out and give her a little peace so she could get some sleep. She should have known better.

Ella and Tess. She didn't want to imagine them together, but she could. Tess was intelligent and curious and beautiful. Ella was intense and magnetic and alluring. Clay didn't have to wonder if Ella would be able to make Tess laugh, she'd seen the light in Tess's eyes earlier. Once upon a time, she'd been the one to put that glow in Tess's blue eyes, but lately, all she'd done was fill them with storm clouds.

Ella and Tess.

She wasn't really surprised. Ella almost never dated, and when she did, she kept the details to herself. She wasn't shy, she wasn't standoffish. She just didn't seem to be taken by anyone in the casual kind of way that was the norm for the life they led. Brief encounters, a love affair to last a month or two. Tess had obviously touched a chord in Ella. Maybe that's what fate was—the simultaneous striking of a note that resonated for two people when they least expected to be captivated.

Clay walked steadily, her gaze unfocused, circling blocks aimlessly, heading away from the few places where lights chased the shadows away. She sought the shadows and hoped the dark would swallow the images she didn't want to see. Ella and Tess.

She'd completed her fourth or fifth circuit around a mostly deserted block of big Victorians set back from the street and shrouded by trees, when she finally turned back toward the center of the village. As she approached the intersection where the tavern was located, the drone of an engine pierced her awareness and she looked over her shoulder. A vehicle—a pickup truck—coasted slowly up the street, shadowing her, keeping pace five yards behind her. The halogen headlights momentarily blinded her, and she couldn't tell make or model or even how many occupants were in the vehicle.

She debated turning the corner and heading away from the upcoming intersection. Maybe she was imagining that the truck was following her. But the neighborhood in that direction was dark, the houses closed and shuttered for the night. Better to take her chances in a well-lit area if there was going to be trouble. Just one more street to cross and she'd be half a block from the tavern, where lights and people would discourage an altercation.

More than likely she was only imagining she was being followed, but she'd learned to heed warning signs. Heart beating hard, she checked over her shoulder again just as she reached the corner. The truck had fallen farther behind her now. She looked across the intersection to the other side of the street. Empty—but far down the block, lights flickered in the tavern.

Clay stepped off the curb, hesitated, listening, and when the night held silent, she hurried to cross. The whine of an engine revving split the air when she was halfway across.

Turn back or go forward?

She made a decision and spun back the way she had come, lunging for the sidewalk and the cover of darkness. She had a split second to think that might have been a mistake before the truck caromed around the corner on two wheels and she went flying into the air.

CHAPTER ELEVEN

A sharp *bang* and the screech of tires froze Tess with her hand on the half-open door of her pickup. Turning away from the yellow-orange glow filtering through the front window of the tavern across the street from where she'd parked, she searched in the direction of the sound. The streetlamps were few and far between this far from the center of town, and all she saw were the flickering red taillights of a vehicle disappearing into the darkness down a cross street half a block away. The night was quiet and still. The wind carried the low notes of a quiet cry—or did it?

She was tired, it was after midnight. She was just imagining she'd heard something. Probably just a garbage can knocked over. But then, what if it was a dog or a cat? Oh please, don't let it be an animal. Fine, she'd check. Better than worrying all the way home.

Pulse hammering, she slammed the door and hurried toward the intersection, dread coiling more tightly in her stomach with every step. Don't let it be a dog or a cat. Okay, not a squirrel, either. Or a possum or a— Slowing at the corner, Tess stared across the street, struggling to make sense of what she saw. Something in the road, partway up on the sidewalk. But it couldn't really be a person, could it? Then she heard the sound again, definitely a moan, unmistakably human.

Every thought, every fear, every emotion left her head except one—the all-consuming need to do something. To help.

Racing across the street, she fumbled in the front pocket of her cargo pants for her phone, staring at the not-quite-recognizable shape in the half-light. Then the darkness seemed to part, and features jumped into sharp relief.

"Oh my God, Clay!" Tess dropped to her knees, barely registering the sharp stones digging into her flesh through her cotton pants. She reached out, jerked back. She shouldn't touch her, right? Shouldn't move her? But oh God, Clay was staring at her as if she wasn't even there. "Clay? Clay, oh God, can you hear me?"

Clay pushed up onto an elbow, her head whirling. Every time she breathed, something jabbed her in the side. Sharp and burning. She heard Tess say her name, but she knew that was a dream. Tess was long gone and far away. "Hurts."

"Lie down, honey, you have to lie down," Tess's voice said, close to her ear. Soft and warm and too cruel.

"I know you're not really here."

"I am. I'm right here. Clay, lie back down. Oh God, there's blood—your head is bleeding."

"Are we at the lake?"

"No, Clay. There's been an accident." Tess sounded upset. And scared.

"I didn't drop my bike, did I?" Clay's insides clenched. She was always so careful with Tess. "You're not hurt? Did I—"

"Stay still. I'm all right, I promise. You didn't crash." Tess cradled Clay's jaw when she tried to sit up.

Somewhere a man yelled, "You need help?"

"Yes," Tess called back, afraid to look away from Clay. Afraid the light in Clay's eyes might disappear. Her phone lay on the ground where she'd dropped it. She'd forgotten to call. Forgotten everything except Clay. "Call 9-1-1. Hurry."

"I'm okay," Clay said, her voice a little thick, but stronger. She braced one arm on the sidewalk and tried to tilt her head back. Her eyes brightened, seemed to focus. "Tess? We're not at the lake anymore, are we?"

Tess's throat tightened. "No, Clay. We're not. Just relax now. Try not to move."

Clay frowned. "Why am I sitting on the sidewalk?"

"I think…" Tess fiercely reined in the tears that flooded her eyes. She had no business crying. She wasn't the one who was hurt. Clay was hurt. And she couldn't bear it. "I think maybe you were hit by a car."

Clay shook her head. The motion made her stomach turn over.

"Fu—damn." She took a couple deep breaths and waited. Some of the fog started to leave her brain. "No. It wasn't a car. It was a truck."

"You saw them?"

"Yeah. Wait, just let me…" The street jumped into sharp relief. Tess knelt by her side. Tiny diamonds glittered on her cheeks. "Why are you crying?"

Tess laughed softly, a faintly broken sound. "I'm not. I'm just—nothing. You're sure it was a truck? I saw lights—but I couldn't—"

Clay's mind cleared along with her vision, and pieces of the last few minutes floated back to her. She'd been out walking, and there had been lights behind her. A vehicle following her. "Tess, call Ella."

"Ella? Oh, of course," Tess said. "I should have thought." Of course Clay would want Ella. Ella was the person she would want to take care of her. Why wasn't Ella taking care of her now? In the distance, sirens wailed. "What's her number?"

"Use my phone. Pants pocket. Here." Clay started to reach into her pants and gasped, pressed her hand to her right side. "You get it."

"Fine. Just hold still." Tess carefully slid her hand into Clay's pocket, felt soft cotton and hard muscle. Closed her fingers over the smooth rectangular object and pulled it out. Her hand was shaking. "Where—"

"Just open the phone app. She's right at the top. ES."

"I've got it." Tess tapped the number for Ella, praying she'd connect to one of the whimsical cell signals that might be available, depending on the wind and the weather and how many people were awake and trying to access it at the same time. She held her breath, heard a ring, a second one, and then the phone was answered.

"Clay?" Ella asked.

"No, it's Tess, Ella," Tess said. "I'm with Clay. She's hurt."

"I see the crowd. I'm almost there. How serious?"

"She's awake, she's talking. But I think she needs to go to the hospital."

"One minute."

The call disconnected. Ella must be running, and she wasn't even short of breath. Tess chased the irrelevant thought away. "She'll be right here. The ambulance is coming."

"I don't need a hospital," Clay said. "I just need a minute or two."

"You've got a gash on your forehead," Tess said, proud her voice was steady. "And you obviously have some kind of concussion. You were confused for a few minutes."

Clay fixed on Tess's face. "I'm not confused now, Tess. I know we're not at the lake anymore."

"No," Tess said, her heart aching. "No, we're not."

"I'm sorry we're not."

"Yes." Tess stood as Ella pushed through the ring of onlookers and crouched by Clay's side. Tess stepped back and whispered, "So am I."

❖

"I'm sorry, Ms. Sutter—"

"Enough with the Ms. Sutter already," Clay snapped. Bad enough she was the center of half the town's attention, spotlighted in the circle of light thrown out from the open bay doors of the emergency response van, without Ella lecturing her while she lay on her back like a helpless turtle. Strapped to a gurney, for Christ's sake. And where the hell had Tess gone so fast? Damn, if her head would just stop pounding for one damn minute she could think. Something she needed to—

"Clay." Ella folded her arms and spread her legs in that *I'm the Secret Service agent and you're the protectee* stance she had when she was about to pull rank.

"What, damn it?"

"I agree with the EMTs. You need to be evaluated at the hospital, and you're going to need stitches for that gash in your forehead."

"A few Steri-Strips will take care of that," Clay grumbled. "And I can tell you right now I've got a cracked rib or two, and it's not the first time. There's nothing they can do for that." She had laid her bike down a time or three, just never when Tess was with her. She recognized the grating pain and the restricted breathing. So she'd be stepping carefully for a few days. She couldn't afford to be out of commission now, and she couldn't appear to be less than 100 percent. In her world, the weak were cut from the pack, and for damn sure there were a few people looking on who would be happy to lend a hand. "As to the rest, bruises and bumps. I'll be fine. Now get me loose."

Tess appeared next to Ella and glared down at Clay. "I know it's none of my business, but Ella's right. Don't be pigheaded, Clay. It's not worth it."

Clay's gaze drifted from one to the other. Ella wore her usual unruffled, unmovable expression. Her I-am-a-stone-wall look. Tess looked half-worried and half-pissed off. She was mad again. And beautiful. Clay sighed. "There's something not right about two against one, especially when I can't move."

"Then don't argue." Ella's eyes glinted with subtle satisfaction. "If you go along with the medical recommendations, I won't file a report with your father. At least, not right now."

If Clay hadn't seen that secretly victorious expression a thousand times, she'd never know Ella was pleased. Ella knew she'd won, and all Clay could do was negotiate her surrender and save some dignity. "If I go, no report. Period."

Tess looked from one to the other. "This is ridiculous. Clay, you need—"

"It's all right, Tess," Ella said gently. "She just needs to define her terms."

"Of course," Tess said, retreating a pace. "You know what she needs—"

"Tess, wait," Clay said. "I need to speak to Ella in private, but… could you stay?"

"Yes." Tess looked uncertain. "But I—"

"Just for a minute. Please."

Tess's expression softened. "All right. Of course."

Clay looked at the EMT, a husky blond with close-cropped hair and the beginning of a beard. "Can I have a minute here?"

"Yeah, go ahead," he said, taping an intravenous catheter to Clay's arm. "As long as we don't get another call."

"Thanks," Clay said.

Tess drifted back and Ella leaned over. Voice low, Ella said, "What happened?"

"I can't swear to it, but I think this was intentional. I saw a vehicle—truck, I'm pretty sure—and thought it might be shadowing me. Whoever it was might just have been meaning to scare me, maybe didn't even intend to hit me."

Ella looked skeptical. "What exactly do you remember?"

"Not much." Frustrated, Clay tried to turn her head to search for Tess, but the EMTs had wrapped an immobilizer under her jaw and she couldn't move. "A pickup like any of the hundreds around here. I couldn't even tell you the make or model or color."

"Driver?"

"Nothing."

"They may not know you couldn't see anything," Ella said. "So let's keep what we know to ourselves."

"Ella." Clay grasped her wrist, pulled her closer. "Tess was close by. She might have seen something—right now she probably doesn't remember. But whoever was driving might *think* she saw more than she did."

Ella let out a breath, slow and steady. As close as she ever got to sighing. "She'll need protection."

"She can't know. She'll refuse." Clay blinked away a trickle of blood. "Get Kelly up here."

"I'll make the call." Ella gestured over her shoulder. A sheriff's cruiser with flashers swirling blocked the intersection. "I should stay here and talk to the investigating officers. They probably won't come up with anything, but if the vehicle has damage and someone brings it in for repair, we might be able to get some information."

"Go ahead," Clay said. "I'm not going to be in the ER very long."

Ella laughed softly. "You know, Clay, there might be some things even you can't control."

Clay grinned, trying not to take too deep a breath. "I'll let you know when I find one."

"I'll be there as soon as I can."

"Don't worry about it. I'll be fine." Clay closed her eyes. She trusted Ella, and this was too important to let feelings she had no business having to begin with stand in the way. "Will you see that Tess gets home okay?"

"I'll look after her." Ella motioned to the EMTs. "She's all yours. Take good care of her."

"You bet," a tall thin redhead with a thick braid swinging down her back said with a smile.

The two EMTs lifted the gurney until the suspension legs locked and wheeled Clay toward the waiting van. After they lifted Clay inside, the blond went to the front and climbed behind the wheel. Just as the redhead hopped in and started to pull the doors shut, Tess jumped in.

"I'm coming with her," Tess announced.

"Okay, sure," the EMT said. "Strap yourself into that jump seat up there."

"What are you doing, Tess?" Clay couldn't see her and held her hand in the air, trying to get her attention.

Tess leaned over her. "Ella's busy with the sheriff, and you're not going alone."

"Tess, you don't have to do this. I'm fine."

"Clay," Tess said firmly. "I'm doing Ella a favor. It's settled."

"Of course," Clay said, and closed her eyes. Tess and Ella. Not her business.

CHAPTER TWELVE

As the ambulance pulled into the space reserved for emergency vehicles behind Saratoga Hospital, the female EMT seated next to Tess said, "Here we are."

Tess released her seat belt. "I want to go in with her."

"Sure," the redhead said, "but the clerk will probably need you to fill out some paperwork first."

"I…" Tess looked at Clay, who had been silent for the twenty-five-mile trip. Only the strain lines around her eyes gave away the discomfort she was trying to hide. "Clay? Do you have an insurance card?"

Clay's eyes opened, the sharp brown Tess was used to smudged with pain. "Wallet. Left back pocket. Behind my license."

"Here," the EMT said. "I'll loosen her chest strap so you can get to it."

"This is getting to be a habit," Tess muttered, leaning over Clay to slide her hand around Clay's hip and into her back pocket.

"I could get used to it," Clay said.

Tess jerked back, wallet in hand, and stared at Clay. Her grin was filled with confidence, despite the tightness in her jaw and the pale cast to her face. Shaking her head, Tess laughed. "Now you're dreaming."

Some of the life came back into Clay's eyes. "Nice dream."

"You ready?" the EMT asked.

"Yes," Tess said, making room for the two EMTs to slide the stretcher out. She climbed down and hurried to reach Clay's side. She grasped Clay's hand as the double doors swung inward and the bright lights of the ER assaulted her eyes. "I'll see you in a few minutes."

Clay squeezed her fingers. "I'm okay. Don't worry."

"I'm not," Tess lied brightly. The last time she'd been here was the night Ray had come in from the field complaining his supper hadn't agreed with him. His face had been gray, his skin coated with sweat. Three hours later, he was gone. Not the same thing this time. Nothing like that. Tess forced her fingers to relax, letting Clay's hand go as two women and a man in medical garb descended on Clay. In seconds, they'd whisked her away. Just like that, Clay was gone too.

"Dear," a woman called from across the empty hall, "you want to give me some intake information?"

Tess jumped, the present snapping into focus. She was letting the past rule the present again, and she had to stop. Tired. She was just tired. "Yes, of course."

"What's her name?" The woman at the counter, a friendly-appearing middle-aged blonde, stared at a computer screen, typing with one hand while whisking a mouse in rapid circles with the other.

"Clay Sutter," Tess said through the open window.

The blonde looked up from her computer. "Sorry. I thought that was a woman."

"What? Oh…uh, it's Roberta. Roberta Sutter. Here," Tess told the clerk, pulling a thin stack of cards from behind the clear window in Clay's wallet, "I have her insurance card."

"Thanks." The blonde held out her hand and went back to typing.

Tess sorted the cards—driver's license, AAA, emergency contact—her breath caught. The photo was creased and worn. Her senior picture, taken right before she'd gone to the lake for the summer. Oh God, her hair had been so frizzy and the harsh makeshift studio light had made her nose too shiny. She hadn't had anything else to give Clay when she'd asked for a picture. They'd been sitting on the dock late one Friday night, just talking as they did so often, listening to the sounds of laughter carrying over the water from some boat passing on the far side of the lake, when Clay had tugged her close and whispered, with her mouth against Tess's ear, "I want a picture of my girl for my wallet."

The girl Tess had been so very long ago.

"You got that card, dear?"

"Yes," Tess said hoarsely, holding out the insurance card, "right here."

The woman took the card from Tess's trembling hand and said sympathetically, "Don't worry, honey. The ER team here is the best."

"Yes. Thanks." Tess smiled fleetingly and tucked the memory back into the past where it belonged.

❖

At three a.m. on a Saturday morning, the waiting room was deserted except for a distraught young mother sitting across from Tess with a screaming toddler in her arms, waiting anxiously for someone to take them back to the treatment area. They'd been there since Tess finished with the clerk, forty-five minutes ago.

"Earache," the young mother said, glancing apologetically over at Tess as she rocked the inconsolable child.

"It's awful when they're so miserable, isn't it," Tess said, "and there's nothing you can do?"

Something like relief appeared in the mother's eyes. "It makes me feel so helpless."

Tess had always thought animals and babies had a lot in common—so helpless, so unable to make their needs known. "Well, they'll take care of her soon. I bet she'll feel better by morning."

"I hope so." The mother patted the baby's back and stared at Tess for a moment. "Um, I hope everything's okay with…your friend."

"Thanks. Me too," Tess said softly.

A few minutes later, a nurse appeared and mercifully took mother and baby away. Tess checked her watch. Almost four. She'd have to call the farm, let Tomas know she wouldn't be there for the morning milking. She'd been waiting an hour—what were they doing with Clay that was taking so long, and why was she so upset? Farm accidents were all too common, and she'd tended to her share of friends, family, and farmhands who had suffered broken bones and lacerations and—thankfully, rarely—crushed limbs or parts thereof without losing her composure. But the sight of Clay bloody and disoriented had shaken her more than she'd imagined possible. As every minute ticked by, the anxious roiling in her stomach grew. What if Clay had one of those delayed internal brain hemorrhages you read about, the kind that kill people unexpectedly an hour or two after their accident? Clay had to have some kind of concussion—she hadn't known where she was at first. Tess's heart twisted.

Clay had thought they were at the lake. Why would Clay even

think of that now? So long ago for both of them. All right, so Tess hadn't forgotten, at least not completely. Weeks and months would go by when she wouldn't think of it—or Clay—and then she'd hear some snippet of music on one of the rock stations and she'd be back in the boathouse, seventeen again, watching Clay lean over the pool table, showing off as she beat some of the local boys at eight ball. Or the sun would glint off the windshield of a passing motorcycle, and the black-garbed rider hunched over the roaring engine would be Clay, turning into the twisting drive of the resort late on a Saturday afternoon to pick Tess up after she was done cleaning to take her spinning around the lake, the wind blowing in her face, her arms wrapped tightly around Clay's middle. Or sometimes, right before she fell asleep, a warm breeze would pass over her face and she'd remember the brush of Clay's mouth on her skin.

Shuddering, Tess stood and peered around the corner toward the treatment area. All of the cubicles were closed, their curtains drawn. Only three charts sat in the rack on the wall, and she heard the baby sobbing from somewhere down the hall. A hand appeared from inside the center cubicle and pushed the curtain back. A woman in blue jeans and a colorful smock decorated with action heroes stepped out and strode briskly down the hall.

"Are you with Roberta Sutter?"

"Clay? Yes. Can I—"

"You can go on back. She'll be ready to leave as soon as her scans are cleared."

"Oh, thank you." Tess hurried to the cubicle.

Clay sat on the side of the stretcher, her arms braced on either side of her hips. They'd taken away her shirt, and she wore a white hospital gown open in the back over her work pants. Her boots sat on the floor beside the stretcher. Steri-Strips covered the three-inch gash on her forehead, the center of each thin white strip dotted with a circle of dried blood.

"Did you get stitches?" Tess stopped a few feet in front of Clay as the curtain swung closed behind her.

"Yes." Clay grimaced. "Twenty-three, the tech was pleased to tell me."

"How do you feel?"

"I'm okay."

"Of course you are." Tess sighed. "And now, how do you feel?"

Clay laughed softly. "My head feels like someone's using it for a snare drum. Whatever they gave me for pain isn't helping, but it's making me sick to my stomach. And I really want to get out of here."

"I think they're just waiting to check your X-rays." Tess frowned. "Where are you staying?"

"The Rice Mansion."

"Well, I don't think they're going to want you to stay alone tonight." Tess flushed. "Although I guess Ella—"

"Ella's room is across the hall from mine," Clay said carefully. "I'm sure she can peek in on me if it's absolutely necessary."

"Oh," Tess said, feeling foolishly relieved. "Well, I imagine it will be. She'll probably be here soon."

"I'm really sorry about this, Tess."

"Why? None of it's your fault."

"Well, I guess that's open to question. Someone obviously has taken a dislike to me."

A chill rippled down the back of Tess's neck. "What are you talking about?"

Clay swore inwardly. She wasn't thinking clearly, or she never would have mentioned anything about the accident. "It's nothing."

"Don't," Tess said sharply. "Don't lie to me."

"I won't. I'm not," Clay said. "But I really don't know anything."

"But you suspect something?"

"I don't know, Tess." Clay wished the jackhammer behind her eyes would ease off for just a second so she could collect herself. She didn't want to pull Tess into her problems, but she'd just said she wouldn't lie to her. "I saw a vehicle behind me, a truck I think. I thought they were following me. Maybe they weren't. But I'm pretty certain they sped up when I stepped into the street."

Tess's face went white. "My God."

"Hey," Clay said. "It's okay. Don't worry—"

"I'm sorry? Don't worry? Someone might have tried to kill you and it's okay?" Tess's eyes flashed. "Is there something wrong with you? Don't you care what happens to you?"

"Most of the time, Tess, I don't think about much of anything except getting the job done." Clay was so tired she didn't even care she'd admitted something she never would have revealed to any other person at any other time. "That's all I have."

"Okay, enough of this," Tess said with odd gentleness. "When you're better, we'll talk."

"There's nothing to—"

The curtain slid back and a man with a five o'clock shadow in rumpled scrubs and a stethoscope around his neck said, "Well, you won't be spending the night with us. You've got bruised ribs, no breaks. Even better, your CAT scan looks fine. No fractures, no evidence of brain swelling. That doesn't mean you don't have a concussion, but the shake, rattle, and roll doesn't look too serious. You might have headaches on and off for a week or two, occasional blurriness of vision, or even a little nausea. As long as none of that persists for more than a few minutes, there's no problem." He held out a sheet of paper to Tess. "Here are the neuro-check instructions. You ought to check her every couple hours for the next ten or twelve and make sure none of the things on this list are a problem. If they are, bring her back."

"All right." Tess took the paper a little uncertainly.

The doctor turned to Clay. "If you're not a hundred percent in a week or two, follow up with a neurologist. You two drive carefully."

He was gone before Clay could thank him. She held out her hand to Tess. "I'll take that."

Tess put the paper behind her back, a defiant expression crossing her face. "And what are you going to do with it? Do your own neuro checks?"

"I was thinking I would give it to Ella."

"I'll give it to her after you're settled in bed."

"Damn it, Tess," Clay said, trying not to snarl. "By the time we get back, it's gonna be five in the morning and you need to be back at the farm. Don't you think I know when you have to start your day?"

"It won't be the first time I've been up all night, Clay. I think I can handle it."

"All right." Clay sighed. "I owe you."

Tess stared at her for a long moment. "No, Clay, you don't." She reached for Clay's shirt and grimaced. "You can't put this on. It's bloody."

Clay grinned. "I'm not going home in a hospital johnny."

"Maybe I can find a scrub shirt."

"It's just for an hour." Clay carefully slid off the stretcher and held out her hand. "I'll wear that."

"If you insist," Tess said dubiously. "Turn around, I'll untie you."

"I'll do it." Clay reached back and gasped. Her bruised rib cage screamed. "Okay. Maybe not." She turned her back. "Go ahead."

"God, Clay." Tess's hands played over Clay's back. "You're all scraped up and there's a huge welt on your side."

Clay braced a hand on the stretcher. The warmth of Tess's fingers bored into her, loosening her muscles and tightening other, deeper places. "Looks worse than it is."

"I hope so," Tess whispered.

The smock fell away and the heat of Tess's hands disappeared.

"I'll wait outside," Tess said abruptly. She dropped Clay's shirt on the stretcher and disappeared around the curtain, leaving Clay alone.

Clay eased into her shirt, the pain a distant echo, buried by the pleasure of Tess's touch. She knew it was foolish, but she let herself enjoy the lingering presence of Tess's hands on her skin. There'd be time enough tomorrow for regret. There always was.

CHAPTER THIRTEEN

The pastel-striped curtain swung closed, leaving Tess alone in the brightly lit hallway. She couldn't quite get her breath. Clay's battered back haunted her. Bruises—scrapes, that was all. They would all heal. Clay would be fine. A trickle of relief loosened the iron band around her chest.

Breathe. She ought to be able to breathe now. She took a few steps, leaned against the cool plaster walls. The pounding in her head eased but the fire in her blood still raged. Her hands burned as if they were living beings, apart from her, unbound by reason. The merest touch of Clay's skin had turned the key on wants and desires she had successfully locked away, until now. And now all she could see, all she could feel, was Clay.

Once, Clay had been reed thin, all sinew and muscle, her hips as narrow as one of the boys, her ass almost too small to hold up the black jeans that had hung low on her hips, bunching over the tops of her heavy black motorcycle boots. Those muscles were still there, more than she remembered even, harder and more defined. Clay's shoulders were wider, stronger-looking. But what had captured her, what enthralled her still, was the subtle arch of Clay's lower back curving into the swell of her hips—hips that offered an invitation to caress she'd barely declined. Clay was a virtual stranger, a woman she did not know. And still she had wanted to explore those curves with the wild abandon that had propelled her into those reckless motorcycle rides over twisting, tantalizing country roads. She'd wanted to let go—of memory, sadness, rejection, and remorse. She'd wanted the unfettered freedom of an unfettered heart. She was losing her mind.

Tess closed her eyes. Clay was a woman she barely knew, she was hurt, and she wasn't her Clay any longer.

"Hey," a soft voice called, and Tess opened her eyes.

No, Clay wasn't hers.

Ella was just coming down the hall, and Tess walked to meet her.

"How is she?" Ella looked as cool as ever, but the icy blue of her eyes flared with intensity.

"She's pretty banged up, but they didn't find anything serious. The doctor just cleared her to go." Tess pointed to the center cubicle. The curtain was still closed. It took almost more energy than she had to resist going back to see if Clay needed help. It wasn't her place to help her. Ella was here now. "She's getting dressed."

"Good. I'll go get her." Ella grabbed a wheelchair from a row of them lined up along the wall. "The SUV is right outside. You look like you could use some air."

Tess smiled wanly. "That bad, huh?"

"No, not really." Ella laughed. "It's been a long night and probably a tough one, considering the patient."

"She's been pretty good, really," Tess said. "But she needs to slow down for a day or two. The doctor said she's probably going to have some aftereffects."

"Post-concussive symptoms," Ella murmured. "Keeping her quiet is not going to be easy."

"I'm glad it's your job instead of mine," Tess said.

"Really?" Ella asked gently.

Tess felt her face burn. Somehow she knew Clay had not told Ella anything about their past relationship, but Ella was perceptive, and she'd been too distracted since the accident, worrying about Clay, to worry about what she might be revealing. She wondered how much was obvious. Not that there was very much to reveal. She and Clay had history, but it was a long, long time ago. She didn't know this Clay any more than Clay knew her. They were connected, if they were connected at all, by memories, and memories were notoriously inaccurate. Tess met Ella's softly questioning gaze directly and answered with total conviction. "Yes, really. You know Clay, I don't. And I'm sure you wouldn't be here if you weren't the best person to look after her."

"Well, I certainly haven't done much of a job tonight." Ella grimaced. "What happened is my responsibility. My fault."

Tess leaned her shoulder against the wall and studied Ella. "I wouldn't bet the farm, but I'd bet a lot that you argued with her not to go wandering around so late, and you lost."

"Your wager would be safe, only the problem isn't who won or lost, but that there was any discussion to begin with." Ella shook her head. "I should know better than to get too close. Friendship impairs judgment."

Friendship. Ella hadn't said *a personal relationship*. She'd said friendship. Of course, Ella was a professional, she wouldn't reveal anything personal about Clay. If there was something personal. Tess shook her head. She was too tired to guess. And what did it matter? "I imagine it's very difficult, spending so much time together, especially if Clay is...difficult, sometimes."

Ella smiled. "I know you two didn't just meet, so I won't bother to protect my boss's reputation and argue that she takes well to being guarded all the time. But I like what I do, and I like doing it for Clay."

"I'm glad she has you," Tess said, all the more confused because she meant it. "She's probably ready by now. I'll go get that air and meet you at the car."

"Thanks, Tess, for stepping in tonight. I needed you. So did Clay."

"I doubt that, but you're welcome." Tess hurried outside. Ella was right. She did need some air. And some distance. Everyone from the EMTs to the young mother in the waiting room to the ER staff had thought she and Clay were together, and at times she'd almost forgotten they weren't. The realization that she could so easily slip into a fantasy world again was terrifying.

The sun was up and Tess blinked, disoriented. The long night had seemed to drift between the present and the past effortlessly, as if the boundaries of time had dissolved and she was simultaneously in two places at once, the feelings she'd had long ago as fresh and vibrant as anything she knew in the present. Everyone seemed to think she and Clay were somehow involved, connected, and nothing could be further from the truth. Every once in a while she'd caught a glimpse of the wild, heart-stopping renegade Clay had been, in the curve of her mouth, the glint of her eyes, the low seductive tenor of her laugh. And when she had, her heart yearned.

But this Clay, the woman who had appeared out of the haze

late on a summer day, was closer to a potential enemy than a friend, and certainly no lover. And not even an old photo Clay had probably forgotten was even in her wallet could change that. Clay wasn't here for her. Clay had come for what lay under the land, and if it hadn't been for that, Clay would not be here. Tess would have gone on with the rest of her life knowing nothing of Clay. This woman who'd stepped out of the past into the present was not the girl she had known, the girl she had loved. Clay was as much a stranger to her as Ella, maybe even more so. Ella seemed to want to know her, seemed to see her as more than an obstacle to achieving a goal. Clay had come to take what was hers. That was not going to happen.

The ER doors whisked open and Ella pushed Clay out in a wheelchair. A light sweat misted Clay's forehead, and every bit of color had leached from her face. She was in pain, another thing Tess could do nothing to change. Sadness, heavy and dark, pulled at her, and she pushed back at the mental clouds by forcing her body to move. She hurried to the SUV parked behind an ambulance twenty yards away and opened the rear door just as Ella maneuvered the wheelchair alongside.

Clay braced both hands on the arms of the chair and started to push herself up.

"Wait." Tess gripped her elbow. "Go slow. Changing position is probably going to make you dizzy."

Clay leaned against Tess as she got to her feet. She swayed. "Understatement."

Ella backed the chair away. "Do you have her?"

"Yes." Tess slid an arm around Clay's waist. Clay didn't argue for once, and that was almost as worrisome as the fine tremor coursing through Clay's body. Tess tightened her hold. "Here, the seat is right behind you. Hold on to me and just ease down inside."

"Why don't you ride in the back with her," Ella said.

Tess started to protest, but Ella was already on her way around to the other side of the SUV. Tess could either argue for no good reason, or follow Clay inside and make sure she was settled. She climbed in next to Clay and pulled the door closed.

Clay leaned her head back against the seat and shut her eyes. "If I find out who did this to me, I may have to run them over just so they know how bad it feels."

"Everyone secure?" Ella asked.

Tess leaned over Clay and hunted around for her seat belt. She clicked the buckle and then fastened her own. She felt a little silly being chauffeured around, but if she'd been sitting in the front seat, she would have spent the entire ride back turning around to check that Clay was all right. She might as well ride back here where she would know. "Ready as we'll ever be."

"Let me know if you want me to stop," Ella said.

The vehicle glided smoothly out of the parking lot, and Clay groaned softly. "The car's going in one direction and my stomach in the other."

"Here. Lie down." Tess loosened Clay's seat belt and drew her down until Clay's head was in her lap. "Try not to move too much. Maybe you can sleep."

"Is it tomorrow?" Clay murmured.

"Yes. About five in the morning."

Clay pressed her cheek to Tess's lower belly and closed her eyes. "I'm sorry, Tess. I really screwed up your night."

Tess laughed at the absurdity of it all. Clay, who had roared into her life and taken her to places she'd never imagined, then dashed her dreams and broken her heart, apologizing for something totally beyond her control. What was one lost night compared to so many of them? "Please don't apologize any more. You couldn't help what happened."

"Maybe. I don't know." Clay sighed, sliding her hand around Tess's waist. "I thought I was doing the right thing, the only thing. It wasn't fair, making you pay for who I was."

Tess froze. "What are you talking about?"

The steady hum of the SUV's powerful engine was the only sound. Clay's breath warmed Tess's belly.

"Clay?" Even through her cotton shirt, the heat of Clay's hand on Tess's back was like a torch flaming against her skin. So hot, when inside she was so cold. She wanted to grab her, shake her. Scream at her to speak, to tell her at last something, anything, *why.* Most of all why. "What did you do?"

"I don't know," Clay said at last. "Nothing. It doesn't matter now."

"Maybe you're right. Don't worry about it now." Ashamed of her own selfishness, Tess rested her hand on Clay's shoulder to steady her against the vehicle's subtle motion. Browbeating Clay when she was barely aware of her surroundings wasn't going to get her any answers.

Clay's breathing softened into the slow, deep rhythm of sleep as the vehicle knifed over the empty roads. Already, heat rose off the soft blacktop in waves that distorted the horizon. The fields and distant mountains shimmered in and out of focus, much like Tess's thoughts. Clay seemed to carry a deep well of sadness, pain she recognized, a reflection of her own. Tess stroked Clay's hair, let her fingers linger on the warm skin of her neck. She'd so rarely had the chance to protect Clay. Clay had always supported her, protected her, made her feel unique and precious. She'd warned off overeager boys who wouldn't accept polite refusals, softened Ray's criticisms of Tess's dreams for the farm by assuring Tess she could do anything, banished her insecurities with whispered words of desire. With Clay she had grown certain, confident, bold.

Tess sighed. So many good things she'd forgotten, buried by anger and hurt. Clay hadn't been much older than her, and she ought to be forgiven her broken promises—most people's pasts were littered with them. Tess ran a strand of sleek dark hair through her fingers. She could try to forgive the girl Clay had been, but that would not change the present. Nothing good could come of Clay being here now.

Tess looked up, caught Ella watching them in the rearview mirror. Her eyes were soft with sympathy. For Tess. For Clay?

"She's all right," Tess whispered.

Ella nodded and turned her gaze back to the road. Tess wondered what had shown in her face. But then, what could show? All she felt was numb.

CHAPTER FOURTEEN

Ella parked the SUV behind the B&B and turned to Tess and Clay. "We're here."

"Clay," Tess whispered. "Wake up."

"Tell Ella to drive around some more," Clay muttered, holding on to Tess more firmly. She'd been to bed with women who hadn't excited her, or comforted her, as much as spending the last forty minutes wrapped up in Tess.

"Why?" Tess asked.

"I like the way you smell. A little bit like clover and sunshine."

"I think that's one of my cows you're taken with," Tess said, her voice oddly husky.

"Cows are nice too." Clay didn't need to open her eyes to know Tess was frowning, two small vertical creases etched between her red-gold brows. Tess wouldn't want compliments from her. So she wouldn't tell her she felt even better than she smelled—firm and smooth under Clay's cheek. Clay wished she could taste her skin. She bet it would be warm as honey. She wouldn't tell Tess that either. "Cows or not, I'm not moving."

"Yes, you are," Tess said, laughter and a tiny sliver of irritation in her voice. "I've got a farm to run, and you need to be in bed."

Clay opened her eyes a fraction. Tess's shirt was a rich, vibrant yellow. Must be why she smelled like sunshine. "What day is it?"

"Saturday."

"Hmm." She closed her eyes again and burrowed closer. "What are you doing today?"

"What? Oh—if I hurry, I'll make it before the end of the milking, so I can get the stats on the morning yield, make sure the herd is all right. The vet is coming at eight to vaccinate the calves. I need to get soil samples for the state—" Tess halted. "God, Clay. You don't want to hear this boring stuff."

"I do, Tess," Clay murmured, envisioning Tess striding around the farm, confident and intense and at home. Tess had made her believe in home, once upon a time. "I've always imagined you on the farm. Happy. I wish I could help."

"You can." Tess's voice had grown distant, lost its gentle warmth. "You can find some other place to dig your wells. Somewhere away from our farms and our water."

"What if there isn't any other place?" Clay whispered, not even sure she'd spoken loud enough for Tess to hear. But she must have. Tess's hand on her back was gone. The soft caress of fingers through her hair only a memory.

The SUV door opened and Ella said, "Need a hand?"

"Yes," Tess said.

"No," Clay said. "Go away."

"Okay," Tess said. "Ella, you take her feet and I'll take her—"

"All right, all right," Clay said. "I'll move."

"Careful," Tess said quickly.

Clay sat up slowly, waiting for her head or stomach to rebel. Neither did. The headache was ferocious, but her stomach had settled, and when she opened her eyes partway and carefully peered out the window, her vision seemed normal until the bright light struck her retinas and transformed into ice picks. She slammed her eyes closed. "Ow, damn it."

"What? What is it?" Tess gripped Clay's arm.

Clay didn't want to get out of the SUV, not because moving was going to hurt—she'd survive that—but because Tess was beside her, and the anger and distrust that had stood between them like a stone wall had tumbled down. A temporary reprieve. Once they left the vehicle, they would both be thrown back into their separate lives, and Tess would be lost to her again. But she couldn't keep her here under false pretenses, either. It wasn't fair to play on her sympathies. Tess's caring nature was just one of the things that made her so special. Tess truly, genuinely cared about all living things—animals, plants, people. She would reach out, offering help or solace or encouragement, to anyone who needed it. Clay didn't want to be just one of the many who was lucky enough to benefit from Tess's tenderness. Not when she knew what it was like to be the only one, the heart of Tess's heart. She gently drew away from Tess's hold.

"I'm okay now, I'm ready."

When Clay opened her eyes, she saw something that might have been regret pass across Tess's face, before Tess smiled fleetingly and slid out of the car. In the next second, Ella leaned in, one hand extended. Clay grasped it and slowly climbed out of the vehicle. As she stood, Ella's hand came to rest on her waist where Tess's had been, respectful and supportive. Ella's boundaries had always been unassailable, but she somehow still let Clay know she cared.

"Thanks," Clay said.

Ella said, "I'm glad the original owner had that elevator put in so he could get upstairs from his car without people seeing him in the main house. Can you make it?"

"If we go slow," Clay muttered. Every breath was a punch in the chest and her stomach was back to threatening revolt. She was not going to get sick in front of Tess.

"Lean on me if you need to," Ella said.

Tess closed the SUV door and stepped away. "I'll be going."

"Tess, wait." Clay searched frantically for some way to keep Tess from walking away. What could she say? *Can you forget why I came—who I am? What I've done? What I will do?* With no words that might not be lies, she called, "Thanks."

Tess looked back over her shoulder. "Listen to Ella. Get some rest."

Clay stood still, letting Ella think she needed another minute to get her legs under her, but really just waiting until Tess disappeared around the corner. Suddenly more tired than she could ever recall, she sagged slightly. Ella was there, her arm sliding more firmly around Clay's waist. Ella was taller than Tess, more muscular, and when Clay let herself lean into her, Ella's scent was cool and crisp, like an ocean breeze. Tess was earth, Ella the sea.

"Did you know she'd be all tied up in this before we got here?" Ella asked.

"No," Clay said. "I knew she'd be here, but not right in the middle of it all. I walked into this pretty much blind."

"Maybe you should walk out again."

Clay tensed and a shaft of the pain pierced her chest. She drew a shallow breath. "They'll just send someone else. At least with me, she'll get a fair deal."

"You might not want to voice that opinion out loud." Ella guided Clay toward the back entrance. "Especially around any of the project people. Their loyalty is to the one whose name is on their paycheck."

"I guess I'm lucky you're not a corporate spy, then." Clay waited while Ella opened the door and held it for her. "Although I imagine you've been asked to provide intelligence on me."

Ella met her gaze. "The corporation provides my paycheck, but I've always considered that I work for you. Not NorthAm Fuel."

"Or my father?"

Ella's gaze didn't waver. "Or your father."

"But he's asked you, hasn't he? To keep him updated?"

"Of course, frequently." Ella smiled. "You have been known to drop off the grid."

"And since we've been here?"

"Yes."

A cold hand reached in and squeezed Clay's heart. "Did he mention Tess?"

The rippling blue seas in Ella's eyes iced over. Polar caps, dense and impenetrable. "Yes."

Clay gritted her teeth. "When?"

"Apparently you weren't answering your phone for anyone last night, not just me. He wanted a progress report. I informed him you'd probably have something for him soon, and I'd pass on the message."

"And?"

"He asked about landowners, and he mentioned Tess." Ella pressed the button to call the small elevator down to their level. "He wanted to know if she presented any kind of special problems."

"Special problems." Clay started to shake her head and abruptly stopped when a geyser of pain shot out the top of her skull. "By that he means am I losing my perspective. Taking my eye off the ball."

Ella regarded her steadily. "Are you?"

The elevator door slid open and Clay stepped inside. "No."

❖

Tess walked quickly through the early-morning streets. At not quite six on a Saturday morning, the usual hustle and bustle of contractors, electricians, and other tradesmen ferrying supplies from the Agway and hardware store to pickups and flatbeds was absent. Farmers were busy with morning chores in barns and fields, and truckers with long-distance hauls had grabbed breakfast in the diner at three or four a.m. and were long gone. A runner or two passed by, barely noticing her, absorbed in the music from their iPods or the beat of their own hearts. An elderly woman being pulled along by a squat, fat dachshund smiled and gave her a wave. Tess waved back and a bit of the fatigue weighing on her shoulders lifted away.

"Beautiful day," the woman said.

"Yes, it is," Tess replied absently, her attention on her truck. The Ford was where she'd left it the night before, three blocks from the bed-and-breakfast, across the street from the now-closed Sly Fox Tavern. She slowed as she approached, eyeing Jimmy Larsen, who leaned against the front of her truck.

"Jimmy?" Tess asked.

The young man spun around, saw her, and smiled broadly. "Hi, Ms. Rogers. I saw your truck sitting out here and thought maybe I should keep an eye on it. It was here all night, right?"

"Thanks, Jimmy." Feeling awkward, Tess halted by the driver's door. "Are you working at the feed store today?"

"Not till noon." Jimmy loped around the front of the truck to join her.

Tess wanted to get home, but he'd been trying to do her a favor and she appreciated the thought, however unnecessary. "How'd you know my truck was here since last night?"

"Oh." Jimmy shrugged. "Everybody heard about what happened pretty quick. I came over to see, but you were busy. When I saw the truck still here this morning, I figured you'd be back for it sooner or later."

"Well, it was probably safe but I appreciate you looking after it." Tess pulled her keys from her pocket where they'd been all night. She'd left the house with nothing but her wallet and keys, not expecting to be out very long. Luckily she'd managed to hold on to both, although she had no memory of putting her keys in her pocket when she'd heard the crash. Her stomach lurched. When she'd heard the truck hit Clay. God, she could have been killed.

"You okay, Tess?" Jimmy asked, moving a step closer.

"Yes, fine," Tess said, smiling to prove her point. "But I'm running late. Thanks again."

"Oh sure, anytime." He gripped the top of her door when she unlocked it, pulling it the rest of the way open, holding it for her as if she were about to enter a fine hotel. She slid behind the wheel and reached for the handle to pull it closed. He looked much bigger standing beside the truck, looming over her, than he had when she was outside. "Bye, Jimmy."

His smile never wavered. "So how is she? The one from the drilling company."

"She's fine. Luckily nothing serious." Tess didn't want anyone thinking Clay was vulnerable, even though she had no reason to believe Clay was still in danger.

"I guess she was lucky this time, huh?"

"This time?" A chill raced down Tess's spine.

"Well, you know, accidents and stuff are pretty common in that line of work."

"I suppose so. Although this had nothing to do with her work."

He was silent for a moment. Then nodded slowly. "I suppose not."

Tess tugged on the door. "Well, I'd better be going. Chores."

"Right." He let go of the door and stepped back an inch. "If you need me to put in some extra hours or want anything delivered special, you just let me know. Anytime."

"I'll do that. Bye now." She pulled the door closed and carefully eased the truck forward, afraid she might run over his feet if he didn't move back a little bit more. Finally he did.

She turned the corner and at last she was free. Heading toward home, she rolled down her windows to let in the morning air and the first heat of the day swept in with it. She wondered if Clay was asleep yet. If Ella was with her. For an instant, she imagined Ella sitting on the side of Clay's bed, her hand resting on Clay's shoulder or her face. The intimacy pierced her and she ruthlessly cut the image from her mind. "It's not your place to wonder. Or to care. Why can't you remember that?"

As she drove the last few miles to the farm, she forced herself to review the things she needed to do that day. By the time she arrived, she'd almost forgotten the worry-filled hours in the hospital, the press of Clay's face against her abdomen, and the way Clay's arm circled her waist—possessively, trustingly. She might have forgotten all of it if she hadn't still felt Clay's hair gliding between her fingertips and the warmth of her breath against her skin.

The sight of her big red barn standing sentry over the sweeping fields of corn and soybeans and hay soothed away the hard edges of the night, and she pulled into the dirt lot in front of the main barn with a sigh of relief. So good to be home. Cutting the engine, she jumped out and hurried inside. Tomas already had the last of the cows in the milking stations.

"I'm so sorry," Tess said. "I couldn't get back in time."

"That's all right, I heard what happened. Everything's all right now, I hope."

"Yes, I think so." She watched the creamy milk flowing through the clear tubes to the vacuum pipes. "How was the yield this morning?"

"About the same. So far, the feed is holding up and they're all looking pretty good. The well is starting to run a little low, though." He shook his head and stated the obvious. "We sure could use some rain."

"Yes. We could."

Tess kept busy in the barn, checking the calves and waiting for the vet. They didn't finish with the examinations, the paperwork, the vaccinations, the tagging, and all the other things she needed to do to certify to the state that her herd was healthy until midday. Finally, with nothing more than lunch and a cool glass of lemonade on her mind, she drove back along the road that bordered the farm and turned into her drive. Pete Townsend's truck was parked in her dooryard. Sighing, she got out and found him sitting on the steps of her front porch. "Hi, Pete."

"Tess," he said, rising. He slapped his cap against his jeans and bits of golden pollen floated into the air. "Saw you truck over to the big barn. Thought you'd be coming in around about now. Heard about the ruckus last night. Any more news about what happened?"

"Not that I'm aware of."

He shook his head. "Can't say that woman's in for anything except trouble the longer she's here."

Tess pressed her palms to her thighs. She wasn't inclined to fight by nature, but her hands wanted to curl into fists. "What do you mean?"

"Well, she's not too popular with quite a few folks. She been around to talk to you yet?"

"Not in any detail."

"I suspect she will. Whatever they offer you for the land, it's probably not going to be enough. I wouldn't be signing anything away—"

"Pete," Tess said, holding on to her temper by a thread. "I appreciate your concern, really. But I'm not about to make any hasty decisions. About the drilling or about selling."

He smiled a little paternally, a little leeringly as his eyes dropped down her body and back to her face so quickly she might have imagined it. But she knew she hadn't.

"I'm sure that's the case," Pete said. "You're not the hasty type. But I hope you give things due consideration…about the drilling and about my offer. I promise you we could work out something that was suitable for both of us."

"I'll do that." As if she would be swayed by the promise of a fair deal from a man who thought she didn't know the worth of her own land.

"See you at the Grange meeting tonight?"

"I'll be there."

"Good. That's real good." Pete settled his cap back onto his head and walked past her, his body nearly brushing hers. She didn't move back when he passed.

Once he'd driven out and left her finally, blessedly alone, she went to the kitchen to prepare her lunch. The folder Clay had left with Ray's paperwork sat on the table like an unanswered invitation. Pausing on the way to the refrigerator, she stared at the folder and picked up the phone. She dialed the number she already knew by heart.

"Hello?"

"Leslie? Hi. It's Tess."

"Hi, Tess! I was just thinking about you. It was so great seeing you."

"Well, you might not think so when I tell you why I called."

"I'm sitting down. Go ahead."

Tess laughed. She'd forgotten how good it was to have a friend. "I think Ray might've gotten me into some trouble with NorthAm. They made him an offer for drilling rights on the land and he was apparently negotiating with them. I think money might've changed hands."

"I think you need representation," Leslie said, the laughter gone from her voice.

"So do I. I want to hire you."

"All right. I'll need to look at the paperwork. Can you scan it and e-mail it to me?"

"I don't have a scanner here, but I can do it on Monday in the village."

"That's probably soon enough. In the meantime, don't worry about it. You need to be prepared, though. You might be looking at a lengthy negotiation here."

"I'm used to waiting," Tess said, squinting out the window into the bright cloudless sky. Not a hint of rain. "I'm a farmer, after all."

Chapter Fifteen

The Grange was a square, wood-frame box sitting at the four corners where a spur of the Delaware & Hudson Railroad had once connected the industrial cities along the Hudson River to the farms upstate. Farmers built their barns along the tracks so the train could off-load goods and machinery and pick up produce, hay, milk, and beef. Now the tracks were paved over, forming one of the main county roads joining the rural communities dotted over the countryside. The narrow two-lane intersecting the former rail line bordered the north hundred acres of Tess's farm.

Tess decided to walk the two miles to the Grange for the meeting. Maybe the exercise would work out some of the knots in her neck and shoulders. The twinges and cramps had gotten steadily worse throughout the long afternoon and evening, reminding her of the sleep she'd missed. Not that a lost night was all that unusual—she'd gone plenty of nights without sleep over the years, waiting on a new calf to show up, watching the weather reports while hoping to beat a ten-day rain with an early haying. Catnapping was her specialty—anytime, any place—curled up in the cab of her truck, on an old shirt spread over a pile of hay in the barn, in the porch swing. Not today, though. She'd tried to nap but couldn't. Even with all the windows open in her shady north-facing, second-floor bedroom, the solid mass of air crowding inside was heavy and hot. Not a breath of a breeze.

She'd tossed and turned on top of the sheets for twenty minutes, reliving the memory of Clay lying in the street, dazed and bleeding, and the sight of her naked back, bruised and beautiful all at the same time, and the way Clay's face had softened in sleep, making her appear at once vulnerable and desirable. She'd lain awake thinking of the many facets of Clay, her skin tingling and her blood racing, excited in a way no other woman had ever been able to arouse her. And what bothered her most of all was knowing it wasn't memory that tormented her, but a woman who loomed large on the canvas of her life right now. Clay wasn't a figment of her imagination or a girl viewed through the cloudy lens of time. She was a handsome, confident, sexy woman whose voice struck long-silent chords in Tess's heart. Irritated with herself for being so susceptible to Clay's charm all over again, she'd finally gotten up, showered, and dressed, killing time until she could leave by reading one of the novels she'd been meaning to get to for weeks. Never mind that she had to keep rereading page after page when she realized she didn't know what her eyes had just passed over. At least she'd kept herself occupied and thoughts of drowning-dark eyes and a seductive grin at bay.

At eight p.m., the sun finally dropped over the horizon and a faint breeze promised a little cooling overnight. She walked along the side of the road, assessing her fields and those of her neighbors. The earth was dusty and cracked, like the parched lips of a lost soul wandering in the desert. The corn was half the height it should be, yellowing at the base of the stalks, the shoots raggedy from insects, the fledgling plants unable to fight both the unending heat and the onslaught of nature's pests. Soybeans were stunted, and hay grew too slowly for even a second cutting when it should have been ready for a third. The cows slumped with heads drooping, tails swishing listlessly in whatever bits of shade they could find under the trees along the edges of the pastures. Every living thing—human, animal, and plant—wilted in the unrelenting drought.

Finally she picked up her pace and stopped torturing herself with images of a woman she didn't want in her life and weather she couldn't change.

Pickup trucks filled the gravel lot in front of the white clapboard Grange building and both sides of the road adjacent to it. The big double doors at the top of the four wide wooden steps stood open, held there by iron planters used as doorstops. The slatted black shutters were folded back from the open windows. Men and women stood outside, talking and smoking. Tess nodded to some and made her way inside. Rows of wooden chairs formed uneven lines in the single large room. A wooden table along with four rickety chairs sat in the center of a makeshift platform stage at the front. The village board members and the Grange president congregated in a cluster in one corner drinking coffee, waiting for everyone to straggle in and sit down. Tess searched for a seat on the side of the room opposite where Pete Townsend held court with several of the larger landowners. Making her way down a narrow row, she said hello to Cliff Wright, her nearest neighbor.

"Keep me company," Cliff said, motioning to the seat next to him, "and maybe I'll stay awake."

"How are things over at the farm?" Tess settled onto the slat-backed chair next to Cliff and tried to find a comfortable position. Cliff was a jovial man in his midfifties, of irrepressible good humor and optimism. Tonight, even he looked a little weary.

"Oh," Cliff said with a hint of his usual good nature, "we're doing all right. Watching the sky and doing what we can. I was thinking I might get Joni to do a rain dance one of these nights if it don't rain soon. You know, one of those moon rites that are supposed to call up the woman spirits from the earth and whatnot."

Tess laughed. "Why do I think you're serious?"

His blue eyes twinkled. "Well, if it doesn't rain, at least it will be a good show."

Tess looked around the room. "If she hears you, you're going to be in trouble."

"She's home—we've got a cow about to freshen. She wants to make sure the baby's all right."

"Well then, you're safe for a while."

"It might work even better if there were two females doing the dance—you're welcome to come and join her."

Tess regarded him solemnly for a moment. "Does this perhaps require being sky-clad?"

Cliff laughed, his ample belly shaking over his faded jeans. "I haven't heard that since Woodstock. And I do believe it does."

"Well," Tess said contemplatively, "I really *do* want it to rain."

"I'll have Joni call you if she gets adventurous." He laughed again and they both looked forward as three men and a woman scraped back their chairs on the plank floor and took seats behind the table facing the crowd.

The room slowly quieted, except for the shuffling of feet and a few people clearing their throats. Once in a while a cell phone chirped, and someone would mutter *sorry*.

Most of the business was the usual affairs of a small town—what roads were on the docket to be resurfaced and which ones would have to wait until the next year, a proposal to ban the dumping of discarded oil and gas tanks and heavy machine parts in the local large-refuse area, another to enforce the long-ignored ordinance against butchering game on private property. The arguments flowed back and forth between those who opposed regulating what a person could do on their own land and those who insisted the practice was a health risk and some who just enjoyed a good squabble.

Finally everyone agreed to table the more contentious items and investigate what neighboring counties had done to resolve similar issues.

Tess listened with half an ear, knowing that nothing major would be decided and any changes would be small and not likely to substantially alter the way of life in the local community. No one really wanted anything to change, at least not the kind of change that might threaten the independence everyone prized. Sometimes progress was slower in coming, but most people valued the benefits of preserving what mattered most—the vitality of the way of life the community had known for hundreds of years. Everyone enjoyed a good gossip about who was doing what where and maybe with whom, but in the end, live and let live was more than an empty aphorism.

Finally, the Grange president, Sybil Worth, a widow who now ran the family franchise, rose and said, "I think it's time we talked about the issue that I know a lot of you are here to discuss. That's the drilling that's about to go on around here. We've debated the pros and cons in the last few years, but until a thing is about to happen, that's all it is—talk. Now we might need to make some decisions."

Pete Townsend stood up. "I don't think there's much deciding that's necessary. This drilling could endanger the livelihoods of most of the people in this room." He looked around, his gaze lingering on Tess for a moment before moving on. "We need to stop them before they get started."

"And how do you plan to do that, Pete?" Herb Brown, the owner of a big brush clearing business, called out from the back of the room. "Shoot 'em?"

"By any means necessary."

"Well, I don't think we all agree with that," said Don Walsh, a dairyman from the eastern part of the county, standing up and facing Pete. "Some of us have made agreements with NorthAm. They're willing to pay us good money for limited access on our land, and I for one think that the money they're gonna bring into the community—and you can bet there'll be a lot of it—is gonna be good for all of us." He turned to Tess. "You've got a big spread right close to NorthAm's main camp. They'll be drilling near you or on your land, if you'll let 'em. What do you think about it, Tess?"

She stood, the gaze of everyone in the room shifting to her as she rested both hands on the back of the wooden chair in front of her. She gazed around at her friends and neighbors before facing the town board and Grange president. Nothing like the looming advent of fracking had divided community sentiment since the move to reforest clear-cut pastureland and preserve some of the mountainous areas a century before. Whatever she said, she'd make some people angry.

"The most important thing to me is that my land stays clean and the water stays safe for my herd and my crops. Right now, I don't know how to judge what the danger really is. I'm no chemist or geologist. But bringing the fuel company into our lives is about more than whether some people make money or whether the community benefits with new roads or if there's a real danger to some of us that might not ever actually happen. We need to make smart decisions now so we don't box ourselves into a corner in the future—for or against drilling."

"Well, how do you expect to get that information?" Pete said, his tone and body language a challenge. "You sure as hell can't expect NorthAm to provide it."

"That's not the case." Tess tried to keep her anger from showing in her voice. If the discussion deteriorated into bickering, they'd get nowhere. "Clay…Clay Sutter, the head of the project, said her team can look at the water table and backflow projections and give me a risk assessment affecting my land. I imagine anyone else who wants to get—"

"And you trust her?" Pete scoffed. "Why in hell should you? Why do you expect Sutter to tell you the truth? All her and her company care about is getting what's under the ground. She won't care about what happens to those of us who have to stay here when NorthAm has its wells and she leaves for the next project."

"I don't think you can automatically assume that NorthAm, or the people who run it, don't care about what happens here." Tess wasn't sure how she found herself arguing for Clay's side of things, but she didn't like being pushed into corners, and she didn't like making decisions without all the facts. And she especially didn't like the way Pete seemed to be singling out Clay, making her the face of the enemy. The decision came easily when she thought about what she wanted—the truth. "I'm going to let them run their tests on my land."

"Well, you can help them out all you want," Pete said, "but there's no reason any of the rest of us have to believe what they say."

"What I would suggest," Clay said from the back of the room, "is that you also get an independent group to verify our findings."

Every head in the room turned toward the back as Clay walked confidently down the aisle. Tess doubted anyone but her, and probably Ella, would know Clay was holding herself stiffly. Her gait never faltered and not a flicker of pain showed in her face. Clay smiled at Tess for an instant before stopping in front of the table and turning to face the room.

"I'm sorry I haven't had a chance to talk to any of you before this. I'm Clay Sutter, and I'm in charge of the NorthAm project here. I know we've taken a lot of you by surprise, and I hope that I'll be able to answer all your questions over the next few weeks." She looked at Pete, nothing showing in her face. "Even yours."

A few people laughed and Pete scowled. Tess slowly sat, watching the cool, confident, commanding woman slowly charm most of the people in the room with her candor and willingness to listen to their concerns. After spending days trying not to think about Clay, Tess finally admitted she wanted to know everything about her.

CHAPTER SIXTEEN

Facing the room full of mostly suspicious farmers, Clay resisted the urge to lean back against the table that sat on the edge of the low platform behind her. Couldn't look tired this early in the game. She stood straight and fielded questions, ignoring the thinly veiled accusations of greed and dishonesty that underlay some of the comments. She answered what she could, admitted what she didn't know, and offered solutions. And she made mental notes on which speakers were the most aggressive in challenging NorthAm's drilling rights and practices. She couldn't help wondering if the driver of the pickup truck was in the room.

After forty minutes, her patience was starting to thin, her head felt as if a platoon of machine gunners were trying to shoot their way out, and the fleeting glimpses of Tess she caught every time she looked in that direction were becoming more and more distracting. Tess always seemed to be looking at her, as if memorizing her face. As if she were a stranger who oddly fascinated her. She hated being someone Tess no longer knew, not that she could expect anything else. She'd broken promises, walked out of Tess's life, and stayed away out of remorse and guilt. No wonder Tess didn't want to meet her halfway.

"When are we going to know where you plan to dig?" a woman asked.

"I can't give you specifics tonight," Clay said, "because I don't know yet. We've only just begun our on-site assessment, and that will take us at least a month. Much of what was done before was based on noninvasive geological surveys—radar, sonar, geothermal imaging.

What we'll be doing now is an intensive physical survey to decide where to set up our drilling rigs. Once we get our project center operational and all our permits and filings taken care of, we'll collect core soil samples and run geochemical profiles, test the composition of gas effluents, and chart underground water flow. That will take some time, and the more of you who let us sample—"

"The more chance we might end up contaminating our own land or someone else's," Pete Townsend shot out.

"One thing I never do, Mr. Townsend, is provide facts before I'm very sure of what I'm saying. There's no room for guesswork in my business." Clay remembered him in the tavern when he'd had his hand on Tess, had loomed over her as if he'd been trying to intimidate her. Tess hadn't backed away from him, but the tension around her eyes signaled she was uncomfortable. Clay didn't like people who made Tess uncomfortable. She gazed at him steadily for a long moment until the room grew suddenly quiet. Men like him would see her directness as a challenge, and she wanted him to. If he planned on bothering Tess, she wanted him to remember her face. And it was time to send the rest of her message to everyone else in the room—she had come to do a job and she planned to do it. "I don't make empty promises…and I don't run from threats, empty or otherwise. I don't ask for trouble, and drilling indiscriminately is the fastest way to run into it." She kept her eyes on Townsend, whose mouth had curled into a snarl. "I don't much like surprises. When I sink my drills, I already know what I'm going to find."

She glanced around the room and saw less animosity and suspicion in the faces looking back than she had before she'd started talking. The decision to crash the meeting had been worth it, no matter how much the cost in pain. "I appreciate you letting me interrupt your meeting. I'll leave my cards at the back of the room with my number. Any of you can reach me if you have questions or anything else you'd like to discuss."

She glanced quickly at Tess, whose brief smile did more to help the headache than any of the painkillers she'd taken earlier, and walked back down the center of the aisle with measured steps. Ella, who'd been leaning against the wall next to the door, followed Clay outside.

Once on the steps, Ella angled close to her and pressed a hand to the small of her back. "How are you holding up?"

"I've been better," Clay muttered. Ella had parked the SUV on the grass close to the front of the building, and Clay didn't have far to walk. Even those twenty paces took most of the energy she had left. By the time Ella opened the back door of the SUV for her, Clay was light-headed. Behind her, people began filing out of the Grange, their voices a low indistinguishable rumble on the air, like thunder in the distance, presaging a storm to come.

Clay gripped the top of the rear door and eased onto the seat. She paused before settling in for the ride, searching the faces leaving the building. Tess came down the steps with a middle-aged man half a head shorter than her, and whatever they were saying made Tess laugh. The gibbous moon, sailing free above the clouds, lit her features clearly. She was more beautiful than she'd been as a teenager, and she'd stopped Clay's heart then. Now the luminous glow of her delicately etched features created such longing, Clay's chest ached with some primitive need to reach out and claim her for her own.

Tess turned her head as if she could feel Clay's gaze, and her lips parted as if she meant to speak. Clay gripped the door handle and pulled herself back to her feet.

Ella, just about to swing the door closed, said, "What are you doing?"

"I'll be back in a minute."

"Clay, you're in no—"

"I'm okay." Clay made her way across the grass to Tess. Strangers she barely noticed streamed by on either side of her. She and Tess might have been alone on the pine-needle-strewn slope leading down to the lake's edge where they'd met so many nights under the moon. The cool breeze off the lake was missing tonight, though, and the distant cry of the loons had been replaced by a symphony of croaks and buzzes and chirps. They weren't teenagers and they weren't at the lake, but Tess was still all she could see.

"Hi, Tess," Clay said, a million other words choking in her throat.

"I didn't expect you'd come tonight," Tess said, although she didn't know why she was surprised. Stubborn didn't begin to do Clay justice, and she was very good at hiding what she felt—at least from most people. But Tess wasn't fooled. Clay's voice had been steady and strong the entire time she'd stood in front of the room, but her eyes had been nearly black with pain, and a fine sheen of sweat had coated her brow. “You shouldn’t be out of bed, let alone walking around. How did you get Ella to let you come here?”

“I threatened to fire her.”

“It would take more than that,” Tess murmured, sliding her hand around Clay’s forearm. She tugged gently. “Come on, you need to get back in the car. Ella needs to take you home to bed.”

Clay’s brow elevated and her quicksilver grin flashed. “What if that isn’t what I had in mind?”

“Stop that,” Tess said, ignoring her skipping pulse. She couldn’t control her biology, and Clay just had that certain something that tripped all her switches. “You’re in no shape to flirt, either.”

“I’m not flirting.” Clay laughed softly, and the low husky rumble was as seductive as a kiss. “What I am, though, is really hungry. I need dinner. Come with me.”

“What? No!” Tess jerked her hand away and glanced around for Ella to bail her out. Ella leaned against the SUV, her arms folded across her chest, a faintly amused smile on her face. When she saw Tess looking her way, she shook her head. Tess glared at Clay. “No.”

“Why not? I bet you haven’t had anything to eat. I haven’t. And I don’t think either of us had breakfast, either.”

“Whether I ate or not is irrelevant. I’m not having dinner with you.”

Clay sidestepped and blocked Tess’s path. “It’s only dinner, Tess.”

Tess had to stop too or run into her. Clay was only inches away in the dark, but Tess felt her along every inch of her body. Nothing with Clay was *only* anything. “What are you doing?”

“I’d like company for dinner tonight,” Clay said. “Your company. We’ll eat and relax. We won’t talk business.”

“Then what do we talk about?”

Clay laughed. “Whatever people talk about when they’re having dinner together. The food, the weather, baseball scores.”

Tess frowned. “I don’t follow baseball.”

“Don’t say that too loudly.” Clay’s eyes danced and some of the darkness in them receded. “Ella is a fanatic. She can quote any statistic for the last hundred years, probably.”

“You’re both very strange,” Tess said.

"Come on." Clay took her hand, surprising Tess so much she didn't pull away. Clay tugged her toward the car, calling to Ella, "Tess and I are going to dinner. We'll drop you at the B and B."

"You can't drive, Clay," Ella said.

Relieved at the opportunity for a buffer between her and Clay's unnerving magnetism, Tess jumped in. "Well, you can come to dinner with us too."

Ella glanced at Clay. "Actually, Tess, you can drive."

"Oh, but—"

"Really," Ella said. "I appreciate the invitation, but some other night would be better."

"It's settled, then." Clay pulled Tess into the SUV with her, and Tess sank into the buttery leather as far away from Clay as she could mange. As the SUV slid away from the Grange into the dark countryside, she wondered what she was doing. No, she knew what she was doing. She wanted to spend time with Clay, as foolish as that might be. She'd wanted to be with her from the instant she'd seen her walking down the center of the room. Before that even, when Clay had roared up to her farm on a shiny black motorcycle. Being around Clay was more exciting than anything else she knew. Just dinner, Clay had said—she could go along, and pretend that's all it was.

❖

Tess drove to a small, casual restaurant in Greenwich where the home-cooked food was excellent and the service unintrusive. Beside her, Clay sighed, leaned her head back, and seemed content not to talk. Tess didn't mind the silence—it gave her a chance to observe Clay unobserved. Fatigue and pain had painted shadows beneath her eyes, but she was still beautiful—her face boldly carved and strong, her body compact and radiating a muscular sensuality. Tess barely resisted the urge to rest her hand on Clay's thigh, instead gripping the wheel even harder. She couldn't trust herself to behave rationally around Clay—her emotions were all over the place—first angry, then protective, then aroused.

"Wonderful," she muttered.

"What?" Clay asked without opening her eyes.

"I thought you were asleep."

"Nope. Just enjoying the quiet."

Tess slowed to park. "We're here."

Clay caught her arm before she could open her door. "Do you think it's as strange as I do that one minute I think I know you and the next I have no idea who you are?"

Tess's throat closed. "Please don't, Clay. Not tonight."

"I'm sorry, Tess." Clay rubbed her eyes. "I'm off my game."

"I'd prefer that to what I'm sure is a very smooth and practiced routine, if I were interested in any game at all. Which I'm not." She tried to keep her tone light. Clay had opened herself up, but she wouldn't make the mistake of leaving herself vulnerable in return. Clay was not herself tonight, she'd admitted as much. And Tess had no idea who she really was or what the next day could bring.

"Okay." Clay smiled weakly. "Just dinner."

After they ordered, they didn't talk about business or baseball or the weather or politics. Clay asked her about the farm, and before Tess realized it, she was explaining to Clay what it took to convert a standard dairy farm to an organic dairy one. When she paused to let the waitress take her plate away, she shook her head. "Wow. I sure monopolized that conversation. I'm sorry."

"No," Clay said, finishing her second glass of iced tea. "It's fascinating. I never realized it took so long to make the transition, but when you outline everything that has to happen, it makes sense. All the animals, of different ages and history, getting certified—it's like a rotation system, right?"

Tess nodded. "Something like that, yes. The calves and ones under a certain age are naturally certified from birth since everything they're ever fed is organic, and presumably everything they're drinking is too. But the older ones—well, it takes time."

"I think it's great, Tess. And jumping on the yogurt thing now is a really smart move."

Tess swelled with pride. So many people had tried to dissuade her, first Ray before he'd become too disinterested in anything to care what she did with the farm, and then a half dozen neighbors including Pete Townsend, who told her the plan was costly, time-consuming, and might not pay for itself. Of course, usually their advice was followed by a lowball offer to buy her land. As if she would just give it away. For the longest time, she'd been completely alone in her dreams. Hearing Clay support her made her happy.

"What?" Clay asked gently.

Tess felt her face flush. "Oh, I'm sorry. I was just—not very many people have been supportive of my plans."

"Well, that's because they don't know you very well," Clay said with conviction. "Or they weren't paying attention. It's obvious you wouldn't start something if you didn't have a pretty good idea it would be successful, and you've clearly researched everything thoroughly, and you'll do whatever it takes to succeed."

"Why are you so sure of that, Clay?" Tess asked, almost daring to believe Clay really saw her, really understood.

"We might not know each other now, but we aren't strangers either. Some things don't change." Clay's face grew solemn. "And I know the things about you that will never change—your determination, your drive, your passion. If this is what you want, I know you'll fight for it, and I know you'll succeed."

"Even if that means fighting you?"

"You don't have to fight me." Clay leaned forward, her gaze so magnetic Tess felt herself being pulled forward, deeper into the vortex of Clay's spell. "Let me help you."

Tess swallowed, pulled away from Clay's intense eyes. "I told everyone at the meeting tonight I was going to let your team on my land."

"I heard you. Thank you."

"I'm not sure I haven't made a mistake." Tess gripped the edge of the table. Steadied herself. "Now I'll have to trust you."

"Is that so hard?" Clay asked.

"Just about the hardest thing I've ever done."

Clay grasped Tess's hand, her fingers, strong and warm, sliding between Tess's as smoothly as a glove.

"I'm sorry that you feel that way," Clay said, "and I'm the reason that you do. But I'm asking you to trust me now. I promise I won't lie to you."

"All right," Tess said. "Just this once."

"It's a beginning," Clay said softly.

"No," Tess said, pulling her fingers away. "It isn't. It's business. I need to know where I stand if and when you start drilling."

Clay leaned back in her chair. "I meant what I said about the independent verification. Getting an outside group to confirm our findings might be the only thing to convince some of your neighbors."

"I was thinking about that," Tess said. "I think I know someone."

"How is that?" Clay asked.

"We aren't the only ones who've changed," Tess said. "Dev Weber works for the DEC. And she studies water, among other things."

Clay laughed. "You're kidding me. Dev?"

"That's not all," Tess said quietly. "She and Leslie are together."

Pain flashed across Clay's face before she could hide it. "Are they."

"Yeah, weird, isn't it? Who would've thought."

"Dev never talked about much of anything personal, and never about Leslie, but I wondered sometimes. When they were together, you could see it." Clay grimaced. "Of course, I was pretty much only ever looking at you."

Tess signaled for the waitress who was clearing a nearby table. "We're ready for the check now." When she was sure she could keep the anger and hurt from erupting, she glanced back at Clay. "Well, I'm glad we got things settled."

"Did we?" Clay asked.

"We did." Tess smiled. "For the moment, we'll do business, but I'll make no promises about the future."

"No," Clay said quietly. "I wouldn't expect you to."

CHAPTER SEVENTEEN

Late in the morning of the twenty-eighth day without rain, Tess stood on her porch and shielded her eyes against the ever-present glaring sun, following the dark shapes of the off-road vehicles and trucks crawling slowly along the crest of the hill that rose beyond her barn. Clay's crew had been prowling about at first light every day for five days, marking drill sites with sonar and boring holes and measuring water pressure in the underground tables and doing whatever else they needed to do to map the configuration of the natural gas pockets and project where the water they pumped down the shafts of the tubes they drilled into the deep shale would come from and go to. As she understood it, the water would be pulled from the local aquifer, millions upon millions of gallons, and forced down narrow channels thousands of feet into the earth to open pathways for the gas to stream upward and be collected. The water and chemical solvents and sand pumped in would flow back out into containment chambers where it could be collected and safely disposed of. She understood the theory, and she understood that theories did not always translate into practice.

The puffs of smoke from the diesel engines, the distant whine of heavy machinery, and the occasional rumble of male voices on the wind were foreign to the usual chorus filling her days. She sometimes felt as if an invading army had camped on her land while she waited behind flimsy barricades for the first volley to sail overhead and shatter the harmony of her life.

She feared the peace she might lose could never be reclaimed, and yet could think of no other course to take. She'd told Clay she would trust her and fretted she might have been a fool to think she could. She hadn't spoken to Clay except in a brief phone conversation two days after the dinner where they'd declared a temporary truce. Clay had confirmed she would be bringing her crew that day, and they'd been at it all week since. Clay had been polite on the phone, completely professional and carefully distant, and Tess hadn't known how to ask her if she'd recovered from the hit-and-run.

She heard the distinctive roar of a motorcycle engine most mornings and saw Clay's Harley parked at the foot of the hill, but Clay didn't pull up to her porch in a spray of gravel and grit the way she once had, offering her a spin into the freedom of the road. Whatever fragile personal connection they'd forged hadn't lasted beyond the dinner they'd shared. She'd made it clear she hadn't wanted anything more, and apparently Clay had heard her.

She should have been happy about that, and she was—or she would be, if the nagging sense of something missing would stop plaguing her. The only thing missing in her life was rain.

Annoyed with her annoyance, Tess turned her back on the activity on the hillside and looked out over the fields as she did almost every hour, as if expecting to see something different. The crops were browner every day, and her feed reserves were growing slim. If she had to supplement by buying feed, she'd need to cull the herd after a few weeks. She simply didn't have the money to feed the number of cattle she had, and she'd have no choice but to slaughter the cows near the end of their fertility cycle or those who didn't produce as much milk as others. She'd lose all the way around if it came to that—dairy cows didn't bring as high a price as beef cattle when slaughtered, their muscle mass being proportionately less, and she'd lose the milk that she would have profited from as well.

Tess sighed and leaned her head against the porch post, wondering if perhaps she ought to consider the rain dance Cliff had suggested. Out of better ideas and not quite ready to bare her behind to the moon, she turned to go back inside and stopped when she saw a black open-topped ATV barreling down the slope toward the house. Ella pulled up a minute later and jumped out.

"Busy?" Ella called, somehow looking fashionable in jeans, ankle-high black boots, and a tan linen jacket over a white T-shirt. Her hair was caught back and clipped at the base of her neck, accentuating the long elegant lines of her face. Despite the heat, she looked cool and, as always, calmly confident.

"I suppose I should pretend to be doing something," Tess said, motioning Ella up to the porch, "but all the pressing work is done and the heat is making me as lazy as my cows. How about you?"

"The crew has another day or two up there, and while the view is beautiful, I think I've had enough of it for a while. I was wondering if you'd like to have lunch?"

Tess's immediate reaction was to say no, her usual response to personal invitations. But watching Ella watch her out of friendly eyes—beautiful eyes—Tess couldn't think of a reason to say no and several to say yes. Ella had an openness about her that made Tess feel safe—and a directness that made her feel like Ella was totally focused on her. That she was beautiful was a bonus, and as Ella slowly smiled, Tess registered a warm stirring that was a pleasant surprise. Impulsively, she said, "Lunch would be great." She hesitated, took a breath, and decided to be daring. Everything in her life was so carefully calculated and controlled—the farm budget, the milking-feeding-vetting schedule, the planting and harvesting schedule. For once, she wanted to just follow her urge. "In fact, if you've got time for more than just lunch, we could drive up to the lake. Ever been?"

"No," Ella said, and the golden timbre of her voice was like honey rippling over Tess's skin.

"My friend Leslie has been asking me to come up, and it might even be cooler up there. Of course, if you don't—"

"I think it's a great idea." Ella glanced at her watch. "Let me make arrangements and we'll go. Say, half an hour?"

Tess nodded, refusing to second-guess her decision. Ella awakened a spirit of adventure she'd lost, and Ella didn't scare her deep down inside the way Clay did. She might lose herself to Clay, but Ella she could trust. The excitement felt good, and maybe she'd even be able to forget about those dark lumbering metal beasts tearing up her land, and the woman who'd brought them. "Yes. That would be perfect."

❖

"Kelly will stay on-site and drive you back when you're finished," Ella said, "if you're good with that."

Clay pulled off her navy ball cap and wiped her forehead on the sleeve of her once-white cotton shirt. Clean that morning, it was streaked with dirt, sweat, and machine oil. "I told you to take the day off—you didn't even need to come over here this morning. Believe me, I'm safe from cows and wildlife. Besides, Kelly is more than enough help if I need any."

Ella didn't bother explaining for perhaps the five hundredth time that being out in the field, even a literal field, was infinitely preferable to sitting around a hotel or even a charming bed-and-breakfast, waiting for a meeting to end or a protectee to decide he or she wanted to go to a movie. She'd had plenty of that endless waiting during her time in the Secret Service. Part of what she liked about this job was the fluid schedule, and the chance to be where she wanted, when she wanted, as long as Clay had adequate protection. Once Kelly had arrived from New York City and Clay'd started working on Tess's property, keeping watch over both Tess and Clay on the outside chance someone would try to threaten them was a simple matter. Tess rarely left the farm, and when she did it was usually for a quick trip to the Agway or the country store, and Kelly easily followed her at a distance. Ella, perched in one of the ATVs with her iPad, stayed with Clay. No one had seemed particularly interested in what the crew was doing on Tess's farm, and nothing out of the ordinary had happened since Clay's accident. Maybe it *was* just an accident and whoever had been involved had run off to avoid an entanglement with the law. Maybe. But Ella was paid to be suspicious and on guard, and she couldn't risk another incident in which Clay or Tess might be injured.

"I should be back by this evening," Ella said. "If—"

"It's your day off," Clay said again. "You don't need to be back until tomorrow morning." She grinned. "In fact, if I were you, I'd try very hard not to be back until lunch tomorrow. I hope you've got something more interesting planned than watching them set up for the balloon festival in the morning."

Ella smiled. "Actually, I'm getting a guided tour of Lake George."

Clay's expression shuttered closed. "Oh? Who's the guide?"

"Tess," Ella said.

"Tess." Clay glanced from Ella down the hillside toward the farmhouse. A few seconds passed, and Clay jumped into the cab of a small backhoe they used to clear scrub before taking a core sample. "Well, she'll be a great guide."

"I didn't think that would be a problem," Ella said slowly, keeping her voice down so those around them wouldn't hear. The day after Clay and Tess had had dinner, Clay had explained they'd known each other in the past but hadn't kept in touch. She'd made it sound as if they were old friends and nothing more, and Ella had been glad. They were likely to be here three or four months, and Tess was intriguing. "Because if I'm misreading—"

A muscle in Clay's jaw jumped. "Ella, you asked Tess out. Presumably, she said yes."

"That's right."

"Then that's between the two of you, isn't it."

Ella respected Clay, more than respected her, liked her very much, and there was more to the story than Clay had told her. All the same, she had no reason not to take Clay at her word, that Clay and Tess had no current relationship. "Okay. I'll have my cell if you need me. Kelly will—"

"Go, Ella." Clay started the engine, the grinding gears nearly obscuring her words. "I'm fine."

Ella didn't argue. She wanted to spend time with Tess and didn't think she was mistaken about the interest she'd seen in Tess's eyes.

CHAPTER EIGHTEEN

Tess ended the call and slid the phone into the pocket of her blue and yellow plaid shorts. "Leslie said they're at her parents' lodge—about five miles up on the right. Her parents are out of town for the weekend, and Leslie and Dev are watching the place. You're sure this is okay?"

"It's beautiful up here," Ella said, smiling over at Tess. "I can't believe how undeveloped it still is. And I'm looking forward to meeting your friends."

Tess looked out the window as Ella drove north on the twisting two-lane road skirting the west side of the lake. Once past the village of Lake George proper, bordering the extreme southern end of the thirty-six-mile-long lake, the tourist areas quickly gave way to less crowded stretches of lakeside homes, cottages, and lodges. Intermittent breaks in the pine forest allowed teasing glimpses of the wide lake with its deep blue waters and hundreds of islands. The temperature was easily fifteen degrees cooler than it had been at home, and the air smelled of wind, water, and pine. Tess's heart ached at the timeless familiarity. "It never seems to change."

Ella glanced away from the road for a second, her gaze sliding over Tess with gentle warmth. "Do you spend a lot of time up here?"

"I worked at Leslie's parents' most of one summer," Tess said. "The place we're going now."

"Did you live there too?"

"Yes, along with a couple of other girls. We'd just graduated from high school. It was pretty exciting at the time."

"I can imagine. Just out of school, alone in a place like this—oh yeah."

"You sound like you would have enjoyed it." Tess grinned.

Ella's expression changed and the calm composure drifted into sadness. "I probably would have. My father died suddenly the summer after high school, so I don't remember a whole lot before I finally looked around and I was in college."

"Oh, Ella. I'm so sorry." She brushed Ella's bare arm. "That's so hard."

"Thanks. It was pretty awful—he was a great guy, a fireman. It was on the job—" Ella cleared her throat and her features lightened as she breathed in slowly. "I was lucky to have had him for a dad."

Waiting for the sadness to drift away on the breeze, Tess finally said, "Well, I was a little too green to really take advantage of being up here, and working too damn hard, but I managed."

Ella laughed softy. "Is this where you met Clay?"

Tess tensed. Ella was very perceptive and maybe Clay had told her more about their past than she thought. "Yes. How did you know?"

"Just a guess. Clay doesn't talk very much about her past, but I know once she graduated from Stanford, she hit the ground running with NorthAm. I don't think she's stopped for a real vacation since." Ella slowed for a long line of motorcycles pulling out of a roadside tavern. "Since the company doesn't have any interests up this way—or didn't use to—I just assumed she'd met you during college."

"Before that. Right before…she left."

"You two do go back a ways."

"So long ago, I don't really know her anymore." Tess tried to keep her tone light. She didn't want to discuss Clay or the past with Clay's colleague. Especially this afternoon, when what she wanted to do most was escape the activity up on the hill behind the house and the constant wondering if one of the figures etched against the sky was Clay.

"I suppose none of us really changes too much, do we?"

"I hope you're wrong." Tess smiled wryly. "I hate to think I'll keep repeating my mistakes."

"I don't think we're destined to repeat ourselves over and over again, but who we are at the core?" Ella shrugged. "I'm not sure we can do much about that except maybe make better choices when faced with similar situations."

"I like your optimism."

Ella shot her a smile. "Good."

Tess studied Ella as she drove. She appeared relaxed behind the wheel but was so clearly aware of everything around her. In control, she radiated strength. Everything about her was attractive. Tess recognized her attraction and sensed Ella's interest. What she wasn't sure of was what she wanted to do about it. "You should know I don't have any real experience dating."

Ella's brow lifted and she glanced in Tess's direction. "I find that pretty hard to believe."

"Why?"

"I would have thought you'd been on plenty of dates. You're smart and interesting and quite beautiful."

Tess laughed softly. "I was thinking something very similar about you."

"Thank you," Ella said quietly, her eyes on the twisting road again. "But having established that you're not a big dater, are you uncomfortable?"

"I'm only uncomfortable because I'm not more uncomfortable."

Ella grinned. "I don't usually make women uncomfortable—at least I don't think I do." She reached across the console and took Tess's hand. "And I certainly don't want to make you uncomfortable. So if I do, just say so."

Tess looked down at their linked fingers. Except for brief exchanges with friends a lifetime ago, she'd never held anyone's hand but Clay's. Ella's hands were different than Clay's. Her fingers were longer, slimmer, but just as strong. Just the week before, she'd held Clay's hand in the restaurant. Her skin didn't tingle now the way it had when Clay touched her, but Ella's hand was warm and gentle and confident, like her. Tess tightened her fingers through Ella's. "All right."

"All right, what?"

Tess laughed. "All right, I'll tell you if something makes me uncomfortable."

Ella drew their joined hands onto her thigh and held them there as she drove. She nodded. "That sounds like a perfect plan."

❖

"We don't have to stay," Ella said softly.

Tess stared at the lodge, frozen on the front seat of the SUV. Lost in time. She was seventeen again, on her own, out of place, unsure of her welcome. She gazed down the long slope to the lake, where the huge two-story boathouse with its big square windows opened wide reigned over the beach, and she was there on the dock in the moonlight, waiting for Clay. Anticipation and excitement made her giddy. The roar of a motorcycle engine set her heart racing. She looked past the log lodge and its wraparound porch to the cabins nestled in the woods and heard Clay come in behind her while she cleaned. They'd tumbled onto the just-made bed and she'd let Clay—

"Tess!" Leslie raced across the porch, her smile electric. The door behind her opened and Dev, older, more handsome than Tess remembered, followed Leslie with a welcoming smile on her face.

"You all right?" Ella murmured.

"Yes," Tess said and stepped out. The scent of the water, the cool fingers of breeze trailing over her skin, the glint of sun on the lake's surface were so familiar, she half expected to turn and see Clay coming down the twisting drive on her motorcycle. Her heart ached at the memory. And then Leslie was down the stairs, calling her name again, arms open for a hug.

Ella stepped up beside her and Tess took her hand. Ella squeezed her fingers, and the past disappeared.

❖

"She seems very nice." Leslie stood next to Tess at the railing an hour after lunch.

"She is," Tess said, watching Dev and Ella tinker with the outboard motor on one of the boats moored at the long dock next to the boathouse. "Thanks for letting us barge in on your day."

"I couldn't be happier." Leslie squeezed Tess's shoulder. "I wasn't sure you'd ever come for a visit."

Tess tightened her hold on the railing, struggling to keep the past from invading the present. While the four of them had sat around a picnic table under the trees sharing the sandwiches she and Leslie had thrown together in the big kitchen in the lodge, she'd let the easy conversation sweep her along like a boat drifting in the current. "I didn't think I would, either, but I'm glad that I did. I had some great times here, and it's nice to remember that." She turned, rested her shoulder against the thick porch post hewn from a massive pine, and smiled at Leslie. "You were one of my best friends. Probably my best friend. I don't know what I would've done without you that summer."

"God, we were young."

Tess nodded. "We were. So many changes, so fast. Everything so intense."

"Everything got so crazy at the end," Leslie murmured, a distant expression on her face as her eyes followed Dev.

Tess had the feeling Leslie wasn't seeing Dev the way she looked now, tall and tanned and strong and laughing, but the lanky, dark-eyed brooding girl she'd been.

"What happened after I left that summer?" Tess asked.

"I made a colossal mistake," Leslie said, her eyes brimming with pain, "and I hurt Dev terribly." She smiled wryly. "One of the major miracles in my life is that she forgave me, and somehow we found our way back to each other."

"From the way she looks at you," Tess said gently, "I don't think she ever went very far away."

"Maybe not, but we lost a lot of years that I wish I could get back." Leslie sighed. "But maybe everything happened when it was supposed to."

"Do you believe in fate?"

"I don't know," Leslie said. "I believe in the connections that we make, and the strength of those bonds to persist over time, maybe even beyond time."

"I wonder what it would've been like if I hadn't gone back to the farm and you hadn't gone away to school, and Dev and Clay hadn't disappeared."

"Maybe we'd be at the same place," Leslie said. "Or maybe we'd be completely different people." She paused. "Why did you leave?"

"It all seems so much less earth-shattering now," Tess said, shaking her head. "Ray—my stepfather—showed up late that afternoon, the day of the party, and said I had to go home. He needed me on the farm. That I had to get my things and leave right then."

Leslie's eyes narrowed. "Did he say why it was so urgent?"

"No. I wasn't used to going against him—never really had." Tess took a long breath. "And I couldn't reach Clay. She was supposed to come for me—we had a date—but she was late. I had her phone number, although I'd never called it. She always was the one to set the time and place where we would meet. If I'd been a little less naïve, I might have questioned that. The whole time I was packing to leave here, I kept calling and calling, but she never answered. For days after—" Tess shook her head. "Well. Clay dropped out of sight, and I went home to the farm. I knew you were set to go away to college, and I was just so lost I just—"

"Hey, I get it," Leslie said gently. "Things were falling apart up here too. Talk about a perfect storm of massive proportions all the way around. But we survived, right?"

Tess shook off the melancholy as Ella turned, looked up the slope toward the lodge, and waved. Tess waved back. The sun slanted through the trees and painted the lawn and lake in glimmering gold. The air vibrated with life, and Tess remembered all the things she loved about this place. She grinned at Leslie. "We did survive, didn't we."

"And I'm really glad you're here," Leslie said.

"So am I."

"Hey," Ella called, standing hipshot with one hand covering her eyes, "everything is in working order down here. Are you ready for a ride?"

"Yes," Tess called down, and she was ready, finally, to take the past back too. So much of what she'd loved had been buried in pain and loss, and she wanted it back. She'd taken back her dreams of the farm, even when everyone said she would fail, and now she was going to take back the memories of the good times she'd let die with her dreams.

"Tess?" Leslie asked. "Are you coming?"

"Yes," Tess said quickly, the image of a dark-haired girl on a motorcycle flickering just beyond the edges of her vision. "Yes, I am."

❖

Clay called a halt at a little after eight when the light started to die and jagged heat-lightning strikes began marching from the west across the ridge toward the hill above Tess's house. Ozone tinged the air, heavy and acrid, and the clouds turned blood red as the angry sun finally slid low in the sky.

Kelly, a hard-bodied blonde with a perpetual smile, joined her as the men began closing down the machinery. "Do you think we're finally getting some rain?"

"I don't think so," Clay said, scenting the hot, dry air. "Not yet."

"I don't know how these people do it. I don't think I could stand having my entire livelihood hinge on something like whether it rained or not."

Clay laughed. "Oh, and your job is so predictable. You just have to chase around after people whose schedules are as changeable as the weather."

"True." Kelly grinned. "I have to say, though, this is one of my better recent assignments. I have to thank you for getting me out of the city. If I have to be hot and sweating, I'd much rather be doing it here."

"Tell me that in a few months."

Kelly glanced around as she and Clay walked toward the Jeep Kelly had commandeered from the job site to drive Clay around. "What are your plans for the night?"

"I'm not sure." Clay stopped by the Jeep and checked Tess's house again. Still dark. Her truck was parked by the barn where it had been all day. Ella hadn't brought Tess home yet. Since she couldn't very well sit up here and wait until Tess returned, which was what she really wanted to do, she needed to do something to keep from imagining what the two of them had been doing all day. "Let's go somewhere and grab something to eat."

"Sounds great." Kelly strode around the front of the Jeep and paused by the driver's door. "Handy that Ella is with Tess—we don't have to worry about covering her for a while."

"Yeah." Clay yanked the door open and dropped onto the seat. Just perfect.

CHAPTER NINETEEN

What's good here?" Kelly put aside the menu and looked around the Sly Fox. "Besides the beer?"

"Probably just about anything on the menu," Clay said. "I can vouch for the burgers. Wings are excellent. So are the fries."

Kelly laughed. "Come here often?"

"Ah..." Clay shrugged and nodded. Like many of the locals, she ended up here most nights for a meal and a beer to purge the dust of the day. Unlike the others, though, she didn't take part in the casual conversation and friendly gossip that went on around her. She recognized most of the faces but she wasn't one of them—and while some gave her a quick glance and nothing more before moving on to the next topic, other eyes lingered on hers, challenging or accusing. She didn't mind—most of the suspicion would magically disappear when the money started flowing in with the gas, and then she'd be on to the next town, all her sins forgiven. Only this time she'd be taking her sins with her. Only Tess could forgive her those, and the time for forgiveness was past.

Tess. She'd caught glimpses of her all week as she'd worked with the crew up on the hill above the farmhouse—early in the morning and late in the evening when Tess walked to the main barn for the milking, at midday when she checked the crops in her ATV, late in the afternoon when she repaired a section of fence out behind the barn. Always from a distance, Tess's features a little too blurred to read what was in her eyes. That's how everything seemed between them now, distant and out of focus, when once the welcoming passion in Tess's eyes had set her heart soaring.

Clay clenched her fists on her thighs as the helpless frustration gnawed a hole through her insides.

"You seem to have a fan at the far end of the bar—big guy, gray hair, midforties, work clothes." Kelly leaned back in her chair, and to anyone who didn't know her, she'd seem relaxed. She probably was. She was also watching everyone in the room. She'd been NYPD before coming to work for NorthAm. Like Ella, she was smart and good company. Clay didn't work with her very often because she rarely needed any more security than Ella could provide.

Clay sipped the beer the waitress had delivered along with the menus and checked the bar. "That's Pete Townsend."

"One of the holdouts on the rights?"

"Yeah. And a vocal opponent."

"He's on his way to pay his respects." Kelly eased her chair back, making room to stand if she had to.

Clay waited until a shadow fell over the table before looking up. "Hi, Pete."

"Sutter." A beer bottle hung from his left hand two inches from Clay's cheek. "How's the work going over at Tess's place?"

"Making progress." Clay didn't even like the way he said Tess's name, as if he had some right to be familiar with her. Clay blinked away the red heat clouding her vision. She'd handled bigger opponents than Pete Townsend before without losing her temper.

"Planning to put a rig up on that hill?" Pete put his foot on the rung of Clay's chair and leaned over her, the innocent-seeming gesture subtly intimidating.

Clay wasn't easy to intimidate. She pushed her chair back, turning to look up at him squarely, forcing him to step back to keep his balance. "When I decide where we'll drill, I'll let everyone know at a town meeting. I'm sure you'll be there."

"Wouldn't miss it."

"I left a few messages with your manager this week," Clay said. "We still need to talk. I'm sorry I missed the last time."

"Busy week."

"Yeah. How about Monday?"

Pete frowned, turned the beer bottle in his big hand. "Sure. Seven thirty?"

"I'll be there."

Pete nodded curtly and strolled away.

"Pleasant guy," Kelly remarked.

"Yep."

"More trouble than just talk?"

Clay thought about the truck coming at her from out of the dark. She couldn't say for sure Pete drove one, but odds were a thousand to one he did. "I don't know."

"Make sure you take company with you on Monday."

"Do I have a choice?"

Kelly pulled her chair back to the table and swallowed some beer. "I'll leave that discussion to Ella."

"Chicken."

Kelly smiled. "You should at least take some time off this weekend."

Clay grimaced. She'd had the paramedic at the job site take her stitches out that morning. The laceration on her forehead was healing well but still bright red, and the bruise on the side of her face was a nasty shade of green-yellow. "That bad, huh?"

"The heat up on that hill has been ferocious all week. I feel like someone's twisted me into a knot and then put me through a wringer." Kelly shrugged. "I could use a break."

"Thanks for giving me an excuse to lay low." She *was* tired, but it wasn't the heat or her lack of sleep. She was tired of trying to fill every waking minute with business or fleeting pleasure that never really reached deep enough to satisfy the empty spaces in her soul. Tired of making do. And ever since she'd first seen Tess again, tired of pretending she didn't want more. She rubbed both hands over her face. "Yeah, you're right. I guess I'll spend some time watching the balloons tomorrow."

"Oh, right. The balloon festival." Kelly grinned. "It sounds like fun."

"Yeah—" Clay's phone rang and she debated ignoring it, but whatever it was, problem or not, wouldn't go away just because she wanted it to. She pulled the phone from her pocket and glanced at the readout. Especially this one. "I'll be back in a minute. The signal is better outside."

Kelly started to rise and Clay held out a hand. "I'll be right out front. There's plenty of people around. Nothing can happen."

"I'll just take a little stroll around out there while you talk."

Clay knew she wasn't winning this one and signaled to the waitress they'd be back. Outside, she found a spot a ways away from the people congregated by the door and called her father back. "Dad? Sorry I missed your call."

"More than one," her father said dryly. "And I haven't had any reports from you all week."

"Sorry." Clay wondered why he was taking such a personal interest in this project—he usually let the project managers handle the day-to-day details. But it was his company, and she worked for him. "I've been getting back pretty late at night and was planning to catch up on paperwork this weekend. I don't have a lot to tell you just yet, but—"

"Where do things stand on those last few contracts that needed completion?"

"There's a little more resistance in the community up here than usual, probably because we haven't been active this far north yet. Before I started pushing on the rights, I wanted to get some of the preliminary data analyzed. The site development is coming along well—we've got all the housing and storage facilities completed. I'm talking to the trucking company next week about effluent disposal."

"Good. You're on schedule, then."

"More or less. The permit applications are in, but the town clerks up here are only in the office a couple half days a week. I'm going to push, but I don't know how long it's going to take."

"I think I'll be able to assist in that."

Warning bells sounded. "What do you mean?"

"I'm sending Darnell up this coming week. I want those contracts sewn up tight, and there's no reason you have to take time away from site prep to do that."

"Darnell? That's a little overkill, isn't it?" Darnell Holmes was one of the corporation's senior attorneys, and he didn't usually attend personally to something as minor as contracts. "What's going on?"

"I don't like loose ends, Clayton. And considering the circumstances, it will be better all the way around if you don't need to handle them."

Clay's stomach knotted. "You mean Tess."

"She's part of it, yes."

"Look, Dad, I'm going to talk to her as soon as—"

"My point, Clayton," her father said with exaggerated patience, "is that we'll have it taken care of and you won't need to deal with her at all."

"These people won't be railroaded, Dad. It's not the right way to deal with this community. That's why you sent me. It's my job, let me do it." Clay walked in a circle, a headache forming at the base of her skull. Why was he so set on keeping her away from Tess? Hadn't she stayed away all these years—hadn't she done as agreed? Tess wasn't a girl anymore—neither was she. Maybe she'd let the past hold her prisoner for no reason at all. "I don't want Darnell—"

"I know your skills and I respect them. This is something that should've been handled before your arrival, and now it will be. Is everything else in order?"

"Nothing new." Clay hadn't told him about her accident. Why would she? He couldn't do anything about it, and his knowing wasn't going to help her recover any more quickly. She didn't share her personal life with him, she never had. She'd used the accelerated work schedule as a reason to bring on more security. Ella couldn't spend every moment working, after all. When would she have time to date Tess? Clay closed her eyes. "I'll get a report out to you as soo—"

"Very good, then. We'll speak again next week when matters have been completed."

"Good night, Dad," Clay murmured into the silent phone.

❖

"You sure this is okay with you?" Tess asked as Ella parked in the lot next to the Sly Fox.

"Absolutely. A burger and beer sounds great." Ella cut the ignition, released her seat belt, and turned to face Tess. "I had a great time today. Thanks so much for taking me to meet your friends."

Tess smiled. She couldn't remember the last time she'd felt so relaxed. Or the last time she'd spent an afternoon not worrying about the weather, the economy, or the price of feed. "I did too. It was fun. Listening to Dev talk about the lake and her work was fascinating."

Ella laughed. "She does have a way of making fish seem like people, doesn't she?"

"She loves what she's doing, that's for sure."

"She reminded me of you that way." Ella caught a strand of Tess's hair in her fingers and ran it lightly between them.

Tess felt her face grow warm. The tug against her scalp was oddly exciting. Her whole body seemed to be on alert, an exposed nerve tingling with energy. She drew a breath, focused on Ella's teasing smile. Bad idea. She glanced away. "Somehow I don't think I could make corn and cows sound quite as interesting."

Ella's fingers brushed over Tess's neck. "Oh, I don't know. I think you would."

The parking lot was dark with only the section closest to the tavern illuminated by the light filtering through the big front window. They weren't visible inside the car, cocooned from the rest of the world. The tone of Ella's voice, the touch of her fingers, wasn't hard to read. She was going to kiss Tess in another second.

"Ella—" Tess swallowed. "We should probably head inside. It's Friday night—going to be crowded."

"Hungry?" Ella murmured, softly stroking the back of Tess's neck.

"Famished," Tess said shakily. A kiss wasn't anything to be afraid of—she *had* been kissed a time or two. But when she looked at Ella, her vision swam until the image resembled someone else. She eased away.

"All right," Ella said softly. "Let's go inside, then."

Tess caught Ella's fingers in hers. "Thanks."

Ella laughed softly. "That's not necessary."

"It's just—"

"There's no need to explain, Tess. Today was great."

"Yes," Tess said. "It was."

Tess held the door to the tavern open for Ella to pass and paused just inside the crowded room, searching for a free table. She froze when she saw Clay sitting close to a pretty young blonde at a table in the corner. Clay wore a typical work outfit—a blue cotton work shirt with the sleeves rolled up past her forearms, jeans, and boots. The blonde wasn't dressed for fieldwork—her dark slacks, pale shirt, and lightweight tailored dark jacket were more office wear. If she wasn't one of the construction workers on Clay's crew, maybe she worked in the office at the work site. Or maybe she was simply a date. Why wouldn't Clay date while she was here? Of course she'd want female company—she was going to be here for two or three months. As Tess stared, the blonde looked over, smiled widely, and waved. Tess's immediate reaction was to turn around and walk out. The last thing she wanted was to see the blonde put a hand on Clay.

"Ella," the blonde called. "Come on over. We've got room."

Clay looked their way and her mouth tightened into a hard line. She didn't echo the invitation.

"Do you know her?" Tess asked.

"Yes, but we don't have to join them," Ella said quietly, "if you'd rather not."

"No," Tess said, refusing to let Clay guess anything about the situation bothered her, "that's fine."

When Tess sat down next to Clay at the crowded table, she was careful not to let any part of their bodies touch.

The blonde sent her hand across the table. "Hi, I'm Kelly Wilcox."

"Tess Rogers."

"Good to meet you."

Kelly was friendly and hard not to like. While she and Ella were obviously friends, Kelly included everyone in her conversation, which was light and smart and funny. Tess contributed when she had to, but Clay drank her beer and said nothing. Clay's silent presence was a force field pulling Tess ever closer even as she struggled to break free. She couldn't help but glance at Clay, and every time she did, Clay was studying her with a brooding intensity that stirred a deep ache inside her.

When the meal was over, Clay took the check and said to Kelly, "You can take the car. I'll walk from here."

Ella shook her head and spoke before Kelly could reply. "That's not a good idea. I need to take Tess home and you shouldn't be—"

"I doubt anyone would be foolish enough to try a repeat." Clay rose abruptly, laid money on the table, and looked down at Tess. "Can I speak with you privately for a moment?"

Caught off guard, Tess glanced at Ella.

"It won't take long," Clay growled, her dark gaze fixed on Tess.

"Go ahead," Ella said. "There's no rush."

"Outside." Clay grasped Tess's hand and pulled her through the crowd toward the door.

"Clay—" Tess protested, tugging to get free. Clay's hold was too tight to break, and when a few people looked their way, she relented and simply followed. If she didn't, she could just imagine the stories that would be going around by morning. As soon as they were outside and away from prying eyes, she yanked her arm free. "What do you think you're doing?"

"Getting your attention for a change."

"What?" Tess shivered under the wave of angry heat rolling off Clay's tense form. She'd never been the focus of Clay's anger before and it was like being buffeted by high winds in a thunderstorm.

"If you hadn't avoided me all week we might have avoided this," Clay said.

The slanting light from the tavern etched the contours of Clay's face in stark black and white, carving out the sharp angles and planes. She looked a little dangerous there in the dark, and Tess's heart beat hard. The night was still hot, and every now and then a slight breeze would carry the scent of earth and sky that clung to Clay. The primal force of her called to Tess, and something deep inside yearned to answer.

"What?" Tess fought the spell and focused on her own anger. She hadn't avoided Clay—well, she'd made sure their paths never crossed, but that wasn't the same thing. If Clay had wanted to see her, she knew where she was. Where she'd always been. Her spine stiffened. "What are you talking about?"

Clay drew her beneath a large maple by the corner of the parking lot. "You need to hire an attorney."

"I'm sorry? What are you talking about?"

"You need to get an attorney, Tess." Clay leaned closer and Tess's back brushed the trunk of the tree. "You're out of time."

"I have an attorney. Why?"

"The company is sending up our attorneys to finalize the rights contract Ray initiated. There might be loopholes in there you can exploit to get out of it, but these guys are good. They're used to getting what they want, loopholes or not."

"Why are you telling me this?" Tess shot out her chin. She wasn't going to run from anyone, especially some high-priced New York lawyers.

"Because I know how they operate." Clay bit off the words as if every syllable was an effort. "If you want a choice in this, you're going to need someone smart and tough to represent you."

"That's not what I mean. Why are you helping me?"

Something hard passed through Clay's eyes, something wild and untamed. She spread her hands on the tree on either side of Tess's shoulders and bent until their faces nearly touched. "What did you say?"

"I said," Tess repeated softly, trapped by the fire in Clay's eyes, "why are you helping me?"

"How can you not know?" Clay grasped Tess's arms and yanked her forward, her mouth coming down hard on Tess's.

CHAPTER TWENTY

Tess jerked as flames shot through her, and she reflexively gripped Clay's shirt in both hands. Twisting the fabric in her fists, she braced her arms to push Clay away, but the *no* forming in her throat gave way to a moan. The ache that had lived inside her for so long exploded into need, and some far deeper instinct compelled her to drag Clay closer, to meet the hot hard heat of Clay's mouth with a hunger of her own. Clay pressed into her, and her back slammed into the tree. She slid her hand upward, over the hard muscles of Clay's shoulder onto the soft skin at the nape of her neck. Her fingers found the silky strands, so sleek and seductive, and she gripped Clay's hair, molded her breasts and her belly to Clay's hard frame, wanting nothing between them. Clay's arm around her waist was a steel band of possession, Clay's thighs stone pillars anchoring her to the earth when she was in danger of spiraling out of control, fragmenting in a million directions. All her carefully constructed caution and self-preservation disintegrated under the demand of Clay's hands and mouth.

Clay was kissing her and she was kissing her back.

She couldn't breathe, couldn't think, could only want. Another soft moan echoed through the roaring in her ears—hers, Clay's? Clay's mouth slanted over hers, demanding entrance, demanding surrender. Tess wanted her inside with a fierceness she'd never known. Helpless longing, a craving so profound her eyes flooded with tears, swamped her.

"Tess," Clay groaned against her neck, "I want you."

Tess's back arched and she bared her throat, the scrape of Clay's teeth sending shock waves deep into her center. Her thighs trembled and she opened, ready to give her anything. She would give her anything, everything, to sate this wild hunger, to staunch this storm of heat and passion. She would lay herself bare for her.

Take me. The words trembled on her lips, bruised and swollen and still famished for the taste of oak and earth and fire. Terror tore through her. Not again. Never again. She pushed at Clay's chest. "No."

"I need you." Clay's voice was a broken whisper, her body immovable, rigid as marble.

Tess turned her head away, gasped, "I can't."

"Please, Tess." Clay's mouth was at Tess's throat. "You're all I can think about."

A sound, half groan, half sob, vibrated from Clay's chest. Her shirt was soaked with sweat. The muscles under Tess's hands quivered, hot and furious. Clay's hips pinned hers to the tree, thrust against her, insistent and insatiable. Tess wanted to spread herself open, take her inside. She wanted the fury of Clay's desire to bring her screaming into the flames until she burned to ashes.

"Oh God, I can't." Tess struggled to get free. "Clay—"

Ella's voice, cool and strong, cut through the insanity. "Everything all right here?"

Clay stiffened, shuddered, a lit fuse ready to ignite.

Tess fought to steady her breath. "Yes," she said, pushing at Clay again.

Clay braced her hand on the tree, her head down, breath rasping like a racehorse pushed too hard to the finish, ready to collapse. Tess ached to stroke her, to soothe her, but she couldn't touch her now. She didn't know what Clay would do. She didn't know what *she* would do. All she knew was what she couldn't do. She couldn't give herself again, not to Clay. Not everything, ever again. Pushing harder, Tess made enough space to slide out from between Clay and the tree. She forced herself to back away, to leave Clay there, alone and vulnerable, and the ache was so huge she nearly cried out.

"Tess?" Ella said quietly.

"I'm fine." Tess ran both hands through her hair, wiped the moisture from her cheeks. "I'll just be a minute."

Hands on hips, Ella's sharp gaze tracked between Clay and Tess. After a moment, she nodded. "I'll be at the car."

Tess turned to Clay, torn between comforting her and raging at her. "Why?"

Clay turned and sagged against the tree. "I lo—"

"Don't," Tess snapped. "Don't you dare." Fury scorched through her as strong as the desire seconds before. "You walked out of my life, without a word, and you say that to me now?"

Tess's whole being vibrated with the urge to slap the words away, to hurt Clay the way Clay had hurt her. She fisted her hands, willed the raging fire to burn out, welcomed the ice slicing through her. "Go to hell."

❖

Tess rolled down the window of the SUV as Ella drove along the deserted roads toward the farm. The air held just the barest hint of a night breeze, a teasing promise of a break in the unrelenting heat that would disappear with the dawn. Just another in a long line of empty promises.

"Is there anything I can do?" Ella said quietly.

Tess's face flamed. She would have been embarrassed at being so exposed to anyone, but knowing Ella had witnessed such a terrible private moment was beyond humiliating. "Sorry about all the commotion."

"That's all right. You've nothing to apologize for."

"It's complicated."

"Most things that really matter are."

Tess glanced over at her and saw only gentle sympathy in her face. "You're amazing. How did you get to be so understanding?"

"Am I?" Ella laughed. "I spend a lot of time watching people. Occupational hazard."

"What have you learned?"

"That sometimes things are simpler than we think, and always more complicated."

"That is very Zen," Tess said softly. "I wish I could tell the simple from the complicated."

Ella reached between them and squeezed Tess's hand. "Tell me to back off if I'm out of line, but I get the feeling that everything between you and Clay isn't past history."

"It's more like unfinished business." Tess wished she could say more, Ella deserved more. But she couldn't betray Clay's confidences even if what they'd once shared hadn't been what she'd believed. She'd held Clay, loved her. She'd *loved* her, and if she turned her back on that, she'd lose part of herself. "I realize this puts you in a terribly awkward position, and I'll understand if—"

"Tess," Ella said softly, turning down the drive to the farmhouse, "I enjoyed today. I'd like to do it again."

"Even after tonight?"

"I like being with you." Ella stopped by Tess's front porch, put the SUV in park, and turned to Tess. "We don't have to make it about anything more than that, right now."

"Are you sure?"

Ella lifted Tess's hand and kissed her knuckles. "Very sure."

"Thank you."

"Like I said, some things can just be that simple."

Tess wasn't so sure, but her heart was weary and bruised, and she let herself be persuaded by the certainty in Ella's voice and the warmth of her touch. She leaned across the space between them and kissed Ella lightly on the cheek. "I hope you're right. Good night, Ella."

Ella cupped her chin, brushed a thumb along her jaw. "Good night, Tess."

❖

Clay watched the lights of the SUV disappear around the corner. Tess was gone. For the briefest of moments with Tess in her arms, she'd shed all the lies and pretenses—she'd felt herself come alive, known the truth of herself again. Tess had always called to the best of her, and without her, she'd been little more than a chess piece on a board game of her father's design. She'd willingly played along, and why not? She had nothing else. Only Tess had ever seen the deepest part of her.

Clay walked back into the tavern and up to the bar. Kelly appeared at her side, sipping a club soda.

"Staying for a while?" Kelly asked.

"I'm taking the Jeep out to the job site," Clay said to her. "I'll drop you at the motel."

"I'll come with you," Kelly said amiably. "The TV reception in the motel room is so bad I was forced to try the pay channels last night, and the selections were, well, interesting."

Clay didn't want company. She wanted to break something. She needed to get the taste of Tess, sweet and tempting, out of her blood.

"What will you have?" The bartender, a redhead in a tight white T-shirt proclaiming *Dairy Maids Are Fresher* in bright pink letters, swiped the wood bar top in front of Clay and gave her a friendly once-over.

Clay noted her nipples created intriguing little bumps beneath the thin cotton and looked away. "A shot of Jameson, please. Make it a double."

"Beer chaser?"

"Why not." When the drink came she downed it in two swallows. The burn helped smother the acid eating away at her stomach, but Tess's taste was still on her tongue, clover and rain. Her hands trembled, and the need rose up so hard and fast she wanted to throw back her head and howl. She chugged half the mug of beer and stared at the empty shot glass, considering another. Alcohol had never helped quench the fire that was Tess, but on rare occasions it had brought her forgetting. She tightened her fist around the glass.

"If it makes a difference," Kelly said after a second, "I'll be driving."

Clay pushed the glass away. "I don't want to forget."

"Sorry?"

"Never mind." Clay left a twenty on the bar and walked outside. The moon had risen—full and bright. The parking lot was lit up as if it were noon. Slivers of dark clouds slashed across the face of the moon as she watched, and were just as quickly gone.

Kelly walked up beside her. "Good night for a hayride."

"Ever been?"

"No," Kelly said, "but up here, it seems like something I ought to try."

"Don't take your clothes off. Hay itches like hell and you can never seem to find every last piece."

"Is that the voice of experience?"

"Once," Clay said softly. "Once I kissed a girl under a moon just like this in her daddy's hayloft." She looked at Kelly, who was staring at her intently. "Best kiss of my life."

"Moon's still up there," Kelly said, her voice so gentle Clay hardly recognized it. "And I bet the loft and the girl are too."

Clay shook her head. "No, not anymore."

"Why don't I take you home."

"Just drive me to the site."

Kelly didn't argue and didn't try to make conversation. Clay looked for Ella to pass them on the one road out of town, returning from Tess's, but the SUV never appeared. Ella must still be at Tess's. Clay focused on the lights marking the entrance to the NorthAm camp up ahead and not the pictures her mind wanted to paint of Ella and Tess.

The site was dark and quiet, the only lights those marking the turnoff to the access road through the woods. Until they were up and running, they only had a skeleton crew on-site at night, and most of them were either out or already asleep in the bunkhouses at the far end of the compound.

"I'll get the gate." Clay jumped out when Kelly slowed and pulled her key ring off her belt to unlock the heavy chain securing the twelve-foot-wide gate. When she got closer, she saw the length of chain dangling freely. The security lock lay in the dirt at her feet. Tensing, she scanned the woods on either side of her. Nothing moved. Here the moonlight was fractured by the tall evergreens, and shadows danced like wraiths. Someone could be standing ten feet away and she wouldn't see them.

Clay backed up to the Jeep. "Someone's cut the lock. Call Ella. Tell her to check the equipment at Tess's."

"You want her to come over here if it's all clear?"

"No. Tell her to stay with Tess." Clay pulled a flashlight from the rack behind the seat.

Kelly cut the engine. "Should I roust the locals?"

"No. I want to check out the place first."

"Clay—"

Clay headed back toward the gate and the road that disappeared into the dark. "Take care of Tess first. I'll be fine."

CHAPTER TWENTY-ONE

Too agitated to contemplate sleep after Ella drove off, Tess walked down to the pasture behind the barn to check the horses. They didn't need checking, but she needed company. If she went inside now, she'd start thinking about Clay. And the kiss. She really didn't want to think about the kiss. The last person she'd kissed had been a teacher she'd met at the county fair in the arts and crafts building. They'd started talking about the dioramas Beth's fifth graders had made and how creative the kids were, making cornfields out of toothpicks and pastures from little bits of indoor-outdoor carpet. The dinner date that followed had been pleasant. The good-night kiss was pleasant too. Warm and tender and safe.

Clay's kiss had been anything but tender and safe. Clay's kiss was volcanic—a rush of molten desire immolating her down to the bone. Thinking about the low rough growl that had escaped Clay's throat when Clay had pressed her to the tree made her hot and wet again, right now. Her thighs trembled, and a terrible urgency pulsed deep inside. She wanted Clay inside her right this minute. Not someone safe, not someone gentle and tender. Not anyone but Clay.

"God," Tess murmured, leaning against the wide metal pasture gate. Would she ever be free? Would she ever want to be? The answers had to be yes or she would lose her mind. She couldn't fight her heart and her body too.

"Hey, guys," she whispered, wishing she could ride away into the moonlit fields and emerge in a world where love made sense and promises were never broken.

The big gelding ambled over, followed by the others. She only kept four, two fat minis who weren't good for much of anything except a smile, and two mustangs she rode whenever she had the chance. The horses stayed long enough for a quick scratch and to confirm she had no treats for them before wandering away to graze in the stubbly grass, tails flicking at flies, graceful, muscular bodies ethereal in the moonlight. One of the barn cats twined around her legs, and she leaned over to pet him. The air lay close on her bare arms, still warm, even going on midnight. Overhead, the moon raced through a blue-black sky, bright and mocking in its perfect solitude.

The sound of an engine rumbling grew louder, and she turned, frowning. No one came out this late at night unless there was a problem. She hurried back toward the house as the familiar SUV pulled up by the porch again. Ella got out, closed the door, and started toward her.

"Did you forget something?" Tess called.

"I'd like you to go in the house, Tess." Ella's tone was flat and impersonal, steely with command. Not quite an order, but not a request.

Tess didn't move. "What's wrong?"

"Possibly nothing." Ella walked around to the rear of the SUV, leaned in, and came out with a large flashlight. "I'm going up on the hill to look around. It would just be best if you waited inside."

"Why?"

"Someone's broken into the job site. Clay wants to be sure everything is all right over here."

"Broken in?" Dread coiled in Tess's stomach. "Where's Clay?"

"She's at the site."

"Alone?"

"Kelly's there. She just called me." Ella flicked on the light, shone it around the yard and barn. A skunk skittered away into the underbrush by the pasture. Otherwise they were alone.

"Shouldn't you go over there? Why would anyone be interested in my place?"

"If it's industrial sabotage, they may be trying to destroy the equipment here. I'll be back as soon as I check things out."

Tess shook her head. "We should go over to Hansen's. Clay might need your help."

"She wants you to stay here."

Tess nearly choked on her anger. "I'm sorry. Clay wants me to stay here? I don't answer to Clay. She's not in charge of my life."

"No, but I answer to her, and she's right." Ella took Tess's arm but didn't try to move her. "There's no point in you being in danger."

"Oh, but it's all right if she is?" Tess had trouble keeping her voice down. The horses whinnied softly and shuffled closer. She took a breath and shook off the image of Clay in the road, nearly killed. Panic would not help anyone, but fear clawed at her throat. "Should I remind you that she's barely recovered from the last time someone tried to kill her?"

"Believe me, I remember. But ignoring a possible threat here won't help her." Ella pointed to the house. "And I can't make sure everything's all right here until you're secured. Please go inside."

"If that's the only way I can get you to go help Clay, fine. But hurry."

"I'll be right back."

Tess headed for the house, and by the time she reached the porch, Ella was gone.

❖

Clay approached the compound along the access road, staying in the shadows of the pines as much as she could. The compound was eerily silent. No lights shone in the bunkhouses or by the big machinery shed on the far side of the camp. The huge yard that would soon be filled with trucks and equipment was dark. They weren't running at full capacity yet and hadn't put up the halogens that would light the space like day once they started running 24/7.

Clay's trailer was the closest to the access road, and a prime target. The big satellite dish on the roof was practically a blinking sign saying *expensive stuff inside*. Chances were this was nothing more than just malicious mischief or at most, burglary—they'd had their share of trespassers at other sites hoping to find some loose tools lying around. Even had a backhoe go missing until it was found abandoned after it got bogged down in a swamp a quarter mile from the yard. The rigs hadn't been assembled yet, and destroying them would take explosives. Vandals would have to be serious and sophisticated to go after them.

Keeping her flashlight on low beam and pointed at the ground, she picked her way over the uneven terrain, doing her best not to kick up rocks or snap branches in the tangle of scrub at the edge of the woods. Once, she thought she heard the murmur of voices, cut her flashlight, and stopped, trying to pinpoint the sound. At night out here, everything was amplified. A car passing on the next ridge sounded like it was around the bend. Maybe some of the crew were still awake in one of the bunkhouses. Or maybe more than one intruder lurked inside the trailer. When she heard nothing more, she resumed her cautious approach until she got within twenty feet and could see more clearly. The trailer door had been jimmied and hung askew. The windows were dark. She stood still again and listened. Nothing. Even the crickets were quiet.

Sweat trickled down her face and she swiped at it with her sleeve. Her breathing sounded so loud in her ears she wondered if it wasn't audible inside the trailer. If anyone was inside, they were doing the same thing she was—waiting and listening. After a minute, she decided to make the first move—taking the aggressive approach usually worked for her. Edging up to the trailer, she slipped along the side until she was under one of the back windows. She didn't want to go through the door and surprise someone ransacking the place, especially with no backup. Rising slowly, she gripped the narrow window ledge and hoisted herself up until she could get a look inside. Her sore ribs protested but she ignored the insistent ache. Enough moonlight filtered through the windows to light the twelve-by-thirty space. Although her lateral vision was obscured, she could see most of the trailer, and it looked empty. She eased down to the ground, caught her breath, and worked her way around to the door.

She was ten feet away from the open doorway when Kelly whispered, "What's the situation?"

Clay managed not to gasp. All the same, the hair on the back of her neck stood up and a shudder ran down her spine. "What are you, part ninja?"

"Used to be SWAT."

"Nice to know." Clay leaned close. "Place looks empty. I don't think anyone's around."

"I'll clear this trailer, then we'll check the rest of the buildings."

"I'm coming in with you."

"Take my backup piece. I know you know how to shoot." Kelly leaned over, and when she straightened, she had a Beretta Bobcat in her hand. She slid the compact .25 caliber to Clay. "Don't shoot unless you have to. Metal trailer—ricochet."

"Don't worry." Clay kept the weapon close to her thigh, pointing down. "Your call."

"I'll go left, you take right."

"Sounds like a plan." Just the way Clay liked it—short and sweet.

❖

Tess paced on the front porch, as close as she could bring herself to going inside. No way could she just sit and wait. The night sounded like every other night—an incredible silence punctuated by the throaty rumble of bullfrogs, the shriek of opossums, and the lonely yip of a coyote searching for its pack. Somewhere, the mournful sound of cows lowing echoed the simmering ache in her chest. She stared at the hill behind the barn until her eyes stung. Ella was up there somewhere, alone. What did it take for someone to face danger so calmly, so matter-of-factly? Tess's heart raced, and she wasn't even in any danger.

Every now and then she caught a glimpse of what might have been a flashlight beam cleaving the dark for an instant, or maybe it was only starlight reflecting off the window of one of Clay's machines. Clay's equipment on her land. Clay was everywhere in her life, when weeks ago she had only been a memory Tess struggled not to revisit. The scent of her still clung to her skin. The imprint of Clay's hand on her hip still tingled. She couldn't breathe without tasting her on her lips. All she wanted in that moment was to see her. Just to know she was all right. Then the terrible pressure in her chest would ease, and her head would stop spinning.

Wrapping her arms around herself, chilled despite the cloying heat, Tess strained to see beyond her fields to the tree line on the ridge bordering the Hansen property. Stark fingers stretched into the sky, spirits rising from the earth, clawing to freedom. Over that ridge, Clay's compound had sprung up like a tent city of nomads in the desert, seemingly overnight. Clay was there, possibly in danger. Clay had always been the perfect picture of danger to her, but she'd never been frightened by her. She'd represented everything Tess had never experienced—independence, rebellion, daring adventure. She still did, only now, Clay seemed less the master of her fate than she had when they were young. She seemed beset from every angle by forces that sought to hurt her.

And now, Tess was one of those who had hurt her. She'd felt Clay flinch when her words had struck like blows. And now that she'd said what she'd wanted to say for so long, she felt no better for it. Whatever had happened that long-ago summer, they had both been part of the play, both of them knowing somewhere in the back of their minds that the dream was only a dream. Clay had broken the fragile fantasy first, but maybe in a few weeks' time, Tess would have been the one to end the perfect idyll. When the summer drew to an end and she'd been forced to choose between riding off with Clay into some unknown future or returning to the farm and the land she knew and loved, maybe she would have been the one to break hearts. She'd held Clay responsible for her pain and disappointment all this time because she needed someone to blame for the loss of innocent dreams.

A streak of light cut through the darkness and she caught her breath. Ella was coming back. Tess hurried down the dirt drive to meet her.

"Did you find anything?"

"No," Ella said. "Everything up there looks all right."

"Can we go to Hansen's now?"

"Clay expressly wanted you safe. Whatever's going on over there, it's no place for—"

"What do you mean, Clay wanted me safe? She said that?"

"Tess," Ella said gently, "do you have to ask?"

Tess jolted. *How can you ask that?* Could even Ella see what she had refused to admit? She narrowed her eyes. "Wait a minute. Kelly just came up this week. But you were here alone until Clay got hurt. Now Kelly is with Clay and you're…you're *assigned* to me, aren't you?"

"Yes, but that has nothing—"

"Clay's idea?"

"I agreed with her, Tess. We don't know what's going on, and you were right there when Clay was injured. So far, no damaged vehicle has turned up, and no witnesses have come forward. No one is admitting to seeing anything at all. Except you."

"So Clay decided I needed protection, and that's what you've been doing? Is that what today was about?"

"You don't really believe that, do you?"

Tess was so angry she knew she wasn't thinking straight. "I'm going to Hansen's. Come with me or not. I don't care."

She marched toward her truck, jumped in, and pulled the keys from the cup holder where she always left them. As she started the engine, Ella climbed in the passenger side and said, "If you're going to do this, follow my instructions. We don't want to go roaring in there and surprise some hothead who's going to start shooting at Clay and Kelly—or us."

"Fine. Tell me what to do, and I'll do it."

"And Tess—about the rest of it—"

"I'd rather you not say anything right now," Tess said. "I've already told one person to go to hell tonight. That's enough."

❖

The trailer was empty. Clay switched on the propane-powered light and surveyed the chaos. File cabinets lay on their sides, their drawers pulled open and dumped upside down. The computer was trashed, and papers, blueprints, and survey maps were shredded and strewn about the room.

"We better check the rest of the camp," Clay said grimly.

"We ought to call the sheriff."

"Let's see if our friends are still around first. If they are, I'd like to talk to them alone."

Kelly grimaced. "We could be asking for trouble."

"No," Clay said. "That's what they're doing." She handed Kelly back her Beretta and shoved the broken door the rest of the way open.

Tess jumped back with a startled gasp. Ella stood beside her, a stoic expression on her face.

"Damn it, Tess," Clay snarled, "what are you doing here?"

"Not listening to you, apparently."

"Go home."

Ella said, "Is the rest of the site clear?"

"No," Clay said, staring at Tess. She looked angry and defiant and so fucking sexy. She sighed. "Fine. Stay. But at least wait inside."

"You'll be careful?"

"Yeah," Clay said, although where Tess was concerned, she doubted that was possible.

CHAPTER TWENTY-TWO

The road forks about twenty feet ahead," Clay called to Kelly and Ella. "Go left—I'll catch up in a minute." She turned to Tess. "You have your cell phone? We'll only be a few minutes."

"Yes." Tess couldn't make out much of the encampment except for the large looming shapes of the buildings on the perimeter, and then only because they blocked out portions of the moonlit sky. Anyone could be out there, hiding or waiting to jump someone who came looking. She grasped Clay's hand. "Why don't you let Ella and Kelly do this? Better yet—the sheriff."

"By the time anyone responded, our visitors would be long gone." Clay smiled, pleased by the frown forming between Tess's brows. Tess was worried about her. Well, at least as worried as she was angry, and either emotion was better than the ice that had crystallized in Tess's eyes when she'd walked away, back at the Sly Fox. Tess on fire meant Tess cared, and right now, Clay would make do with any little connection she could find. Being the brunt of Tess's temper was far better than being frozen outside, locked out of Tess's life. Maybe she'd have to fight Ella for a place by the fire, but she would if Tess gave her the slightest hint there was a chance. Right now, though, she had to be sure Tess was safe. "The three of us together can cover more ground, and Ella and Kelly aren't as familiar with the layout as I am."

"But they're trained for it."

"There's probably no one here, Tess." Clay clasped Tess's hand and squeezed. "I won't be long. If you see or hear anything that frightens you, call 9-1-1. Stay in the trailer until one of us returns. I don't want you wandering around out here in the dark."

"Oh, but it's all right if you do?"

"Yeah, it is. I'm the tough one here, remember?" Clay grinned at the barely muffled snort of indignation. Tess never liked being left out or left behind—especially if Clay hinted whatever they were planning—"borrowing" one of Leslie's boats for a quick trip to the island and a little privacy or sneaking a beer or two out of the boathouse fridge for a private party all their own—was too difficult for Tess to pull off.

Tess almost laughed. Even in the shifting moonlight, an arrogant spark shone in Clay's eyes. "You are so obnoxious sometimes."

"Yeah," Clay said, running her hand up and down Tess's arm, "but that's what you like about me."

"You wish," Tess said, but she couldn't smother her smile. The old exchange, one they'd often had when Clay was being particularly overbearing, sometimes just to get a rise out of Tess, ought to have hurt, but it didn't. Clay was right. One of the things Tess had always found so attractive about Clay had been her confidence, her absolute certainty, and her refusal to pretend she felt otherwise. "All right, go ahead, but if you get hurt again, you're on your own."

"I know you don't mean that," Clay said in a low teasing tone that made Tess's heart skip into hyperdrive. "You wouldn't let me suffer, would you?"

"Maybe, maybe not. Do you really want to find out?"

"I just want you to be here when I get back." Clay's tone turned serious, and the intensity of her expression might as well have been a hand caressing Tess's bare skin, setting her alight.

"Where else would I go? It's black as pitch out here, and since I walked in with Ella and she has the flashlight, I have no idea how to get back out again. So I'm a captive."

"Good, then your only hope of getting home before dawn is time off for good behavior." Clay gave her a little push toward the trailer. "As soon as I get back, I'll spring you."

Tess climbed the first step and looked down at Clay. The moonlight played cruel tricks sometimes—for an instant, Tess almost got lost in the look of desire in Clay's eyes. "Don't get hurt."

"I won't, not if you're here." Clay didn't care who was watching—right then there was only her and Tess, and she wanted Tess to keep looking at her as if she were the only woman in the world. When Tess gave her that little secret smile she could do anything. "What do you say?"

"Don't be a hero." The ice was cracking under Tess's feet, and she was in danger of falling through into frigid reality. She couldn't flirt with Clay like this, not when she was flirting with almost certain heartache too. Clay hadn't changed, and neither had she. She was still far too susceptible to Clay's charm, and if she wasn't very, very careful she'd start imagining something Clay had already proved she couldn't deliver.

Tess tensed, watching the burn in Clay's eyes grow hotter. Any second, Clay was going to kiss her again, and this time, Tess wasn't certain she'd be able to say no. They stood there, poised on the edge of no return for what seemed like hours before Clay sucked in a breath and backed away. She held up a finger, pointed it at Tess like a gun. "Stay put. I'll be back."

"I'll be here," Tess said, not caring how thin the ice had become.

❖

"Everything all right?" Ella asked when Clay caught up to her and Kelly.

"Things would be better if you'd kept Tess at her place like I asked."

Kelly muttered, "I'll check the skids and ATVs over here," and disappeared.

"I had two choices," Ella said mildly. "Sit at Tess's while she drove over here alone, or come with her and at least keep her from walking into something."

"The machine shop is on the right up here. If anyone really wanted to hurt us, they'd go for that. I'll take a look."

"Why don't I—"

"I can handle it."

Ella swung around in front of Clay, blocking her path. "Before you get yourself in trouble because you're pissed at me, why don't we sort this out."

Clay flashed to the image of Ella and Tess walking into the tavern, looking good together. Looking like a fucking couple. She ground her back teeth. "There's nothing to sort out."

"Isn't there? Come on, Clay—I'm not blind. I *was* there tonight."

"I know." Ella had been there all right, witness to Clay losing control and practically forcing herself on Tess. But Tess had kissed her—for just a second, Tess had been right there with her. Her gut clenched remembering the sweet sensation of Tess in her arms. Her throat tightened and she couldn't breathe.

"Plus Tess about tore my head off for not rushing over here to help you," Ella said. "All of which makes the old-business story kind of suspect."

"We have some unresolved issues."

"I noticed that," Ella said dryly. "Clay, if you have something to say, now is the time."

Clay had plenty to say, starting with *stay away from Tess*, none of which she had any right to voice. And on top of that, she was up to her neck in business entanglements with Tess that were about to get a lot worse when the attorneys showed up and her father started pushing for the drilling to begin. What she ought to do for Tess's sake was back the hell away. "What Tess chooses to do is none of my business."

"That's not an answer."

"It's the only one I've got." Clay pointed to the path Kelly had taken. "Let's get this done."

❖

Tess paused on the step, straining to penetrate the dark that closed in around the trailer, leaving the faint light inside as a fitful beacon. When she could no longer see or hear the three of them, she climbed inside. And jerked to a stop on the threshold of the broken door.

The interior was a mess—trash and shredded papers and bits of broken computer parts littered every surface. She didn't like feeling helpless while everyone else was doing something about what had happened, but she couldn't clean up until the sheriff came.

She checked the window, still saw no one outside, and surveyed the chaos on Clay's desk. More paper, various pens and paper clips and scraps of paper. A sticky note with random scribbles clung to the edge of a pad of lined paper, probably something Clay had doodled while she spoke on the phone. Idly, Tess tilted her head to read the crumpled square and jerked as the aimless scribbles took shape. TAR.

Throat suddenly dry, hands shaking, she stared at the damning evidence. Perhaps it was something else. Maybe Clay used tar in some part of the drilling process or maybe it was a toxic by-product of the fracking. She studied the box around the letters, the heaviness of the lines, the way the letters were outlined and filled in with precise cross-hatches. Someone, Clay probably, had focused a lot of energy writing those three letters. TAR. Tess Ann Rogers. She touched the note, traced the heavy inked design. Clay had been doodling her initials. The idea, ridiculous and inconsequential, was thrilling.

The door opened behind her and Tess looked around. Clay stood in the doorway, taking in the room and then Tess. Her gaze landed on the sticky note under Tess's hand.

Tess moved to block the foolish note from view. But she'd seen it and couldn't un-see it now. She could spin so many fantasies from a silly little thing like that—just what she couldn't afford to do. If only her heart would listen to reason. "Did you find anything?"

"Not so far. There are some ATV tracks coming out of the woods. It looks like we either had some curious visitors recently or that's how the vandals left. Nothing else appears to be disturbed. All the guys are bedded down already. Once these guys go down for the night they usually don't even roll over until it's time to get up again. The work out here is tough and lonely—add physical exhaustion to a couple of drinks and most of them are under well before this time of night. Nobody who's awake enough to communicate noticed anything."

"Why would someone do this?" Tess asked.

Clay shrugged and lifted a stack of papers from the pile on the floor onto the small sofa under the windows. "Maybe they think it'll slow us down. Maybe they think we won't want to proceed if we're not wanted here." Clay shook her head. "Hell, maybe it's just a message that something more serious will follow if we don't clear out."

"You won't, will you?" Tess ought to be glad Clay might leave. All her problems would be solved. But as soon as she thought it, she knew that was more fantasy. Clay disappearing again wouldn't solve her problems. She'd still have to find out what Ray had done behind her back with NorthAm. She'd still have to decide what she intended to do when the company returned, because they would. And she still needed to put her feelings for Clay in a place where she wouldn't be opening herself up to more hurt.

"No," Clay said, watching Tess carefully. "I'm not leaving."

A weight lifted from Tess's chest. "Does this happen often?"

"Often enough. Usually in any given community there's at least one person who's opposed to what we're doing, even when the majority understand the procedure and welcome us."

"So resistance isn't that uncommon?"

"I wouldn't call it resistance as much as hesitation. Naturally, people don't want to commit to something they don't really understand or have heard negative opinions about. Our job at this stage is education because without community support, the project becomes much more difficult. We need local labor to build our infrastructure. We bring in our own technicians for the expert work, but we rely on locals for ninety percent of the rest of our needs—and there are plenty—construction, utilities, housing, food, clothes, medical care, entertainment."

Tess pictured all the empty storefronts on Main Street and the For Sale signs crowding every block. NorthAm's operation would be like having a huge new factory spring up in town almost overnight. And that didn't even touch on what landowners would get for drilling rights. She understood why some places would welcome the fracking companies. "That's got to be great for the local economy."

"It is. That's why once we get going, most communities are happy to have us."

Tess rubbed her eyes. She was so tired. Too tired to make sense of all the conflicting feelings. "Where are Kelly and Ella?"

"We need to file a police report to document what happened for the insurance. Ella's waiting for the cruiser up at the highway. Kelly is taking a last walk around to make sure we're all secure."

"I'm sorry, I wanted to straighten up in here—" Tess held both hands up helplessly.

"Thanks—that's okay. I'll sort through everything in the morning and then have the office fax me up whatever I can't resurrect." Clay held out her hand. "Come on, I'll take you home. I want to check your place again too."

"What about Kelly and Ella?"

"They can ride back to town together whenever they're done with the sheriff."

Tess looked around at the disheveled office. "If you're sure?"

"It's late, and you're tired. I'm sure."

"I'm sorry about this," Tess said softly.

Clay took her hand. "It's okay. It's not your fault."

"Maybe not," Tess murmured, letting Clay lead her from the trailer, "but it feels as if I'm part of it somehow."

"You're not."

"It's my community."

Clay held the truck door open for Tess while she climbed into the passenger side. "You live here. But you're not responsible for what everyone does."

Their faces were only inches apart. Clay's jaw was a perfect ivory arch that Tess ached to trace with her fingertips. If she leaned out just a fraction, their mouths would meet. Clay's scent, smoky and dark, swirled in the air, and Tess's nipples tensed. She was so very tired of always doing what was reasonable. "Do you follow your own advice? About most things?"

Clay swallowed, her gaze riveted to Tess's mouth. "Not usually."

"Do you think for one night you could forget about NorthAm?"

"Can you?"

Tess couldn't see the morning and didn't care. All she could see was Clay. "Yes."

CHAPTER TWENTY-THREE

Tess held her breath the entire way from the job site back to the farm. The two-minute ride felt like an hour while she deliberately kept her mind blank, denying the nagging voice in her head the chance to tell her she was being foolish, self-destructive, and outright insane—denying reason the opportunity to make her change her mind. She didn't want to change her mind. She wanted Clay.

Clay pulled up in front of the farmhouse and took her hand. "I can walk you to the door and say good night."

"Can you?" Tess had never heard Clay quite so subdued.

Clay's chest heaved. Her hand trembled in Tess's. "I don't know—I'll try if that's what you want."

The only light in the yard came from the big security light over the barn, but it was enough to illuminate Clay's features. The strong bones in her bold face stood out sharply, the fine muscles along her jaw were sculpted steel, her eyes reflected starlight like sword points. Her body was completely still, but Tess felt the tension spiraling down Clay's arm and into her hand. Clay was anything but subdued—she was a live wire waiting to electrify the unsuspecting. But Tess wasn't stumbling into a force field unawares. She was walking in with her eyes open and her step steady.

"I already told you what I wanted," Tess said. "I don't change my mind easily."

The corner of Clay's mouth twitched and she slowly turned her head, meeting Tess's gaze. "But you think I do."

"Prove me wrong." Tess knew she was playing a dangerous game. Clay might have a leash on her temper, and her desire, right this instant, but she was a jungle cat with nothing more than a thin veneer of domestication keeping her in check. Push her a little, and she'd take what she wanted. Tess had been on the receiving end of that hunger and she liked it, but tonight she wanted something else. She wanted to be the one to bite.

"Just give me the chance and I will." Clay, fixing Tess with that predatory stare, clasped the back of Tess's neck and drew her across the space between them, one slow inch at a time.

Tess resisted letting their bodies touch, but she couldn't fight the pull of Clay's eyes. When their lips touched, Clay kissed her, as softly and slowly and sweetly as her mouth had been hard and fast and rough earlier that night. The fire was no less hot for having banked all evening. The breath in Tess's lungs scorched. She gripped Clay's shirt as she had earlier, in no danger of falling, but every bit as likely to lose herself in the swirling blaze. She whimpered softly and nipped at Clay's lip, as hungry as Clay. When Clay's hand skimmed the underside of her breast, Tess pulled back.

"I don't want to do this here," Tess whispered. "I want you properly."

Clay laughed, her fingers trailing over Tess's nipple as her hand dropped away. "What is properly?"

"In bed. Naked. At my bidding."

Clay shuddered and bowed her head for a long second. When she looked up, even the veneer of civilization had fallen away, leaving nothing but raw need. "Tell me what you want, and it's yours."

"I will," Tess said, because tonight she was taking what she wanted with no worries about tomorrow, and no regrets. She opened the truck door, jumped down, and started for the house without looking back. By the time she reached the front steps, Clay was there. Without saying more, Tess grabbed her hand and led her across the wide front porch, through the door that opened into the parlor, and up the central stairs to her bedroom. She didn't stop at the threshold, didn't pause until she reached the side of the big four-poster bed that had been her mother's, and her grandmother's before that. The wide-open window next to the bed admitted a fitful breeze that did nothing to cool the fire in her blood. "Stand still."

Somehow knowing she shouldn't speak, Clay watched, her hands at her sides, determined to let Tess set the pace. Tess's play, Tess's rules.

Besides, if she touched Tess now, she was likely to break and go too fast, too hard, too far. The pounding in her head matched the pounding in her groin and obliterated whatever reason and restraint made her human. Right now, she was nothing but hunger and want and the wild raging need to take and claim and own. She shivered in the heat.

In a pool of moonlight, Tess unbuttoned her shirt, let it fall to the floor, and slowly unclasped her bra. She dropped it on top of the crumpled shirt and cupped her breasts—offering them to Clay like a gift she would never deserve.

"You're so fucking beautiful," Clay groaned, her nails digging into her palms. Tess's breasts were firm and upright, her pale nipples tight in the moonlight. Clay wanted her lips on them, her hands on them, her mouth filled with them. Her belly and thighs and ass tightened, and the pressure in her groin had her pelvis rocking forward. She ached to fuck and be fucked. Her chest heaved, her breath barely more than a sob, and still Tess kept away. "I want you so much."

"Do you?" Tess smiled, flicked her fingertips over her nipples. For an instant her neck arched and her eyes closed, and then her gaze bored into Clay's. "Prove it."

Clay threw her head back, growled deep in her throat. "How?"

"Watch," Tess whispered as she unbuttoned her jeans, drew the zipper slowly down, and pushed the rest of her clothes off.

Clay remembered every inch of Tess's body, remembered every time they'd kissed, every time they'd played together and teased each other, removed each other's clothes, come together. Tess had always been beautiful, but now she was beyond description, sculpted into graceful curves and lush planes and toned muscle from age and her life on the farm. "Let me touch you?"

"Soon," Tess murmured, starting to open the buttons on Clay's shirt. "First, we need to get you naked."

No one had ever commanded Clay in bed, not even Tess very long ago when Tess could have told her to open a vein and she would have. But Tess could have whatever she wanted right now. Clay forced herself to breathe around the knifing need that pulsed in her depths. Tess parted her shirt, ran her hands over Clay's breasts, and Clay groaned. When Tess's fingernails scraped down her belly, Clay's hips rocked again and the tight knot of need in her clitoris pulsed. "I can't promise how long I can stand still."

Tess stepped back, her palms flat against Clay's chest. "I don't want you to move."

"I'm trying."

"You can do better than try. I know how strong you are."

"I'm not. Not anymore. Not with you naked."

Tess smiled, kissed her lightly. "Good."

Clay watched Tess's hands, every cell burning, as Tess unbuckled her belt, opened her pants, slowly worked them down her thighs. She kicked off her boots and Tess removed the rest of her clothes. When Tess knelt before her and kissed the inside of her thigh, she almost fell. "Christ, Tess. I can't do this anymore."

"Mmm. Sure you can." Tess lingered with her mouth on Clay's skin, breathing deep and waiting for her heart to steady and the dizzying desire to settle enough so she could keep going. She loved the power she had over Clay, the first time ever she'd really been in control. She loved the way Clay tasted, the way she smelled, the way her hard body trembled every time Tess touched her. She'd never felt so powerful, or so damn lucky. She stroked Clay's thighs, traced the etched lines of muscle, losing herself in the sculpted columns until she caressed upward over the arch of Clay's hip bones to the softly curved muscles of her lower abdomen. She pressed closer until her breasts brushed Clay's thighs, her nipples contracting painfully with the light contact. She kissed Clay's stomach and wrapped her arms around her, filling her hands with the tense mounds of Clay's ass. She closed her eyes, rubbed her cheek against Clay's belly. "I want to lick every inch of you."

Clay's fingers came into her hair, tightening against the back of her neck. "I want to come in your mouth, Tess. Please. Please let me."

Tess laughed softly. "I might. Later." She tilted her face up, marveling at the beauty of Clay's naked body and the unholy anguish in her face. Need so pure she felt blessed. "But first, you're going to make me come."

Clay's other hand came into her hair, cradling her head. Clay smiled down at her. "Yes. I am. So hard."

The arrogance rushed back into Clay's eyes, the glint of satisfaction that said Tess was hers and all she wanted, everything she wanted. Tess quickened, ready for Clay to take her right there on the floor. Before she begged, she rose quickly, grabbed Clay's hand, and pulled her to the bed. She shoved the covers aside, stretched out on the sheet, and yanked Clay over her. "Now then. Come to me now."

Clay straddled her on all fours, her thighs on either side of Tess's hips, her arms caging her shoulders. She gazed down, a feral grin making her mouth look deadly and dangerous and delicious. "Tell me what you want."

Tess grinned back and licked her lips. "Fuck me." The hunger flashing across Clay's face almost made Tess come. She broke. "Oh my God. Hurry."

Clay laughed, hearing the need she'd lived for once, could live on now. She leaned down, slicked her tongue over Tess's swollen lips. "Yeah? Is that what you want? Me inside you?"

Tess's eyes flashed and she caught Clay's lip, bit hard enough to make Clay groan. "Yes, damn you. I want you to make me come."

Clay cupped her center, teased her fingers along her cleft, circled her entrance. Her arm trembled. Her throat was so tight she could barely form words. "Sure?"

"I'm going to come if you don't do it now." Tess raised her hips, grabbed Clay's wrist, and took her inside. A sob tore from her chest and she bowed off the bed. "God. Yes. Right now."

"Wait, baby," Clay groaned, pressing her face to Tess's throat. "Let me have you a while first. Please." Ignoring the pressure pounding in her pelvis, she stroked through the tight sheath, pushing deeper with every thrust. Tess's legs clamped around her ass as Tess's teeth found her shoulder. "That's it baby, ride me."

"I am going to come all over you any second," Tess gasped.

"Yes you are." Clay straddled Tess's thigh, ground her clit into Tess's sweat-slicked satin skin. "Yes you are."

"Oh fuck. God. I'm going to come so hard."

"Okay, baby, okay. You come for me right now." Clay gloried in the beat of Tess's heart around her fingers, drowning in the pleasure swimming in Tess's eyes. When Tess cried her name as she went over, Clay knew beyond all doubt she'd never want for more.

CHAPTER TWENTY-FOUR

Tess couldn't move, couldn't speak, but she knew what she wanted. More. She wanted more. More of the incredible freedom of being in the moment and *only* the moment—not the past or the future—without thought, with only sensation. More of Clay. "Oh my God."

"I'm not going to answer to that because I can't defend myself right now," Clay muttered.

Tess laughed and caressed the length of Clay's back until her hand rested on Clay's ass. Clay covered her, her weight unfamiliar but welcome. The room was hot, their skin sweat-slicked, but she wouldn't have had Clay move for anything in the world. She slid her leg around the outside of Clay's, draping her calf in the bend of Clay's leg, tethering her. "I wasn't talking to you."

"Someone joined us while I wasn't looking?"

"I'm not going to feed your ego and tell you that was wonderful."

"I don't mind telling you it was incredible." Clay pushed up on her elbow and propped her head in the cup of her hand. Playing with Tess's hair with her other hand, she grinned down at her. "I think—no, I know—I've never had an orgasm just from making someone come before."

Tess narrowed her eyes and squeezed Clay's ass, letting her nails dig in just a little. "Talking about other…*experiences*…might not be a very good idea at the moment."

"How about…" Clay nipped at Tess's chin. "You're amazing. Unbelievable. You fry my brain. I want you again."

"That's better." Tess tightened inside, felt herself swell again. "Because I want you to have me again."

"Mmm. Good." Clay pushed up on both arms and started to slide off Tess's body. "This time I plan to make you—"

Tess gripped her around the waist, holding her in place. "But not just yet."

"Why not?"

While Clay was off guard, Tess lifted her hips and managed to roll her over. She laughed at the look of consternation on Clay's face when she landed on top of her, pinning her down. "You don't think we're going to do everything on your timetable, do you?"

"To tell you the truth," Clay raised her head, brushed her cheek over Tess's breast, and kissed her nipple, "I can't think of much of anything at all. Except I can't get my fill of you."

"You'll have plenty of time to try before the sun comes up." For an instant, a curtain fell in Clay's eyes, preventing Tess from seeing beneath the solid brown surface. The barrier was a shock after what they'd just done—what she'd just experienced—and she wanted that shield gone. She kissed Clay hard, delving into her mouth, calling her back, demanding she be with her. With her in the moment. When Clay's arms came around her, firm and possessing, she gentled the kiss, teased a little along the edge of Clay's lower lip until Clay groaned. "Any complaints?"

"None," Clay murmured, cupping Tess's breast. She brushed her thumb back and forth over Tess's nipple, making it pucker and pulse. She smiled a satisfied smile when Tess caught her breath. "None at all."

"So for the time being…" Tess kissed Clay on the mouth, on the edge of her jaw, on the slope of her neck. Clay tasted of forest, rich and pungent. A drop of sweat beaded in the hollow between her collarbones, and Tess caught it on the tip of her tongue. Tangy and sweet, uniquely Clay. "This is where you lie still."

Clay grimaced, her eyes flashing. "I already did that."

"No," Tess murmured, circling Clay's nipple with her tongue, "you were *standing* still then. This is the next stage."

Clay tangled her fingers in Tess's hair. "How many stages are there?"

Tess grinned, resting her chin on Clay's chest. The pressure of

Clay's thigh between her legs was making it hard for her to concentrate on words. All she wanted was taste and touch and smell and the sound of Clay out of control for her. "Not sure yet. I'm making it up as I go along."

Clay laughed, a deep resonant sound that vibrated into Tess's chest. She loved the sound, wanted to hear it again and again. "Laughing at a woman in bed could be dangerous."

"Oh no, baby. You're doing great as far as I'm concerned," Clay said.

"And that's all that matters." Realizing how much she meant that, Tess pushed away thoughts of what would happen in the morning. For tonight, there was no tomorrow.

Inching down, kissing Clay's breasts and abdomen, she settled between Clay's spread thighs. She tugged on the skin around Clay's belly button until Clay hissed and her thighs tightened against the outside of Tess's hips. Clay was wet and hot against her belly, and Tess forgot what she had intended to do. Slow, that was it, she was going to go slow and tease her, but God, she wanted her now. She wanted to taste her, to swallow her, to fill herself with everything that was Clay.

"Damn it," Tess gasped, "I can't wait."

"Good," Clay said, her voice raspy. She pushed herself up on her elbows and looked down at Tess. "Neither can I."

"Just one more minute. You look so gorgeous right now." Tess stroked Clay's breasts, her belly, and the base of her clitoris until Clay's thighs trembled and her eyes glazed. The glory of Clay in need threatened to stop her heart. Cradling Clay's hips in her hands, Tess took her into her mouth. She was slick and sweet and hot and hard and everything she desired. Everything.

Clay watched Tess take her, forcing her arms to support her as her muscles melted and her control shattered. Devastated by pleasure, she fought to memorize everything about the moment—the silvery glow of Tess's face in the moonlight, the fall of her tangled blond hair over one shoulder, the way she murmured softly in her throat as she took Clay deeper into her mouth. If morning was the end of this miracle, she needed every minute to last a lifetime.

"I love watching you make me come," Clay whispered and Tess jerked, moaning softly. Tess's eyes were nearly closed, her expression possessive and fierce. "I like when you own me."

Tess looked up, her lips brushing Clay's clitoris. "I like owning you."

"I'd like it even better if you came while you were making me come."

Tess kissed her clit and Clay jerked. Tess grinned. "Is that what you want? Me to come with you in my mouth?"

"Yes. Yes." Clay shuddered, sensing the last of her control snap, one strand at a time. "Fuck yes."

"Like this, then?" Tess's pupils flickered, her lids lowered, and she slid one hand down the bed under her belly and between her legs. She caught her breath as her hips involuntarily lifted.

"Oh yeah," Clay said, scarcely breathing. "That's exactly what I want."

"This will drive me crazy," Tess said.

"Then I won't be alone." Clay cupped the back of Tess's head and pressed up against her mouth. "Take me deep. I'm ready for you."

Heat flooding through her, Tess cupped herself and closed her lips around Clay again. Easing her fingers on either side of her clitoris, she stroked lightly. Pressure built deep inside as Clay rocked faster and faster against her mouth. She was no stranger to making herself come, but never like this, never having Clay inside her mouth and about to explode. The sensation of Clay on the verge of coming pushed her to the edge faster than she meant to come. She pulled away, cried out, "Oh God, I'm going to come."

Clay gripped her head in both hands and pushed up against her mouth. "So am I. Don't stop. I want to be in your mouth when you do."

Tess closed her lips around Clay's clitoris as pleasure broke over her. She came in waves as Clay pulsed inside her, giving her exactly what she wanted. Everything.

❖

Clay lay awake watching the sun come up with Tess curled against her front. Tess's ass was cradled in the curve of her pelvis and her back against Clay's breasts. Clay lightly stroked her belly and thighs, not wanting to wake her, but needing to touch. She hadn't slept much, too hungry for Tess to do more than doze between orgasms. Each time awareness returned, the need came with it, a wild mindless thing clawing inside her, demanding Tess's taste and scent and heat. Clay took her, again and again, with her hands and mouth and heart, devouring, consuming, reveling in the possession of her. She'd finally taken pity on Tess and let her sleep even though the need still pounded through her.

Carefully, Clay feathered her fingers over the soft delta between Tess's thighs. Tess's breathing changed and Clay knew she was awake. She kissed the tip of her shoulder. "Morning."

"Good morning," Tess said quietly. She'd been awake a few minutes, absorbing the sensation of being in Clay's arms, of the way Clay touched her—reverently, as if she were precious, and with an unapologetic sense of ownership that made her want to be filled. She reached down, caught Clay's hand, and entwined their fingers. She drew Clay's hand up to her breast and her nipple hardened against Clay's palm. Clay squeezed her, her clit tingled, and somehow, unbelievably, she was ready again. "What time is it?"

"A little after five."

Tess sighed. "I can't believe I slept so late. I need to go help with the milking."

"If I help, can you stay here a little longer?"

"Clay—you don't know anything about cows."

"I learn fast." Clay sucked the juncture of Tess's neck and shoulder, and Tess shivered.

"You don't have to." Tess had a little trouble catching her breath. Clay did things to her she couldn't control and didn't really want to. All the more reason to get up and get some sense back into her addled brain.

"The air smells like rain," Clay said.

Tess shook her head. "Not in the forecast."

"Forecasts are wrong sometimes. Unpredictable."

"I know."

Clay nuzzled Tess's neck, kissed the spot just below her ear that made Tess moan. "How you doing?"

"I don't know."

Clay tensed, waiting for the recriminations and the regret. "Tess—"

"I'm pretty sure I'm going to be sore in unusual places for a day or two, and"—Tess rolled onto her back and kissed Clay's throat—"I'm also pretty sure I want you to fuck me again."

"Yeah?"

"Yeah."

Clay almost sighed out loud. Tess was still here, with her. The hand that had been fisted around her heart, slowly crushing the life from it as the hours of the night had bled away, let go and she could breathe again. She still had time. She kissed Tess lightly and caressed Tess's belly and cupped between her legs. Tess was wet, open for her, and she gently eased inside.

Tess sucked in a breath, her lids fluttering.

Clay kissed her. "Good?"

"Amazing." Tess covered Clay's hand and held her motionless inside her. "Just stay right there for a minute. If you move, I'm going to come too soon."

"It's never too soon. But I'd stay here like this forever if you wanted."

Tess's eyes glazed, and she caught her lower lip between her teeth. "I love feeling you make me come."

Clay kissed her breast, brushed her mouth over Tess's nipple, and returned to watching her face. "I love making you come."

"If you fuck me just a little right now, I will."

"Anything you want." Clay gathered her close, one arm around her shoulders, and held her tight against her chest. Tess slid her leg over Clay's hip, opening herself, giving Clay room to move. Clay stroked long and slow and deep, her thumb just brushing Tess's clitoris each time she entered. Tess's hips set the pace, and she followed. When Tess pushed harder against her hand, she picked up speed. When Tess's teeth grazed her shoulder, she kissed her, drinking in Tess's cries of pleasure as Tess's orgasm flooded around her fingers. When Tess sagged in her arms, she buried her face in the curve of Tess's neck. "God, Tess, you're so beautiful. I lo—"

"Clay, don't," Tess murmured. "Just—don't."

Silently, Clay nodded. She understood. Tess wanted her in bed, at least right this moment, but that's all she wanted. She didn't trust her for more. And Clay didn't blame her. Tess didn't have any reason to trust her, and the knowledge was a knife in her heart.

A cracking boom split the air and Tess pulled away, half sitting. "Oh my God. I think that was thunder."

The sky outside the open window turned black as night. Tess jumped from the bed and raced to look out. "You should see the sky. Lightning everywhere."

"Something big coming," Clay said, knowing the storms of change had arrived.

CHAPTER TWENTY-FIVE

I'm going to take a quick shower," Tess said, turning from the window.

Clay sat on the side of the bed, waiting to be dismissed. Tess had warned her the night would end at sunrise, but she wasn't volunteering to leave just yet. Visions of Tess in the shower made it difficult for her to think of what her next step should be, anyhow. The only thing she knew for certain was she didn't want to say good-bye, and she feared once she walked out Tess's door, good-bye might be very final.

As if suddenly realizing she was naked, Tess hurriedly gathered up the clothes scattered around on the floor and dumped them on an old-style navy-blue demi-sofa pushed up to the foot of the big mahogany bedstead. Without looking at Clay, Tess sorted through the jumble of their entangled shirts, pants, and underwear. Such a telling activity, with those shed coverings the undeniable testament to their previous intimacy, although Tess looked as if she wanted to avoid thinking of what they meant. Her expression was remote, turned inward, undecipherable.

Clay waited, heart pounding.

"I'd offer to share the water, but to be honest," Tess said as she straightened and finally looked at Clay again, "I don't trust myself in there with you, and I have things to do. If there's a storm coming, I need to check the heifer barn and bring in extra feed for the cows. I have to go."

"That doesn't sound too bad to me. The shower part, I mean." Clay grinned, she couldn't help it. The frown forming between Tess's eyes suggested laughter wasn't a great idea at the moment.

"No, I don't imagine it does." Tess pulled on the shirt she'd been wearing the night before. "And part of me thinks it's a great idea too. But in case you haven't noticed, we're really not teenagers anymore, and I've got a business to run. I haven't been doing a great job of that lately." She shook her head and sighed. "Maybe I haven't been doing a good job of it ever."

Clay grabbed her pants from the pile, pulled them on, and stood. "That's not true, and you know it. This is a great-looking farm and I may not know much about cows, but from the looks of things around here, you're doing everything right."

"Yes, so right that I didn't even know Ray had signed over drilling rights to your company." Tess scrubbed her face. "God, I must look like an idiot. I am an idiot."

"Bullshit. You can't be responsible for what you didn't know."

Tess, wearing only her shirt, jammed her hands on her hips and gave Clay a hard stare. "Okay, maybe you're right about that. But it seems that the things I don't know keep popping up in my life and redirecting it, and I'm tired of not being the one driving the bus."

Of all the directions the morning after might have taken, this was the one Clay had hoped to avoid. For a little while longer, at least. She stepped toward Tess and stopped at the cool look Tess gave her. "Do we have to do this now? Last night was—"

"Last night was last night. But great sex doesn't make the problems go away, and NorthAm is a problem."

"I'm not NorthAm," Clay said quietly. She picked up the T-shirt she'd worn under her work shirt and pulled it on.

"No, you're not. But you walked back into my life and suddenly I discover I may not have any choice but to let you tear up my land." Tess yanked on her jeans and crossed to the window again, keeping distance between them. Her gaze moved past Clay to the bed and she sighed. "I never seem to have any choice where you're concerned."

"You did last night."

Tess closed her eyes. "Yes, I did. Thank you."

"Damn it, Tess. I don't want your thanks." Clay jerked down her fly and stuffed her T-shirt into her pants. She'd been avoiding this conversation practically half her life, and maybe the time had come to stop. Tess couldn't seem to look at her without seeing the past, and maybe the only way to put the past to rest was to dig it up first. "I know I didn't leave you any choice that summer. I don't have an excuse, but I do have a reason. I thought I was doing the right thing."

"You understand I have no idea what you're talking about." Tess leaned a shoulder against the window frame and folded her arms across her chest. "How can I, since I still have no idea what happened back then."

"It's compli—"

"I don't want to hear it's complicated. I know just how complicated it was." Tess pushed a hand through her hair. "How hard would it have been, Clay, to just call me and tell me you had to leave? Even if you didn't want to tell me why—just to say good-bye?"

"I was afraid if I did I wouldn't be able to go," Clay said, her voice so low Tess could barely hear her.

"I don't understand."

Clay sat back down on the bed and gripped the mattress on either side of her hips to keep from pounding it with her fists. She forced herself to meet Tess's confused, angry, and hurt gaze. "My father made me leave. He didn't give *me* any choice."

"Mine did the same thing, but I tried to call you. Over and over." Tess fell silent, clearly expecting more.

"My father was wrong. I was wrong. But it happened a long time ago, and—"

"And you've forgotten it?"

"No," Clay snapped. "Never. Jesus, Tess, I wasn't lying when I told you I loved you."

Tess's expression subtly shifted, anger and confusion giving way to sadness like the march of shadows across a still pond. The hurt still lingered as she said, "You know, I don't hold you to that. How could I? Sometimes we say things we mean in the moment, and then life changes and we change and—"

"No, God damn it, that's not what happened." Clay shot to her feet. "My feelings for you didn't change. They never changed."

Tess had never seen Clay this upset. She'd expected irritation, defensiveness, maybe even dismissiveness, but not this. Clay was hurting. That, more than even the night before, when she'd doubted she could feel any more for Clay—or anyone—than she did right then, pushed Tess to crack the shell she'd built around herself. She gripped Clay's shoulders and caressed the tight muscles beneath her fingers. "All right, slow down."

"I can't stand you thinking I didn't care."

Tess forced herself to remember the way Clay had touched her. She stroked down the outside of Clay's arms, found her hands, and entwined their fingers. "I know you did. Now slow down and just tell me what happened."

"I want to, I've always wanted to. But it's not just about me, Tess." Clay's dark eyes swam with frustration and unhappiness.

Tess wanted to kiss the misery away, but that wasn't what they needed. One kiss and they'd be back in bed. The sex between them was too good, too incendiary. Too cleansing in the moment. But when the passion ebbed, the shadows of all that had been and still might be would remain, and sooner or later, they'd reach this impasse again. She squeezed Clay's fingers, smiled faintly. "I don't understand. You said your father made you leave. Some family matter—some secret?"

Clay looked away. She couldn't figure out how to get through this without hurting Tess, and she refused to lie. She had lied by omission all these years, and she wouldn't keep doing it. "My father wanted me to break up with you. He had his reasons, and I went along with them."

"Your father? But how did he even know?"

"You don't know my father." Clay grimaced. "There isn't anything he can't find out if he wants to."

"Yes, but who? The only ones who ever saw us being friendly were Leslie and Dev, and even they didn't know we were together." Tess slowly accepted she'd never known the whole picture, never known all of Clay. How much of her life had been a lie, partly of her own making. "I never saw anyone else with you—a bodyguard or anything. But you had one, didn't you? Someone like Ella. That's why you could never be sure when you'd be coming to see me, always told me you might be late. You were sneaking around, weren't you?"

"I thought of it as stealing my freedom." Clay stroked Tess's cheek. "That's what you always were to me, Tess. Freedom. The only things you knew about me were the things I showed you, the secrets I told you, the dreams we shared. You gave me a place to be myself, to be free."

"I think that might be the nicest thing anyone's ever said to me."

Tess feathered her fingers through Clay's hair, aching to heal the wounds she heard in Clay's voice, erase the pain she saw in her eyes. "You were my dream, Clay. Maybe that wasn't fair, but that's what you were."

"I'm sorry," Clay whispered.

"So who told your father about me? That you were consorting with a commoner. Your bodyguard?"

A muscle jumped in Clay's jaw. "Damn it, Tess, it wasn't about that."

"Then what was it about?"

The silence stretched and Tess waited. Clay was hiding something, and she couldn't for the life of her imagine what it was. Even if Clay was embarrassed that she had given in to her father's demands, that was no great sin. Most teenagers, no matter how independent and strong they thought themselves to be, had trouble bucking their parents' wishes. That day Ray showed up out of the blue and told her he wanted her back on the farm, she'd gone, no questions asked. Sure, she'd thought she'd have a chance to see Clay again. Talk to her again. Figure out a way to be together, but she hadn't fought him when he'd told her she had to lea—

"Ray," Tess said slowly, something cold and alien slithering through her mind. Something she didn't want to look at but knew she must. "Ray showed up the same day you left. He never did tell me why I had to come home in such a big hurry. Just things had changed and he wanted me home." Her gaze sharpened, bored into Clay. "Did your father call him? Is that it?"

"Tess," Clay said wearily, "Ray's dead. It's behind us now. What—"

"It matters, Clay. It matters because I was part of it, but no one gave me a chance to make any of the decisions. Everyone, including you, decided for me. And I want to know why."

Clay pulled free of Tess's grip on her hand, breaking the last connection between them, and went to the window. Clouds rolled through the sky like angry waves on a deadly ocean, blocking out the sun. "The wind's picking up. Rains will be here any minute. You should get down to the barn."

"I don't need you to tell me how to run my farm," Tess said from behind her. "And I can get back to doing that sooner if you'd stop hiding."

Clay spun around. "All right, if that's what you want, then here it is."

Clay's eyes grew cold and hard, and Tess braced herself. She was no stranger to pain, but when the hurt came from Clay, she feared she might not be strong enough. "All right. Yes. Tell me."

"Ray saw us the night we were having sex up in the hayloft. I'm not sure how he figured out who I was, but he did."

"He knew your name, it wouldn't have been that difficult to find out the rest of it," Tess said. "It never occurred to me to try to find out anything about you, but it probably wouldn't have been that difficult. I bet there were even articles about you in the newspapers."

"Sure there were. I wasn't in hiding, just pretending I was," Clay said bitterly. "Easy enough to read about the Sutter heir if anybody really wanted to look, and I guess maybe he did."

"What did he do?" Tess said, ice freezing around her heart.

Clay looked directly into Tess's eyes. Hers were dark as the storm sky outside. "He contacted my father and threatened to sell a story to the tabloids about us. He claimed I seduced you, took advantage of you."

The air punched from Tess's lungs and for a second she couldn't breathe. "What? How could he—that's ridiculous!"

"You were right about the newspaper articles about me and my family—my father is a very powerful man with a lot of enemies. We make good gossip, and the tabloids love stories about sexual indiscretions."

"But I would've denied it, of course. I would've told everyone—" She stopped, stared at Clay. "I would have told everyone I was with you because I loved you."

"That wouldn't have changed anything. If Ray had gone through with it and the story got out, the press would have had a field day, my father would have set his lawyers on both of you and torn you to shreds," Clay said softly. "But not before everyone in this county would have heard from my father's spin doctors how *you* seduced me and your father tried to blackmail mine. You would have been front-page news, Tess. Your life would have been the topic of gossip in the diner and the Grange and every other place, forever."

"So you decided the best thing for me was for you to disappear? To keep me in the dark about Ray? Your silence let me go on trusting him, and look what he did—he went right on stealing my life." Hands trembling, Tess ordered her shaking limbs not to sway. "Damn it, Clay, why didn't you trust me? Weren't we worth believing in?"

Clay clasped her shoulder. "I know it looks that way, Tess, but—"

"I'll tell you how it looks." Tess jerked away. "It looks as if you took the easy way out. The way that wouldn't embarrass your father or your family name with a scandal. I suppose I even understand that."

"That's not true. I thought I was doing the right thing for you."

"Maybe I didn't want you to decide that, Clay, but you never asked. You were right when you said it was a long time ago. It doesn't matter now. It's over. It's been over for a long time, I just didn't know it." Tess walked to the bedroom door, questioning herself and everything she'd ever known. Ray had manipulated her life for years and she'd never known. She would never let herself be that vulnerable again. She looked back at Clay, afraid she'd made a huge mistake. Clay touched the heart of her so easily and so deeply she couldn't think rationally about anything. "Now you're back, and I've got another decision to make. At least this time, I'll be responsible for what happens to me."

"Can we at least—"

"I don't know." Tess laughed humorlessly. "The only thing I know for sure is I can't decide anything with you in my bed."

Clay nodded. "I'll clear out."

Tess's vision swam with confusion and regret, unable to trust anything she felt. Only the pain was real. "Good-bye, Clay."

CHAPTER TWENTY-SIX

Tess stepped out into a morning as dark as night. As she left the porch, the rain started, slanting sheets of needle-sharp pellets, ominously cold. She squinted into the murky haze. Not rain, hail.

"Oh Lord," she muttered, dashing to her truck. A hailstorm could strip the shoots from the cornstalks, shear the hay off at the ground, and strip fledgling leaves from the soybean plants. A storm like this could take all the crops with it. Tearing down the drive, she bumped off the gravel surface and onto the dirt tractor path skirting the largest of her fields. Straight ahead, the square windows in the cow barn glowed like unblinking yellow eyes in a curtain of black. She pulled up as close to the door as she could and jumped out. Tomas was inside, seeing to the morning milking. The bulk of the herd was under cover, leaving only the heifers, who wouldn't give milk until they'd calved, and the dry cows out in the pastures. She rotated the milk cows over her fourteen pastures every twelve hours, but the non-milkers were scattered in half a dozen different pastures.

"Is Jimmy here?" Tess called. "Looks like we're going to get worse weather before this ends, and we need to bring the rest in."

"He just went out," Tomas said, adroitly removing the suction tubes from one cow and moving the milking machine to the next cow in line. He washed down the udders of the cow he'd just finished milking, swabbed the next one, and set up the suction lines.

"I'll go help him," Tess said. Tomas didn't need her help—he could do the whole barn almost as fast as the two of them together.

"Why don't you let me do it, Tess. No sense you getting soaked out there."

"That's all right. I need to check on the heifers anyhow." Tess grabbed a rain slicker from a hook next to the door and a feed bucket from a nearby shelf. Right about now a little ugly weather suited her mood just fine. Maybe the icy rain would cool her off enough that she could think straight. "You take care of this. I'll be back after I give Jimmy a hand."

"All right, but watch for trees. After all this drought, the roots are going to be loose. More than a few will be coming down."

"I will. Thanks."

She ventured out into the storm, and the ferocity of it took her breath away. The wind howled, and bullets of hail the size of marbles pummeled her back and shoulders. She tied the slicker hood tightly under her chin and raced toward the pasture where the dry cows had been left to forage. As she came closer to the big metal pasture fence, she caught flashes of red and finally made out Jimmy, bending into the wind to keep his footing on the slick, muddy ground, coming from the other direction. What had been a dry gulch the day before was now a slippery slope.

"I'll get the gate," she yelled, cupping her hands around her mouth when she was close enough to be heard. "Let's get them in the small barn."

Looking white-faced and ghostly in the unnatural gloom, Jimmy shouted, "The storm's got them all riled up. I'm afraid they'll scatter if we let them out of here."

"Chance we'll have to take." Tess released the chain on the gate. "Hopefully they'd rather be dry and safe than running around out here in this mess."

Tess opened the gate, pulled it wide, and swung the feed bucket in a big arc, hoping to catch the attention of the closest cows. When they focused on the familiar object, she started leading them to the barn while Jimmy herded the wanderers back into line. The jostling animals, agitated and frightened, ambled past her in an uneasy clump. The barn meant food, water, and warmth, and fortunately, that was enough to keep them all moving steadily toward safety.

Inside the L extension off the main milking barn, two long rows of open stalls stretched the length of the building. Tess and Jimmy tied the cows up to the big rings mounted on the walls, forked straw for bedding, and shoveled feed into buckets. As they worked, the uneven drumbeat of hail on the roof continued.

"If the rain keeps up like this," Tess said, "it's going to be more damaging than the heat."

"Sure hope not," Jimmy said. "We've got enough trouble to worry about with the oil people. Don't need more weather problems too."

The vehemence in his tone was surprising, but probably he was echoing the sentiment of a lot of the locals. Before long, Clay and NorthAm would be getting blamed for everything that went awry in the whole county. She squelched her immediate desire to defend Clay.

"Hopefully this will let up soon," Tess said. Be careful what you wish for. That seemed to be the message of the day, possibly for her whole life. She had wished for a love of her own, a romance to last a lifetime, and when she'd met Clay, she'd thought she had it. She'd spun visions of the future for the two of them that included everything she'd ever wanted—the farm, the challenge of going organic, a life of her making, all wrapped inside an envelope of love and passion. And now she was faced with the reality that her stepfather, a man she'd never deeply loved but had depended upon and trusted as a parent, had used that dream and her very real love for Clay to manipulate her life. And continued to betray her long afterward.

Tess cut the baling twine on the last bundle of straw and slid her utility knife back into the pocket of her jeans. She tossed handfuls of straw into the last stall, thinking about Ray and what he'd done.

Why? What had he really gained by keeping her and Clay apart? He got her to come home where she provided free labor, but she would have done that anyhow if he'd told her he couldn't run the farm without her. She would have come home—she would have sacrificed her plans to go to college for however long it took to get the farm on solid footing, but he hadn't said that. He hadn't told her much of anything. So why—

Tess shivered in her rain-soaked shirt and pants. She was cold, but the chill that overtook her had nothing to do with the weather. What had Clay said? That everyone in the county would've heard that she had seduced Clay and her father had blackmailed Clay's. No, that just couldn't be true, could it? Ray wouldn't have done that.

"Can you handle things, Jimmy?"

"Sure, Tess." Jimmy straightened, his face eager. "Anything you need. Anytime."

"Thanks for getting over here early today—you were a big help." Tess hurried to the far corner of the barn where she usually had good luck getting a cell signal and pulled out Clay's card—the one she'd picked up at the Grange and tucked into her wallet—and punched in Clay's number. The call went right to voice mail. She disconnected the call without leaving a message. This wasn't something she wanted to discuss on the phone.

"Is everything all right, Tess?" Jimmy said from a few feet away.

"What?" Tess jumped. He'd gotten close without her knowing it and that wasn't like her. She shook her head and forced a smile. "Oh, yes. Everything's fine." She waved toward the open doors and the steady pounding of water that kicked up muddy mini-fountains all across the yard outside. "This damn storm. I'll have to keep an eye on the creek—if we get much more of this, it's going to flood."

"I've got the ATV up here. I'll take a look around in a couple of hours. Make sure none of the trees come down and back it up."

"I don't want you out in the storm," Tess said. "If one of those trees comes down, I don't want you getting caught under it."

"I'll be fine, Tess." He blushed and stuffed his hands in his pockets. "When do you figure those oil people will be done up on your hill?"

"Oh—soon, I think." Tess smiled. "Well, thanks again. I'll see you later."

"Sure, Tess. If you need me to come back out for anything, just call me."

"I'll do that." Tess dashed across the soggy yard toward the main barn, thinking of Clay's card in her pocket and the questions she had to ask. No one could help her with what she really needed. She was going to have to do that herself.

❖

Clay had waited for Tess to leave before clearing out, as promised. She'd stood at the window and watched as Tess's truck tore down the drive and cut across the fields toward the big barn. She'd lost sight of her in the haze of hail and rain after a minute, and had no excuse to linger.

She found her boots, pulled them on, and contemplated the tangle of sheets and pillows on the bed. She left it all as it was, deciding she didn't want to erase her presence, even though Tess probably wanted to. Tess seemed ready to erase everything—past, present, and future. In some ways, she understood.

Now that she'd put the past into words for Tess, she was forced to look at them through the lens of time. Back then, she'd had only her own perspective, as Tess had had hers. They'd experienced the same events very differently, and that was mostly her fault. She supposed in some ways, Tess was right, she *had* taken the easiest course—she hadn't defied her father, she hadn't given Tess a choice, and in all the years that had followed, she hadn't given Tess the satisfaction of knowing all the details. She didn't deny her reasons—she hadn't wanted Tess dragged into some public display by Ray or her father. And she hadn't exaggerated what her father would have done if Ray threatened them. To him, the family name was synonymous with power, influence, and always coming out on top, and he would do anything to win. She hadn't wanted Tess to be a casualty of that war, and she hadn't wanted it for herself, either.

If she were Tess, she'd be angry and distrustful too. And the present situation only made things worse. If she'd come back into Tess's life for no other reason than to tell her all of the truth about the past and admit what she hadn't been willing to acknowledge to herself—that she'd never been happy a single day of her life after leaving the lake that summer—maybe they could have gone forward. Instead, she'd reappeared as a representative of NorthAm, a potential threat, if not an outright enemy. No wonder Tess couldn't sort things out. She hadn't been doing a very good job of that herself.

Clay walked downstairs, closed the front door carefully behind her, and strode through the driving rain to the SUV. She had come here to do a job, and as much as she hated to admit it, her father had been right. She'd let the personal cloud her professional judgment, and in the process, she'd damaged her nascent relationship with Tess and hadn't been a particularly good representative of the company, either. That she could change, at least. And then maybe she'd have a chance to repair her relationship with Tess.

Driving one-handed down the empty country roads, she tried to raise Ella on her cell phone. The signals fluctuated on a good day, and she got nothing today. When she came to a crossroads, she hesitated before turning right and heading into Cambridge. Instead, she turned left. One good thing about dealing with farmers, they were always up early.

❖

The house was eerily quiet when Tess returned to change into something dry. Clay's SUV was gone, and she ignored the unexpected ache Clay's absence carved within her. She put the kettle on to boil, went upstairs, and stripped down in the bathroom. Walking naked to the bureau in the adjacent bedroom, she caught sight of the bed in the mirror. The image of Clay shimmered into crystal clarity. For the first time in her life, the memory of the younger Clay didn't eclipse the present. She had a new memory now, one of a powerful, beautiful, devastating woman. She turned to the rumpled bed, and the memory didn't fade. The outline of Clay's body stretched out above her, beside her, beneath her, was as sharp as the desire curling in her depths. The scent and taste of her were as potent as they had been when they were deep inside each other. Her skin vibrated with the sensation of Clay's hands moving over her. She ached for the cool, silky splendor of Clay's mouth on her flesh.

Clay Sutter was no memory. She was a living presence stamped on her every cell.

"Great," Tess muttered. "Just great."

She pulled on jeans and a T-shirt and went downstairs to finish making the tea. Sitting down at the kitchen table, she made a call. If she knew Leslie, she'd be up by now.

"Hello?" Leslie said.

"Les, it's Tess. Sorry to bother you so early, but I need to talk to you about the situation with NorthAm."

"That's all right, I was going to call you too. I've been going over the papers and I've come across a few things that seem odd." Leslie murmured something Tess couldn't hear, probably to Dev, then came back clearly. "Tell me why you called first."

"Clay tells me that her father's planning to send his legal team up to close the remaining contracts. I wanted you to know right away."

"Did Clay say when?"

"Soon."

"I wish I had better news," Leslie said, "but I don't think you're going to have much wiggle room in these negotiations, Tess. Ray signed some fairly binding agreements. Even though you are now his heir, these kinds of things are difficult to reverse. We can certainly try, and I'm willing to do it, but you need to know going in it could be pricey, and there's no guarantee."

Tess squeezed the bridge of her nose. "That's my quandary. I'm not even sure how I feel about the drilling. NorthAm is still surveying and testing and we're supposed to get more information soon. Either way, though, I'd like to have the choice once all the information is available."

"I totally understand and I agree with you. We'll do the best we can. Ray never talked to you about this?"

"Ray didn't talk to me about a lot of things," Tess said.

"What's going on?"

Tess gave her the bare bones of the story Clay had told her that morning, and as she did, she saw the two of them again, young, innocent, untested, and caught in a moment out of time that was destined to vanish. "I can't believe Ray did that—or I guess I don't want to believe he did that, but Ray was always the kind of person who felt the end justified the means. I guess he did that time too."

"I didn't know him," Leslie said, "and I certainly have no desire to defend him. Using you that way was unconscionable, and to go on keeping you in the dark all this time just as bad. That must've been really hard for you, and Clay too."

Tess closed her eyes. She hadn't been the only one hurt. "Yes."

"There's something really strange about these contracts too," Leslie said. "Some of the riders are relatively recent, but the original agreement isn't. Ray signed these rights over years ago, well before NorthAm moved into your area in full force."

"How long ago?"

"As far back as that summer, Tess."

"But that doesn't make any sense," Tess said.

"It might, if Ray didn't think he was actually giving anything up but was forcing NorthAm into buying something they might never use."

"I'm not following."

"Considering what you just told me, this deal could be a well-camouflaged payoff," Leslie said quietly. "If Ray demanded money from Clay's father but could show that NorthAm had actually paid him for something, legally he'd be in the clear."

Clay's words came back in force, and Tess had the answer she was looking for. "You mean Ray might've blackmailed Clay's father but made it all look like a transaction?"

"It's possible. I've done a little research, and the price NorthAm paid Ray was triple what drilling rights in the Northeast were going for at the time."

"How could this have happened," Tess whispered.

"Money changes hands all the time under the guise of legitimate business deals for a lot of reasons. For greed, for power, for influence, and sometimes just to preserve the status quo. It's ugly, and when you're caught in the middle like you and Clay were, it's immoral. Unfortunately, it's not illegal."

"Then why do I feel so dirty?"

"You shouldn't. You were a victim. Both of you were."

Tess straightened in her chair. "I know you're right, but I refuse to be anyone's victim. I might have been then, but I won't be now."

"I'm glad. And I'm here, no matter what you decide to do."

"Thanks, Les. I appreciate it."

Tess said good-bye and cradled her cup of cooling tea. She sipped it, trying to digest everything she'd heard that morning. Unraveling the past was an impossible task, and maybe an unnecessary one. What mattered now was what she was going to do. And the first step was dealing with the woman she'd slept with the night before, the woman in her life now, whose touch wouldn't stop haunting her. She'd meant what she said to Leslie. She wouldn't be a victim ever again, not even of her own pride.

Chapter Twenty-seven

Clay, barely able to see through the deluge, crept down the winding drive to Pete Townsend's farm with the windshield wipers on as high as they would go. She slowed next to the rambling white clapboard farmhouse, trying to discern if anyone was up yet. From the front the place seemed quiet, but a window in the barn was alight. When she reached the first of half a dozen long, low cow barns, she pulled to a stop, jumped out, and ran through the downpour to the big sliding doors. Easing inside, she wiped the rain from her eyes and looked around. As she'd anticipated, the barn was modern and expensive-looking. Townsend, unlike Tess, raised beef cows, and most of his stockier, heavier-coated cattle were probably outside in the pastures. A few cows with young calves occupied several of the stalls. At the far end of the building, a man in a yellow slicker forked hay into a wheelbarrow. Walking down the center aisle, she called, "Mr. Townsend, it's Clay Sutter."

Townsend leaned on his pitchfork and watched her approach, his big florid face appraising. "Not much of a morning to be out."

Clay pulled her wet shirt away from her shoulders. "I agree with you there." She laughed. "And since I was in the neighborhood enjoying the day, I thought I'd come by. Sorry I'm early."

"No problem. I can't do much but kill time until this rain lets up, anyhow." He hung the pitchfork on a hook. "What can I do for you?"

"I was hoping we could discuss the shale project—find some neutral ground."

"Not sure there is any, but why don't we walk up to the house. I could use some coffee. You?"

"That would be most welcome."

She hunched under the short overhang outside while he took care of closing up the barn, and then they both sprinted across the wide drive to the back door of the farmhouse. Inside the large country kitchen with its wood-burning stove, massive wood trestle table that would easily seat twelve, and eight-burner commercial-grade cookstove, she stamped the water from her boots and nodded to a blonde frying eggs and bacon at the stove.

"I'm just going to get a dry shirt," Pete said and disappeared.

The blonde, who looked to be a decade or more younger than Pete, smiled at Clay, her expression questioning.

"Sorry to barge in," Clay said. "Pete didn't tell me you were in the middle of breakfast. I'll come back later—"

"No need to go unless you're not hungry," the woman said with a warm smile. She put down the spatula, wiped her hands on a brightly colored dish towel, and held out her hand. "I'm Mary Townsend. Pete's wife."

"Clay Sutter."

Her eyebrow rose. "Ah. I missed the Grange meeting—one of the kids was sick. But I've heard about you."

"I'm sure you have." Clay grinned wryly. "I hope I can improve on the impression."

Mary laughed. "Oh, no need to work at that. Mostly folks said you were respectful and seemed reasonable. High praise."

"Well, then, I'm happy."

Pete walked in and handed Clay a hand towel. "Thought you could use this."

Clay toweled her hair and wiped her hands. "Thanks. Listen, I really can come back—"

"I told Ms. Sutter I had plenty to spare," Mary said.

"Always do." Pete gestured Clay toward the table. "Sit down. If I don't have help eating it, I'll just do it all myself."

"Well then, it smells great and I'm starving." Clay had learned quickly that negotiating with people out in the field bore no resemblance to boardroom power games. And she'd learned that timing was critical—strong-arming locals never worked. So she'd take things at Pete's pace and enjoy a home-cooked meal. And maybe for a few minutes she wouldn't think of Tess. The hollow ache in her stomach wasn't hunger—and no meal, no matter how fine, was going to fill it. Only Tess's forgiveness and a little bit of welcome in her eyes would do that.

Pete sat down at the head of the big wooden table and Clay sat beside him. Mary set plates piled with bacon, ham, potatoes, and eggs in the center and slid into a chair across from Clay. A teenage girl who seemed too old to be Mary's and a boy who looked to be about nine joined them. The girl smiled shyly at Clay and spent the rest of breakfast reading on an electronic device she propped against her plate. The boy rattled on about baseball tryouts at summer camp, and Clay mostly enjoyed the casual conversation that kept her mind off Tess for entire seconds at a time.

Any time there was a lull in the conversation, she was back in the bedroom with Tess beside her, closer than she'd ever dreamed of being to anyone. The intimacy they'd shared had been nothing like what she'd experienced as a teenager. Tess was every bit as special now as then, but the moments they'd shared the night before had been emblazoned with the reality of loss and the wonder of rediscovery. And then the rain had come and washed the slate bare again, leaving yet another chapter to be written. If only she knew where to begin.

"More coffee?" Mary Townsend asked.

Clay jolted, realizing Mary had asked her the same question a few seconds before. "Yes, thanks. Sorry."

Mary smiled softly. "No need to apologize. You sure you don't want more eggs?"

"No, I've already eaten well past my limit," Clay said. "But it was so good I had to. Can I help you clean up?"

"Absolutely not." Mary laughed. "The last thing I need is you two anywhere around, disrupting my system. Take your coffee and go somewhere else, both of you."

Pete laughed, looking chagrined and a little bit pleased at being ordered around by his wife. He signaled for Clay to follow him, and she grabbed her coffee cup and followed through the beautifully restored farmhouse to what she took to be Pete's office.

The room with floor-to-ceiling windows looking out on the drive was lined with bookcases on two walls and sported a modern wet bar in one corner and a big oak desk that commanded the center of the room. Pete gestured to a comfortable-looking captain's chair in front of the desk while he sat behind it.

Clay sat, crossed her legs, and balanced her coffee cup on her knee. Townsend had closed the door behind them. Maybe his business arrangements were something he didn't discuss with his wife in general, or maybe this discussion was something he particularly wanted to remain private. She regarded him steadily, waiting for him to open the conversation.

He sipped his coffee and studied her in turn. Finally, he said, "I imagine things would be a lot easier for you and your company if you had the support of the major landholders."

"It's always nice for the locals to be behind us. It's important to NorthAm that we not disrupt the lives or the livelihood of the community."

"I guess things have been a little rocky starting out."

Clay said nothing. He was going somewhere and she figured she would just let him get there.

"When do you expect to be done with your assessments—up at Tess's and elsewhere?"

"Shouldn't be much longer. Some of the initial work was done by the advance team. We're making progress at the Hansen parcel and almost finished at Tess's. It'll be another week before I can pinpoint the most likely areas for productive drilling."

"Still looking at our three places?"

Clay smiled. "Well, I'm not actually looking at yours yet, since you haven't given me permission."

Townsend took a sip of coffee and set his cup down on a stone coaster. He leaned back in the big leather chair behind his big oak desk, looking just like every CEO she'd ever had the pleasure of jousting with.

"What if I told you I could bring the community around to supporting NorthAm. If I pushed to accept what you needed to do hereabouts, that would carry a lot of weight." He smiled. "I might even be able to help out with those permits that seem to be hung up in red tape somewhere."

Pete had influence, apparently. As one of the county's largest landowners, that was no surprise. Clay nodded and smiled pleasantly. "Well, we certainly would welcome the support."

He smiled thinly.

Clay waited. She wasn't about to make the offer.

"Double the per-acre price for drilling rights," Pete said.

"That assumes I even want to drill here."

"You sign the preliminary agreement, you can bring your rigs in here and punch whatever holes you need to." Pete shrugged. "I'm betting you'll find what you want."

"What about your concerns for your water and livestock?"

"That's why I've got insurance."

His offer to sell his rights at an inflated price wasn't surprising. He wasn't the first landowner to hold out for what he hoped would be a better deal than his neighbors had negotiated. She was authorized to pay what she wanted for rights, using her best judgment as to the potential value. Townsend's land bordered half of Tess's, and with his rights secured, she could probably avoid direct drilling on Tess's farm. She named a figure a little bit under her top limit. He appeared to think it over, then countered higher as she'd expected he would.

They went back and forth a few times until Clay got tired of the wrangling. "That's the best I can do. If I have to, I'll drill elsewhere and set charges to open veins that will drain your gas without touching an inch of your land."

"I think that price will work," he finally said, a hard glint in his eyes.

Clay was glad she'd gotten breakfast first. She had a feeling she'd be going hungry otherwise. Townsend had held out and she didn't blame him, but he was wrong to think she could be pushed into making a bad deal. She couldn't be pushed if she was willing to walk away, and she always was. "I'll have the attorneys draw up the paperwork. I'd like to move my equipment in as soon as we have a signed agreement. That'll take a couple days."

"Good enough," Townsend said.

"In the meantime, I'll speak to the town board and ask the Grange president to call another meeting. I should be able to lay out our plans then, and your vocal support will be appreciated."

"You'll have it," Pete said.

"I don't suppose you know anything about the break-in over at my construction camp last night?"

Townsend's brows drew down. "Should I?"

"Well, it occurred to me that some of your acquaintances might have been a little eager to see us change our minds about setting up operations here."

"If I'd gotten wind of anything like that, I would have put a stop to it. Even if I was completely opposed to you being here, I don't support that kind of activity."

"Fair enough." Clay wasn't sure she believed him, even though his end game had apparently been to sell his rights, just for more money than everyone else. He'd obviously stirred up resistance to make his eventual support more critical. It wasn't a new game, and she'd seen plenty. Still, he might be telling the truth and the break-in was nothing more than some of the locals looking for an easy score. Clay stood and put her cup on his desk. "Thank your wife for the coffee and breakfast. It was excellent."

Townsend stood. "I'll tell her."

"You should have the paperwork beginning of the week."

He held out his hand. "Pleasure doing business with you, Ms. Sutter."

"I'll be in touch." Clay shook his hand. Business was business, but she'd never trust Pete Townsend.

❖

The rain hadn't lessened as Clay left Townsend's farm and headed back to Cambridge. She pulled in behind the bed-and-breakfast and took the elevator up to her floor. When the door opened, Ella was waiting in the hall.

"I saw you pull in. You're not answering your phone," Ella said.

Clay held up a hand. "I tried." She tossed her phone to Ella. "Check the call record yourself."

"Really. You think I'm going to do that?" Ella laughed shortly and handed the phone back. "I've been trying to get you ever since this storm broke. Roads are already washing out. I almost drove out to Tess's to make sure you were all right."

"What makes you think that's where I was?"

"Because there's nowhere else you would've been. Kelly already checked the trailer."

"Come on, I want to get out of these wet clothes." Clay motioned Ella into her room, stripped off her shirt and pants, and re-dressed in a T-shirt and jeans. "Since my whereabouts last night don't have anything to do with business, I'd rather not go into it."

"I'm not asking you to." Ella leaned back against the closed door. "But you are my business, and if you're going to insist on going rogue, I'm going to head back to New York. I can't do my job like this."

"Hell, Ella," Clay muttered. "I need a little room right now. It's… complicated."

Ella smiled fleetingly. "I'm hearing that a lot. From where I'm standing, it doesn't look that way. Maybe you and Tess need to settle the business issues first so you can figure out the rest of it."

"Yeah. About that—I'm working on it." Clay told Ella about Pete Townsend and the pending rights deal.

"Damn. I should have figured that angle earlier," Ella said. "I'm still not ruling him out as being behind the attacks."

"Neither am I. Any news from the local law?"

"No. The sheriff thinks last night was just random vandalism, and the hit-and-run investigation is stone cold."

Clay sighed. "Well, hopefully we've seen the end of it."

"You staying put for a while?"

"I need to get out to the camp, see what shape the files are in. But first I need to make a call."

Ella gave her a long look. "I'll leave you to it, then. But when you get ready to leave, I'm driving. Deal?"

"Deal—and Ella, thanks." Clay waited until the door closed and then placed her call. Miraculously she not only had a signal, but the call was answered on the second ring.

"Hello?"

"Tess, it's me," Clay said.

CHAPTER TWENTY-EIGHT

Tess stood at the kitchen window, her back to the wood-burning stove, watching the rain scour trenches into the drive and collect in pools in the pastures. When she'd checked the creek on her way back to the house, it had already risen a couple of feet, and broken branches and other debris swirled in the roiling muddy water. If the storm kept up at the rate it had the last few hours, the creek would overflow and the fields would flood. Already, parts of the drive looked on the verge of washing out. Their prayers for rain had been answered, but God or someone was laughing.

"Tess?" Clay's voice was staticky but strong.

"I'm here," she said wearily. "Did you make it back all right?"

"Yeah, fine. How are things out there?"

"All right for now. Ask me again in twelve hours." Tess hadn't expected Clay to call—she hadn't known what to expect. Part of her thought she'd driven her away, that she'd never see her again, and that part of her wept for all they'd shared and for the loss of all the magical moments that might have been. She couldn't deny—didn't want to deny—the hours they'd spent so deep inside one another there'd been nothing else—no past hurts, no present questions, no future fears. And the other part of her, the one that wanted to push her away and wanted her gone, resisted the rapid beat of her heart and the tingling that started in her throat and streamed through her like an electric charge at the mere sound of Clay's voice. If she locked Clay out of her heart, she would be safe and her life would go on as it had been—hard but rewarding, solitary but fulfilling. After all, she wasn't a teenager any longer—she was beyond taking risks and challenging the fates. Wasn't she? "I think I might owe you an apology."

"I can't imagine why."

"I didn't handle everything you told me this morning very well. I'm afraid I let my feelings get in the way of my judgment." Tess thought about the stories she'd told herself all her life—of who she was, who Clay was, and who was to blame for writing an ending that broke her heart. "I was wrong to put it all on you. I—"

"No, you weren't. I screwed up. Look, I'm headed out to the construction camp. I need to come by and talk to you."

"Today?" Tess scanned the sky. The sun was a memory, buried behind a wall of dense black cloud. The rain gauge clamped to a post in the yard was filling fast, and the rain showed no sign of letting up. "That's not a great idea. We're getting an inch an hour, maybe more. That's flood level, Clay, and the kind of flash floods we get around here can take a car under pretty fast."

"I've got a big SUV," Clay said with bravado that came clearly down the line. "But I'll be careful. Can I see you?"

She should say no—even if Clay was crazy enough to travel in this, and of course she was, she should say no until she had more time to absorb everything she'd learned about Ray. Until she could find solid ground again. "The ground has only ever been solid with you."

"What?"

When she wiped the clouds of disillusionment away, Tess knew with absolute certainty she'd never been more secure, more confident, and more ready to take on any challenge than when she'd been with Clay. She'd been managing just fine on her own, but the world had grown smaller and a little darker. "There's something I want to talk to you about too. So if you can make it, you're welcome to come by."

"I'll be there in an hour. Do you need anything?"

Tess smiled wryly. There were a lot of things she needed, but nothing she could ask Clay for. To rewrite the past was never an option for anyone, and she'd finally accepted that. To undo the secret dealings Ray had had with Clay's father? Not Clay's fault or problem to fix. To stop the rain before the crops drowned? Beyond anyone's powers. To give her the strength to trust again? Only she could do that.

"Just get here safely," Tess said, and as she spoke, she realized that was all she really wanted. She wanted Clay. "Just be safe."

❖

Clay texted Ella that she was leaving, and by the time she reached the SUV, Ella was behind the wheel.

"I've been listening to the weather and road reports," Ella said. "A couple of the smaller roads are already closed—bridge washouts. I told Kelly to stay put at the trailer."

"How are things out there?"

"A lot of the guys are out of the area for the weekend, so there's only a skeleton crew on-site. Besides being wet and bored, they're fine."

"Kelly?"

"Dry and bored."

Clay laughed. "Tell her she'll get hazard pay."

"Huh. I'm not sure that will be enough. She's grumbling about not being able to sleep—too quiet."

"Things *have* been quiet. Maybe we can let her head back."

"Maybe." Ella sounded cautious as she maneuvered carefully around a slew of branches, leaves, and bits of trash littering the road. "I was talking to the innkeepers this morning. They say this kind of storm always ends up bringing down a lot of trees—power outages and flooding are common."

"We've got enough propane to run the generators for a week if the power goes down. Hopefully, we'll be able to stay on schedule."

"I think the guys are going to be grounded awhile."

"I ought to be out there with them—if there's a problem, I want to deal with it." She hesitated. She had nothing to hide, and Ella wasn't the type to make assumptions about anything—including relationships. But she had Tess's privacy to consider. She'd let her down too many times, and she wasn't going to continue. "First I need to talk to Tess. When we get to camp, I'll take the Jeep over to Tess's. You can keep the SUV in case you and Kelly want to leave."

Ella turned her head, stared hard. "Clay—look out the window. Can't it wait?"

Clay shook her head, her gaze locked on Ella's. "It's already waited fifteen years too long."

"It's not my business," Ella said, turning on the county road leading to the job site, "but why the hell did you wait all this time? It's pretty clear you still have feelings for her."

"I told myself lots of reasons," Clay said, "most of which were honorable and downright heroic. But the truth of it is, I was ashamed to face her. I didn't deserve her then and I don't deserve her now, but if I can figure out what to do so that I will, I want to."

Ella shook her head, her laugh short and a little bitter. "I don't think love has much to do with whether you deserve it or not. Maybe you just need to be lucky enough to recognize it and not blow it when you have the chance."

"Voice of experience?"

"Something like that." Ella sent Clay a fleeting grin that was humor mixed with a little bit of pain. "You, though—you've always struck me as being really lucky."

"I thought my luck had run out the summer I lost Tess. Since then, I haven't really cared how my risks paid off."

"Well, I hope this time the odds are in your favor."

"Thanks," Clay said. "Is there anything else you and I need to settle?"

"I was considering a duel at dawn, but the weather kind of put an end to that idea." Ella concentrated on the road. "I'll tell you what I told Tess. I think Tess is a great woman. I've liked getting to know her. She never suggested we were going anywhere, so I'll be glad if we can be friends."

"So will I," Clay murmured. She hoped there would be more than friendship for her, but Tess might not agree.

CHAPTER TWENTY-NINE

"Hi," Tess said, holding the side door open. "Come on in."

"I'm pretty wet—maybe I should leave my boots out here," Clay said, feeling awkward all of a sudden. Seeing Tess again was a punch to the chest. Even with worry in her eyes, Tess looked beautiful, her hair still damp, wearing a plain light-blue shirt, worn work jeans, and fuzzy gray socks.

"Don't worry about it, everything is wet." Tess followed Clay's gaze down to her feet and laughed softly. "Just take everything off inside here. I've got a fire going in the kitchen, and you can dry out a little bit. Want some coffee?"

"Yeah, I could use some. Thanks."

Tess backed up, still facing her. "Come on in, Clay. It's safe."

Clay realized she was still standing out on the porch, dripping onto the mat that said *Welcome*, hoping that she really was. She wanted to see the warmth of welcome in Tess's eyes more than she'd ever wanted anything. If she could only have that, she'd be grateful, even if she did ache for more every day of her life.

"Unless you're scared," Tess teased gently.

"Terrified."

Tess laughed, and grinning, Clay stepped into the parlor, a big room facing the front of the house with an antique rug the colors of the fields covering most of the random-width wood floor, a couple of big sofas, a fireplace that looked like it worked in winter but was barren now. Hand-hewn exposed beams framed the ceiling, crowning a room that spoke of history, of generations one with the land. "This place looks like you."

Tess's eyes widened slightly. "Thanks. It feels like me, but that always seemed like a funny thing to think."

Clay took off her rain slicker, draped it on an iron coat rack next to the door, and kicked off her work boots. She set them on a tray next to a similar pair that must have been Tess's. "I don't think it is."

"Well," Tess said, all of a sudden not knowing what to do with her hands or any other part of her. What she wanted to do was grip Clay by the shirtfront, drag her closer, and kiss her until the rain disappeared and the only storm she knew was the one they made upstairs in her bed. Clay was like the land to her—alive and vibrant and powerful, filling a hunger as old as her soul. And she had the most kissable mouth.

Clay stared at her, as if reading the want burning beneath her skin.

Afraid to move too quickly, afraid of what she might do if she let up on her control, Tess slid her palms into the back pockets of her jeans and rocked slightly in her ridiculously unsexy gray work socks. Now was not the time to be thinking about escaping her life. What she needed was to get it set on the right course. "We should talk."

Clay grimaced. "Now there's a statement you never want to hear from a woman."

Tess laughed and relaxed a little. Clay always seemed to be able to make her laugh, even when she was angry at her. "You know, sometimes you walk a very thin line."

Clay shot her a brief but cocky grin. "I know. I was hoping you might like that."

"There are a lot of things I like about you. I just wish there weren't so many things in the way."

Clay's expression suddenly turned serious. "I'm hoping I can change that this morning—get rid of some of the baggage…past and present."

"All right." Tess let out a long breath. She wasn't angry any longer, and the absence of the dark fire that had been a constant companion for far too long was exhilarating and a little frightening. She understood now how a person could come to depend on anger to give some kind of meaning to life, but that was not what she wanted to build the rest of hers upon. Tess hesitated, then held out her hand. "Come with me. You're leaking on the floor."

Clay took Tess's hand without the slightest pause, her grasp firm but gentle. Tess rubbed her thumb over the top of Clay's hand as she led her on a winding path through the house to the kitchen. The subtle rise of Clay's knuckles and the valleys between her tendons reminded Tess of the rolling countryside around her, enduring and endlessly beautiful. Clay's skin was warm and slightly rough across the palm. She didn't just manage the drilling operations, then. Apparently, she did some hard work too.

When they reached the kitchen, Tess pointed to the cast-iron wood-burning stove. "A couple of minutes in front of that will dry out the worst of it. Are you hungry?"

"No," Clay said, turning her back to the stove. "I had a huge breakfast at Pete Townsend's not that long ago."

Surprised, Tess paused getting the cups down from the cabinet. "You met with Pete this morning? After you left here?"

"Yes." Clay shrugged. "I was too keyed up to sit in the B and B and listen to it rain. Couldn't take the bike out for a run. So I figured I'd take a run at Pete instead."

"How did it go?" Tess asked, more conflicted than she'd expected to be. On some fundamental level, she wanted Clay to succeed merely because she was Clay. And she didn't like the idea of Pete making Clay's job harder, which of course made no sense, since Pete was essentially standing up for everyone who didn't want NorthAm drilling in their county. And that included her, at least, she thought it did. "Damn it."

"What?"

"Oh, nothing. You just muddle my head."

Clay looked annoyingly pleased. "Sorry?"

Tess laughed. "Never mind. You're an awful liar."

"My meeting with Pete is part of the reason I'm here," Clay said.

Digesting that news, Tess poured coffee into two big ceramic mugs and carried them to the table. Even though Clay had said she wasn't hungry, it was well after noon, and she suspected Clay hadn't had lunch. Clay looked tired and drawn, and Tess had an overwhelming urge to erase the shadows from beneath her eyes. If she couldn't do that, she could at least feed her. She quickly assembled a platter of cold cuts and put a loaf of bread in the center of the table on a breadboard along with a knife to cut slices for sandwiches. "Just in case."

Clay reached for the bread knife. "Come to think of it…"

"Here, I'll do it." Tess assembled a couple of sandwiches, enjoying the simple act of preparing a meal for Clay. She could easily get used to it, and for once, she didn't deny herself the pleasure. They ate to the sound of rain on the slate roof.

A few minutes later, Clay pushed back from the table and sighed. "Thanks for seeing me, Tess."

"Somehow after last night, thanks seems unnecessary." Tess folded her napkin carefully and placed it beside her plate, giving herself time to find the right words. "Last night was…I've never experienced anything like it. I felt so damn free."

"I don't quite know how to describe it, but you've always made me feel that way—free." Clay rubbed her face. "Last night was even more than that…something special, something all unto itself. I felt like we were somewhere out of time—where no one could touch us."

"I know," Tess said softly. "I feel the same way, and now it's gone."

"Is it?"

Tess stared at her hands. "I don't know."

"I think we could find that place again—every time we touch." Clay reached across the table and clasped Tess's hand, entwining their fingers. "I know you don't want to hear this, but I love you. I have always loved you and always will. I know I fucked up—"

Tess looked up sharply. "Don't. I don't want to keep dragging the past around with me, at least not the parts that keep hurting. So I don't want to hear 'I'm sorry' from you again."

Clay nodded, her gaze searching Tess's.

"There are a lot of things I want to say to you." Tess took a shuddering breath. "But first I have to know—did you know Ray blackmailed your father?"

Clay grew very still. "I suspected there was some kind of deal…" She shook her head. "My father doesn't share all his dealings with me. In fact, he doesn't share a lot of things with me. He tells me what he wants me to know, and I suppose I'm partly responsible for not pushing back more."

"Well, you couldn't have been responsible for any of this."

"What did you learn?" Clay asked.

"According to Leslie, who's representing me legally, by the way, Ray signed the rights to the land away a long time ago. For quite a lot of money."

"I didn't know."

"Even if you had, that wouldn't have been your fault. You were taken advantage of just as much as me."

Clay let out a breath. "Thank you."

"I want to pay it back."

Clay's brows came down. "Pay what back?"

"Whatever money Ray took for the drilling rights. I want to pay it back and I want your father to tear up the contract—or whatever the legal term for it is."

"No."

Tess straightened, the anger she thought she'd conquered surging through her. "Excuse me?"

"No," Clay said, her jaw set. "Whatever Ray did, it's not your responsibility to undo. My father paid Ray, and the money is gone now. Ray either spent it or put it into the farm. You're not going into debt to pay back what my father willingly paid—he could have fought Ray. *We* could have fought Ray."

"If I pay it back," Tess said, hating the idea of owing anything to Clay's father even by association, "can you convince your father to return the rights?"

"That's not going to be necessary."

"I don't understand."

"Townsend and I came to terms, and he signed over the rights to his land. I'm not going to drill on your farm, Tess."

"Pete?" Tess couldn't wrap her mind around it. "But I thought he was so opposed."

Clay shrugged. "Money is a great motivator. He changed his mind when the price was right. I'm certain that was his plan all along."

"Pete…God, Pete always has an angle." Tess shook her head. "He's probably going to keep hounding me to sell him the farm now, especially since he knows what's under the ground."

"Well, you just keep saying no."

"NorthAm is going to drill in this county, isn't it?" Tess said.

"I told you I wouldn't lie," Clay said, hoping she wasn't driving another wedge between them. "We will. The fuel is down there, the state wants it, the country needs it, and the locals will benefit more than they'll risk. It's inevitable, Tess."

Tess looked out the window. The ridge behind the house was

obscured by rain, but she could still see the machines in her mind—foreign creatures she didn't trust and didn't want. "But you don't need to be here?"

"We can get what we want elsewhere."

"At what cost?" Tess narrowed her eyes. "What aren't you telling me?"

"In the greater scheme of things, not a whole lot greater expense—a few more thousand feet of pipe, a few more drill heads to tap the deepest reservoirs—nothing we haven't done elsewhere." Clay touched Tess's hand. "We'll still be close when we drill, though, Tess. I'll do everything in my power, I promise you, to see that we have clean wells. I'll make the same promise out loud to everyone in the county in another week."

"I believe you. But what is your father going to say? What about the attorneys he's sending up here?"

"I'll talk to him. In the meantime, you can go ahead and tell Leslie to pull out her big guns if she needs to. But I don't think you're going to have a fight."

"And what about you? How do you feel about all this?"

"I'm not my father," Clay said quietly, "and I'm not NorthAm. And I meant what I said earlier—I would never do anything to hurt you. I'd quit first."

"There's something I need to say to you," Tess said quietly, grasping both Clay's hands and holding them in her lap. "I've blamed you unfairly all these years, and I'm sorry for that." Clay started to protest and Tess stopped her words with a brief firm kiss. "Let me finish. I loved you so much, and I didn't realize I was doing it, but I made you responsible for making all my dreams come true. We were young, I know, but what we had was real. Real enough that it's lasted all this time."

Clay's heart leapt and she couldn't catch her breath. "What are you saying?"

"I'm saying I'm done looking back. I'm saying that I'm really glad to meet you, Clay Sutter."

Clay cradled Tess's face, kissed her softly, and drew back. "Very glad to meet you too, Tess Rogers."

Tess slid over into Clay's lap and put her arms around her neck.

She kissed Clay again. “I love the way you taste. You have the sweetest kisses.”

Clay’s arms came around Tess’s waist and she nuzzled her throat. “I love everything about you.”

Thunder boomed and Clay laughed. “The earth just moved.”

“Clay?” Tess jerked away. “Wait.”

“Okay,” Clay murmured against her throat. “Whatever you want, Tess. This is enough if it’s—”

“No.” Tess jumped up. “Look!”

Clay looked out the window. An orange glow mushroomed over the rise behind the farm. Clay bolted to her feet. “Jesus. That was an explosion. That’s our camp.” She raced for the door, Tess behind her. Clay jammed her feet into her boots and yanked the door open. “I’ll be back. I—”

“I’m coming,” Tess said.

“No, you’re not.”

Tess pushed Clay out the door and slammed it closed. “Don’t argue. Let’s go.”

Chapter Thirty

I'll drive," Tess shouted, pointing to her pickup truck parked next to the barn. "I'm used to these roads in this kind of weather."

"All right." Clay raced across the drive, barely keeping her footing on the muddy ground. By the time they reached the truck, her pants were soaked through from the thighs down, and water streamed over her face and down her neck. She jumped into the passenger seat, yanked the seat belt across her chest, and punched in 911. After three rings she lost the signal.

"Damn it." Clay texted Ella. *What's happening?*

Beside her, Tess buckled up and threw the truck into gear.

"Hold on," Tess cried. "The roads will be a mess."

"I'm good. Go. Go!"

Tess pointed the truck toward the road and hit the gas, punching through rain so heavy they could have been driving on the bottom of the lake. The headlights reflected back at them as if from a murky mirror. Clay kept trying to call with no luck.

"Ella's not answering," Clay yelled over the pounding rain. "Can't get emergency services, either."

"Couldn't have happened at a worse—oh!"

The truck swerved violently, and Clay's head bounced off the side window. Her stomach lurched as the truck fishtailed. She grabbed the handhold over her head as Tess fought to keep the big truck on the road.

"Tree down," Tess shouted. The truck steadied off and Tess laughed unevenly. "Sorry. Should have expected that. Are you all right?"

"I'm good." Clay fingered a tender spot above her ear. "You?"

"Fine. We're almost there." Tess gripped the wheel, her face set in concentration, her eyes glued to the road ahead. "What do you think it is?"

"That was gas—had to be one of the propane tanks." Clay had seen plenty of well fires on the job, but they weren't drilling now. Every one of the tanks at the camp was in proximity to the barracks or the operations trailers, where she had people. Ella and Kelly had probably been in her trailer, and she couldn't raise either of them. She pushed the sick feeling away as a black cloud of anger filled up her chest. "And my guess is it's not an accident."

Tess caught her breath. "More sabotage? But this is crazy—who would go this far?"

"I don't know," Clay said, "but I will before I'm done. How much longer?"

"A minute or two."

Clay gripped Tess's thigh, squeezed lightly. "When we get there, I want you to stay in the truck. If one of the tanks exploded, the others might be rigged to go too. I don't want you anywhere near—"

"Clay," Tess said mildly, "I haven't sat back and let anyone handle my problems in a long time. I'm not going to start now."

"Damn it, Tess," Clay growled, "I'm not trying to control your life, just trying to keep you from getting hurt. I know what these things can do. We've got a couple dozen wood-frame buildings sitting right next to a lot of propane tanks. It's a situation designed for disaster once a fire gets going."

"And what do you plan on doing by yourself?"

"We plan for these contingencies—but first I have to make sure all my people are safe. Then I can contain the fire and shut down the gas lines." She pointed to the rain-streaked windshield. "We're right up there. The turn—"

"I've got it." Tess swung onto the dirt access road, and a wall of trees and water instantly enclosed them. She leaned forward, squinting through the brief clear area as the wipers labored with the volume of rain. "I know you want to save your equipment and your buildings, but they're not worth you getting hurt."

"As soon as I know all my people are safe, I'll assess the fire situation—I don't plan on being a hero."

Tess glanced at her. "Good, because I just got you back. I don't plan on losing you again."

Clay covered Tess's hand on the wheel. "I don't think I've ever heard anything quite as good as that."

"Just remember it, then." Tess slowed, the rear wheels hydroplaning as she braked. The truck skidded and slid fifteen yards toward the woods before she got it under control. They passed the open access gate, and up ahead, flames leapt into the sky. "How far—"

"This is close enough—we don't want you getting stuck," Clay said. "Turn the truck around so it's pointed toward the road. If we have injured, you might need to take them to the hospital."

"All right," Tess said. "I'll get the truck ready to evacuate any injured, but I'm not taking them. I'm not going anywhere without you."

Clay jumped out, holding the door open as the rain lashed her face, and stared in at Tess. "I don't remember you being this stubborn."

"I wasn't." Tess smiled. "I'm tougher now. You're going to have to get used to that."

"I can handle that. If you're not going to stay here, you have to promise to follow my lead. Can you do that?"

"Yes." Tess shut down the engine and left the keys in the ignition. She jumped out and ran to the front of the truck to meet Clay. "I'm very sure. Because wherever you're headed, I'm going with you."

"Stay close!"

Tess grabbed the back of Clay's shirt as they ran, afraid she would lose her in the otherworldly orange haze. The fire was bright, but the air was so heavy with smoke and rain, visibility was practically zero. Beneath the roar of the flames and rush of water falling all around them, she thought she heard shouts. The rain, a cold, dense wall, suddenly shimmered and broke apart as a wave of heat speared through it. Recoiling, she finally made out the silhouettes of burning buildings writhing against an ominous sky. Two buildings, storage sheds or barns of some kind, were fully involved. Flames leapt twenty feet into the air as if trying to escape their own fury. The trailer door stood open as she remembered it had been after it had been vandalized. It wasn't burning but appeared dark and deserted.

"Wait here," Clay said. "I need to get the men organized and find Ella and Kelly."

"I'll check the trailer," Tess called and took off running as Clay's protests were quickly swallowed by wind and flame. She jumped up onto the top step and grabbed the side of the trailer for balance. The metal was scorching and she yanked her hand back. "Ella! Kelly! Are you in here?"

She heard nothing but had to be sure no one was lying unconscious inside. Carefully, she stepped inside, checking her footing and testing the air. Nothing appeared to be burning, but the power was out just like everywhere else. Venturing a few feet farther, she could tell almost immediately the trailer was empty. She pivoted back to the door and nearly ran into Clay.

"Oh!" Tess's pulse jackrabbited with a rush of adrenaline.

"Damn it!" Clay grabbed her shoulders. "Whatever happened to following my lead?"

"I was—you went to check in with the men, and I went to look for Ella and Kelly. They're not here. They must be with the men." Tess grabbed Clay's hand. "Come on, we need to find them."

"Just be careful. Please."

"I will."

Back outside, they ran toward the nearest burning shed. As they got closer, Tess could finally make out human forms, a half dozen figures dragging equipment and loaded pallets away from a wall of flames.

"I don't see Ella…Wait"—Tess pointed—"I think that's Kelly."

Tess raced toward Kelly as Clay was stopped by a big man in an undershirt and work pants. Kelly's face was smudged with soot, her shirt and pants drenched and covered with smears of oil and grime.

"What happened?" Tess said.

"Not sure—it looks like a gas leak. Looks like the fire started over near the big storage building."

"Where's Ella?"

"I lost track of her when we went to check on the men in the barracks."

"Is everyone accounted for?"

Kelly shook her head. "There's no way to tell. The guys bunking in one building didn't know who had stayed in the others. We located the crew foreman before Ella disappeared. He's trying to get a head count now. It could take hours before we know for sure." Kelly wiped her forehead, smearing the soot into long dark streaks like war paint. “Any chance help is coming?”

Tess shook her head. “I doubt it. Not in time, anyhow.” A chorus of engine roars brought her spinning around in time to see Clay climb into the operator’s station on a large track-type tractor, engage the plow, and head directly toward one of the burning buildings.

“What is she doing?” Tess started to run.

“Wait.” Kelly grabbed Tess’s arm. “She’s going to take the building down. It’s the only way to contain the blaze and keep it from spreading.”

“What about the gas?” As Tess watched, other men jumped into tractors and backhoes and started for the second burning building.

“The men already shut down the lines from the uninvolved tanks. They’ll be all right,” Kelly said.

Tess jerked around, fury making her voice quiver. “How exactly do you know that? They’re driving right into the middle of that fire.”

“They know what they’re doing, they’ve done it before. This is part of the job.”

“It’s a ridiculous job,” Tess yelled, knowing *she* probably sounded ridiculous, and not caring. Clay had disappeared behind a wall of flames and she was terrified.

“Trust her,” Kelly said. “Clay knows what she’s doing.”

Trust. Why did it always come down to that? Clay might know what she was doing—but not even Clay could control nature. Tess knew what formidable foes wind and rain and fire could be.

“I can’t just stand here and watch,” Tess said. “I’m going to check the rest of the buildings and make sure that they’re all empty, just in case.”

“Good idea,” Kelly said. “I’ll come with you.”

Tess trotted toward the nearest uninvolved building. “I don’t think you need to be on duty tonight, but I appreciate you looking out for me.”

“Right now, I think we all need to look out for each other, at least until we find out if this was an accident or not.”

“Clay doesn’t seem to think so.”

“No,” Kelly said, her usual good humor gone and a hard edge to her voice. “Neither do I.”

Running from building to building, they cleared them all in less than five minutes. All were empty with no sign of any injured workers anywhere. The fire was concentrated near Clay's trailer and the storage sheds. If there was an arsonist, he seemed to have targeted buildings that were unoccupied.

By the time they crossed back across the wide expanse of the camp, Clay and the others had knocked down both burning structures and were heaping mounds of dirt on the flaming debris. Tess searched for Clay, but in the swirling smoke and embers, she couldn't tell one person from another. Despite Clay's promise she wouldn't try to be a hero, Tess couldn't think of any other name for it.

"When she gets off that tractor, I'm going to kill her," she muttered as she paced.

"I don't know," Kelly said. "If it was me, I'd kiss her."

Tess shot her a glance.

Kelly grinned. "Well, you know, if I was into hot sexy women."

"I don't plan on asking for details."

"I'm going to check the perimeter for Ella—she's got to be out there somewhere."

"Text me every few minutes so I know you're all right," Tess said.

"Will do. You should be fine if you just stay here."

"Fine." Tess squinted through air thick as sawdust and about as easy to breathe, searching for Clay, trying to make herself believe everything would be all right. She thought maybe Kelly was right. When she saw Clay again, she planned on kissing her. Until then, there was work to do.

As Kelly disappeared from view, Tess ran toward the closest tractor.

CHAPTER THIRTY-ONE

Clay pulled her T-shirt up over her nose and mouth to block out the worst of the smoke and soot. Her eyes burned, her vision blurred through the veil of tears. She'd lost track of time, aware only of the heat and noise and the inexorable beast that slashed and roared and fought to annihilate everything in its path. Propelling the tractor back and forth in sharp, short bursts, she knocked down the burning metal buildings, uprooting their timber supports and shoveling earth onto the piles of rubble to smother the flames. Periodically she directed her men to the edge of the forest to trench a firebreak and prevent the fire from spreading into the adjacent woods. Catching sight of a line of flames licking toward the underbrush, she maneuvered next to the vehicle on her right to send him in that direction.

"Hey," she yelled, her voice raspy and her throat burning after hours of breathing smoke. The driver turned in her direction and Clay shook her head, certain she was mistaken. Her low-level headache skyrocketed with the motion, but her vision cleared up. She hadn't been wrong. "What the hell are you doing?"

Tess sent her a grin, looking like she was having a fabulous time. "Following your lead."

Irritated, impressed, proud, Clay worked on frowning. "Not what I meant."

"What do you need?"

You. You and nothing else. Clay debated finding someone else to take care of the problem, but everyone was engaged and Tess clearly knew how to handle a tractor. "Over there to your right—about two o'clock—dig a trench and outflank that finger of fire headed for the woods. Be careful it doesn't come around behind you. If it does, plow a path through the woods if you have to, but don't let it trap you."

"I'll be careful. You too, okay? The wind is making this monster unpredictable."

"I will." Clay hesitated. "Hey!"

Tess stared back, her gaze so intense Clay felt the world drop away—as if they were back in bed with all the time in the world to show each other what mattered. "I love you."

"I love you too."

"I'll see you later," Clay said, wanting to say so much more. Wanting every night, every morning.

"Yes. You will." Tess smiled, and somewhere beyond the wild, angry night, Clay's world righted itself.

Clay pushed the tractor into gear and went back to plowing the burning debris into the center of a cleared area of the yard, building a giant bonfire that would eventually burn itself out. By the time they'd managed to contain the conflagration, the sky was lightening in the east. Dawn was coming, and the rain had eased off to a steady drizzle. The long night was over.

Piles of twisted metal and thick beams smoldered all over the camp, dark smoke roiling in the air. Clay was covered in soot and sweat. When she climbed down from the tractor, her legs trembled, and she had to lean against the big machine to keep her balance. Around her, the men congregated in small weary groups, their faces all alike—dirt covered, sweat streaked, exhausted, and triumphant. She went from group to group, thanking them, checking that none of the crew had significant injuries, instructing them to check in with the crew foreman to facilitate a head count.

Tess stood a little ways away, waiting for her. She looked as bedraggled and weary as any of the men, but she was smiling, the smile Clay had thought she'd never see again and knew now she could never do without. When she reached Tess, she wrapped her arms around Tess's waist and rested her head on her shoulder. Somehow Tess still managed to smell sweet. "I'm going to have to be more careful about what I say in the future."

Tess welcomed Clay's weight against her, liking that she could hold her up, that Clay would lean on her when she needed to. She stroked Clay's sweaty hair. "What do you mean, baby?"

"I didn't expect you to take me literally—about following my lead."

"I would've done it anyhow—I've been driving a tractor and moving earth since I was seven." Tess kissed Clay's temple. "But it was nice knowing you approved."

Tess laughed softly when Clay grumbled. She was discovering she enjoyed teasing her. All she wanted was to drag Clay away where they could finally be alone, but they weren't done here yet. "We've got to find Kelly. Ella was missing last night. I'm worried."

Sighing, Clay straightened and slid her arm around Tess's waist. "Let's go to the trailer. That's where they'll be."

They trudged through ankle-deep mud, and Tess turned her face up to the sky, letting the cool clean rain wash away some of the grime on her hair and skin. "I want to stand in the shower for an hour when we get home."

"Does that mean I'm invited to shower with you this time?"

"You might want to let me get the first coat or two of grunge off first," Tess said, "but yes. You're invited. Although I have to warn you, my body feels like I've been carrying the damn tractor on my back for a week."

"Yeah," Clay muttered, "me too." She laughed. "But I think a shower with you might just make me forget about being tired."

"I just might let you make me forget about it too." Tess loved that Clay wanted her—the desire in Clay's eyes stirred her in ways that made every problem seem solvable. Clay's desire filled her with strength. "I want you again."

Clay's arm on her waist tightened. "I can't think of much else."

"I hear voices," Tess said as they reached the trailer where the door still hung askew. Relief kicked through her. "I think they're here."

Clay grabbed her hand. "Let's find out."

Tess hurried inside after Clay and abruptly halted. Ella and Kelly stood side by side in front of Clay's desk in nearly identical postures—legs spread, arms crossed, hard impassive expressions—both staring at the man sitting opposite them on the only chair.

"Jimmy?" Tess said. "What are you doing here?"

Ella glanced at Tess and Clay. "It seems our friend Jimmy here was trying to drive his ATV out through the woods and managed to flip it over. Which is why he didn't get away after he opened the gas lines and conveniently dropped a match. Isn't that right, Jimmy."

Jimmy looked at Tess as if waiting for her to answer. She didn't want to believe Jimmy was behind the arson, but he had no business being at the camp. "Jimmy? What's going on?"

"I know you don't want them anywhere near your land. I was just trying to get them to move."

"Oh, Jimmy." Tess glanced at Ella. "I think we're going to need to get the authorities involved before we talk to Jimmy any further."

Ella nodded. "We haven't been able to raise them yet, but Kelly and I will be happy to babysit him until we can get someone out here to take him into custody."

Jimmy's eyes grew huge and his head swiveled from Tess to Ella and back again. "What do you mean, custody?"

"We'll need to talk to the sheriff, Jimmy," Tess said. "Until then, you need to stay here. This is serious—do you understand?"

For a minute, he looked as if he might try to bolt, but his gaze flickered to Ella and Kelly, and he slumped back, his hands between his knees, his eyes on the floor. "Doesn't look like I'm going anywhere. I got it."

"Tell the sheriff to call me when you get a hold of him," Clay said to Ella. "Are you both all right?"

"I could use breakfast and a shower." Ella grimaced and indicated her mud-caked boots and soiled clothes. "Chasing Jimmy in the storm was ugly, but otherwise I'm good. You?"

"We're fine." Clay ran her hand down Tess's back. "I want to get Tess home, but I'll come back and relieve you as soon as I've had a shower."

"We're good here," Ella said, "and you've both been working all night. Get some sleep first."

"Thanks. Call me if anything else develops."

"Will do." Ella raised a brow at Tess. "Get her out of here, would you? And keep her away for a while?"

Laughing, Tess grabbed Clay's arm and pulled her toward the door. "I'll try."

As they slogged toward the truck, Tess said, "I can't believe Jimmy did this. I'm so sorry, Clay."

"It's not your fault, Tess. You didn't ask him to do it."

"But he did it because he thought that's what I would've wanted."

Clay stopped by the front of the truck, pulled Tess into her arms, and kissed her. "It wasn't, and I know that."

Tess pressed her palms against Clay's chest and kissed her back. Clay felt so good against her, under her hands, under her lips. "People need to understand what you're doing here, and what it means for them. I'm finally getting it and I know you can explain it to all of us. Give us the good and the bad, and we'll be able to handle it."

"I will. I promise." Clay ran her fingers through Tess's hair and kissed her, deep and slow. She didn't care about the rain, or the acrid smell of smoke in the air, or the weary trembling of her muscles. The taste of Tess, the softness of her skin and the warmth of her body drove every other thought and sensation from her being. Tess was all she knew and all she wanted to know.

After a minute, Tess looped her arms around Clay's waist and leaned back. "Are you paying any attention at all to what I'm saying?"

Clay kissed her throat, nibbled along the angle of her jaw. "I am, I'm paying total attention to everything that matters. You."

Heart pounding, Tess gripped Clay's shirt harder, wanting to have her naked, above her, inside her. Right that instant. "We have to go. I need you."

Clay shuddered. "I need you too. More than I can say."

"Then all you have to do is take me home, and take me."

CHAPTER THIRTY-TWO

Clay took Tess's hand as they walked from the truck to Tess's front porch, unable to remember a time when she'd been as happy. The sunrise blossomed over the treetops to the east, splashing the same blazing reds and oranges across the morning sky as the fire had painted the night's. The rain had fled at dawn, and only a faint mist shrouded the tall stalks of corn in the fields. The creek running adjacent to Tess's house was swollen nearly to the tops of its banks, rushing to drench the bordering pastures, finally bestowing the crops with the nourishment the farmers had been awaiting so long.

"Looks like it's going to be a beautiful day," Clay said, sliding her arm around Tess's waist.

"Mmm," Tess murmured, slowing to lean her head against Clay's shoulder. "It already is."

Clay kissed the corner of her mouth. "You look beautiful. I like seeing you at sunrise."

Tess blushed and kissed Clay's throat. "Do you remember our first?"

Clay chuckled. "You mean the morning when I couldn't get the outboard's engine started, and we were stuck on the island until a fisherman came by and gave us a tow?"

"Yes," Tess said, laughing too. "I was so worried I was going to lose my job when I didn't get back to the lodge until nine, but Leslie had covered for me."

"She never did find out you were with me, did she?"

"No," Tess said. "I told her I went out boating and got stuck for a ride back, which was technically true." She shook her head. "I'm not sure why I didn't tell her about you, but I always had the sense we were a secret."

"That was my fault." Clay sighed. "I should have told you who I was right away and maybe none of this would've happened."

"Oh, if it was going to happen, it would have whether you told me or not. Maybe even sooner."

"I would have told you, you know," Clay said, "before summer ended, but we ran out of time. I just had this feeling that summer was the last thing I'd ever have that was all my own. And you were a big part of it. I knew what my father had planned for me, and it's not like I didn't want to take on the responsibility of working for the company, but I knew I would always be following his path."

"Are you sorry?"

"I like the work—I know it's hard for you to understand, but I believe in it. We're not perfect, we make mistakes, but we're trying to get it right, and in the end, I think we're going to do something good on a lot of levels."

"And what about for you, personally?"

"NorthAm is my job. But I found something at the lake no one else could touch, something all my own." She kissed Tess softly. "Was I right?"

Tess turned into her, threading her arms around Clay's neck. The press of Tess's body, the soft swell of her breasts, and the perfect fit of her hips sent a shiver of recognition and sublime contentment arrowing to Clay's heart.

"You're very right," Tess murmured against Clay's mouth, sliding her lips slowly over Clay's and teasing her with the tip of her tongue. "I'm all yours if you want me."

"I love you. And I want you every second of the day." Clay cupped Tess's ass and kissed her again. "And I don't mind saying it over and over, because it sounds really good to me."

"To me too," Tess said. "But you know, I think I'd like to hear it upstairs after a shower. In bed."

❖

Tess pulled Clay down the hall to the mudroom. "Toss your clothes directly into the washing machine. I'll get the shower started."

"Okay," Clay said, unbuttoning her shirt.

Tess paused, half-undressed, distracted by Clay's naked body coming into view. Even soot streaked and dead tired, Clay was the most beautiful woman Tess had ever seen.

Clay grinned at her. "What?"

"I don't even care that we're all kinds of grimy right now," Tess said softly. "I want you."

Clay's eyes went from playful to smoldering in a heartbeat. "Anything."

"Shower. Hurry." Tess quickly shucked her jeans and the rest of her clothes. "Or I might have to start without you."

"Not a chance."

"Oh yeah?" Tess raced for the stairs.

Clay followed at a gallop seconds later, and Tess, laughing, careened around the corner into the bathroom. She yanked open the shower door, flipped the dial to hot, and shrieked when Clay caught her around the waist and dragged her into the still-ice-cold spray.

"Wait, wait," Tess cried, trying to escape the icy needles.

"You'll be warm enough soon," Clay said and kissed her.

Clay was right. As soon as Clay's mouth covered hers, she didn't feel the water anymore. She didn't smell the smoke in her hair or the lingering odor of burning wood and rubber and other things. All she tasted, all she knew, was Clay's essence drenching her mouth, saturating her psyche until she overflowed. Her thighs softened and she leaned into Clay, growing wet and hard and needy in a heartbeat. She wrapped one arm around Clay's neck for balance, kissing her more deeply, and searched for Clay's hand. Finding it, she drew it between her legs and pressed Clay's fingers high between her thighs. "Don't make me wait. Not this time."

Clay turned her until her back was against the tiles, never relinquishing her mouth, and filled her up in a swift easy glide. The pressure was exquisite, too perfect to contain.

Tess pulled her mouth away and gasped. "Oh my God. You're so good. I already want to come."

"Good." Clay's mouth was on her neck, sucking, biting gently.

Her breasts were pressed hard against Tess's, her stomach and thighs gliding over hers. Clay's thumb rested on her clitoris, massaging it with every deep, sweet stroke.

"I *will* come," Tess warned breathlessly, "if you keep doing that."

"Then I guess you will," Clay muttered, kissing down the center of Tess's chest until she reached her breast.

Clay's lips tugged at Tess's nipple and she gripped Clay's shoulders, needing to fill her hands with Clay's warmth, needing to surrender to Clay's strength, needing her—needing to be hers.

The storm gathered, the fire raged, and her orgasm broke with the ferocity of dawn shattering the dark. Her hips surged on their own, taking Clay deeper, and she cried out, again and again. When she finally stopped coming, she was dizzy, ecstatic, shuddering with pleasure. "I love you so much."

Clay buried her face in Tess's neck. "I want you too. I need you too."

Tess gripped Clay's ass, urging her to straddle her. "I want you to come all over me. Hard, so you can't think of anything except me."

"I don't. I can't." Clay braced her arms on either side of Tess's shoulders, pressed her mouth to the angle of Tess's neck, and thrust against her. "I love you. I always will. I promise."

"You're mine," Tess whispered fiercely, burning with an ancient need to claim, to hold, to own and be owned. "Mine."

"Yes," Clay groaned, slick and hard and so vulnerable. "Yes. Please."

"That's it, that's right," Tess urged, lost in power that blazed like white lightning through her mind. "That's just what I want. You. Just you."

"So good, baby, so good." Clay's arms trembled.

Tess dug her fingers into Clay's ass and tensed her thigh between Clay's legs. "I love you."

"I'm going to come," Clay warned.

"Harder," Tess said. "I want to feel you all over me. Harder."

Clay threw her head back, her face tight with pleasure. Hips pumping, she came with a shuddering cry.

"Oh yes." Tess held her tightly, kept her from falling. "I have you now."

"Always," Clay gasped. "All yours."

❖

Tess lay with her head on Clay's shoulder, stroking the center of her abdomen, entranced by the way Clay's muscles flickered at her touch. "I love your body."

Clay laughed softly and stretched, curling one arm around Tess's shoulders. She kissed her temple. "I'm glad. I love your hands on me."

"I want you again." Tess pushed up on her elbow and kissed Clay softly.

Smiling, Clay tugged Tess on top of her. Their legs automatically entwined as if their bodies knew they belonged together. "Anytime. Always."

Tess rested her forehead on Clay's for an instant, her eyes hazy and satisfied. "We should sleep, but I don't want to."

"I need to get back to the job site," Clay said. "Things are a mess there, and I don't know how long it's going to take to get it straightened out."

"I know you need to go. I just don't want to let you out of my sight."

"Believe me," Clay said, running her hands up and down Tess's back, arousal stirring again, "I don't want to leave. But I can come back, right?"

Tess's stomach tightened for an instant, then she reminded herself the future was theirs to write. "I want you to come back." She nipped Clay's lower lip. "In fact, I insist on it."

"I know it's probably too soon to talk about the future—"

"Really? You can say that?" Tess shook her head. "I've waited for you almost all my life. It's not too soon."

Clay ran her fingers through Tess's hair. "I love you. I always want to come back here, to you."

"I'll always be here, and as far as I'm concerned, you belong here." Tess's brow furrowed. "Will you be happy here?"

"Yes," Clay said instantly. "You're here, and I love you. And I love this farm, this place, this land that's yours and part of you."

"Even when your job here is done?"

"Then I'll go to the next job, and I'll be away for a while, and I'll miss you so much. And when I come home, I'll show you how much every minute for a month."

Tess shook her head and Clay's heart sank.

"No?" Clay asked softly.

"Two months."

Laughing, filled with the joy she'd thought she'd lost, Clay rolled Tess over and pinned her hands on either side of the pillow. She kissed her mouth, her neck, pushed her down on the bed and kissed her nipples.

Tess arched beneath her, moaning softly. "Stop unless you don't plan on leaving anytime soon."

"I don't know how long I'll be gone. I need to find the sheriff and talk to him about Jimmy. We can't just let him go, but maybe we can work something out so the charges aren't too bad."

"He needs to be held accountable," Tess said.

"I know. I'll do what I can." Clay pushed lower and kissed Tess's belly button, settling her breasts between Tess's thighs. "I'll call you when I know how long I'll be gone—if there's any service yet."

"You'll be careful, won't you?" Tess cupped Clay's chin and tilted her face up until their eyes met. "I don't want anything to happen to you."

"Nothing will."

"Are you sure—about the agreement with Pete, and my land, and—"

"I'm sure. I'm sure about everything." Clay kissed the curve of Tess's inner thigh, moved up beside her, and pulled Tess into her arms. "One of the things I'm going to do after I get things organized back at the camp is call my father and tell him he doesn't need to send his attorneys up here. Then I'll get Ella to set up another town meeting and talk to the community about our plans. We might not win them all over right away, but it will be a start."

"What do you think your father will say to your decision about my land?"

"He won't like it, but I don't think he'll fight me. I closed the deal with Pete, we'll get what we need to drill, and he owes me."

"I don't care about the past."

"I know, but I didn't stand up for us then, and I will now. It's important to me."

"Then it's important to me too." Tess stroked Clay's chest. "But just know, all that matters to me from here on out is us. What we mean to each other and what we do about it."

"I love you. I want to be yours every day for the rest of my life," Clay said.

Tess smiled. "Then all you have to do is come home to me."

About the Author

Radclyffe has written over forty-five romance and romantic intrigue novels, dozens of short stories, and, writing as L.L. Raand, has authored a paranormal romance series, The Midnight Hunters. She is an eight-time Lambda Literary Award finalist in romance, mystery, and erotica—winning in both romance (*Distant Shores, Silent Thunder*) and erotica (*Erotic Interludes 2: Stolen Moments* edited with Stacia Seaman and *In Deep Waters 2: Cruising the Strip* written with Karin Kallmaker). A member of the Saints and Sinners Literary Hall of Fame, she is a RWA/FF&P Prism award winner for *Secrets in the Stone*, a RWA FTHRW Lories and RWA HODRW winner for *Firestorm*, a RWA Bean Pot winner for *Crossroads*, and a RWA Laurel Wreath winner for *Blood Hunt*. She is also the president of Bold Strokes Books, one of the world's largest independent LGBTQ publishing companies.

Books Available From Bold Strokes Books

Homestead by Radclyffe. R. Clayton Sutter figures getting NorthAm Fuel's newest refinery operational on a rolling tract of land in upstate New York should take a month or two, but then, she hadn't counted on local resistance in the form of vandalism, petitions, and one furious farmer named Tess Rogers. (978-1-60282-956-5)

Battle of Forces: Sera Toujours by Ali Vali. Kendal and Piper return to New Orleans to start the rest of eternity together, but the return of an old enemy makes their peaceful reunion short-lived, especially when they join forces with the new queen of the vampires. (978-1-60282-957-2)

How Sweet It Is by Melissa Brayden. Some things are better than chocolate. Molly O'Brien enjoys her quiet life running the bakeshop in a small town. When the beautiful Jordan Tuscana returns home, Molly can't deny the attraction—or the stirrings of something more. (978-1-60282-958-9)

The Missing Juliet: A Fisher Key Adventure by Sam Cameron. A teenage detective and her friends search for a kidnapped Hollywood star in the Florida Keys. (978-1-60282-959-6)

Amor and More: Love Everafter, edited by Radclyffe and Stacia Seaman. Rediscover favorite couples as Bold Strokes Books authors reveal glimpses of life and love beyond the honeymoon in short stories featuring main characters from favorite BSB novels. (978-1-60282-963-3)

First Love by CJ Harte. Finding true love is hard enough, but for Jordan Thompson, daughter of a conservative president, it's challenging, especially when that love is a female rodeo cowgirl. (978-1-60282-949-7)

Pale Wings Protecting by Lesley Davis. Posing as a couple to investigate the abduction of infants, Special Agent Blythe Kent and Detective Daryl Chandler find themselves drawn into a battle over the innocents, with demons on one side and the unlikeliest of protectors on the other. (978-1-60282-964-0)

Mounting Danger by Karis Walsh. Sergeant Rachel Bryce, an outcast on the police force, is put in charge of the department's newly formed mounted division. Can she and polo champion Callan Lanford resist their growing attraction as they struggle to safeguard the disaster-prone unit? (978-1-60282-951-0)

Show of Force by AJ Quinn. A chance meeting between navy pilot Evan Kane and correspondent Tate McKenna takes them on a roller-coaster ride where the stakes are high, but the reward is higher: a chance at love. (978-1-60282-942-8)

Clean Slate by Andrea Bramhall. Can Erin and Morgan work through their individual demons to rediscover their love for each other, or are the unexplainable wounds too deep to heal? (978-1-60282-943-5)

Hold Me Forever by D. Jackson Leigh. An investigation into illegal cloning in the quarter horse racing industry threatens to destroy the growing attraction between Georgia debutante Mae St. John and Louisiana horse trainer Whit Casey. (978-1-60282-944-2)

At Her Feet by Rebekah Weatherspoon. Digital marketing producer Suzanne Kim knows she has found the perfect love in her new mistress Pilar, but before they can make the ultimate commitment, Suzanne's professional life threatens to disrupt their perfectly balanced bliss. (978-1-60282-948-0)

Trusting Tomorrow by P.J. Trebelhorn. Funeral director Logan Swift thinks she's perfectly happy with her solitary life devoted to helping others cope with loss until Brooke Collier moves in next door to care for her elderly grandparents. 9978-1-60282-891-9)

Forsaking All Others by Kathleen Knowles. What if what you think you want is the opposite of what makes you happy? (978-1-60282-892-6)

Exit Wounds by VK Powell. When Officer Loane Landry falls in love with ATF informant Abigail Mancuso, she realizes that nothing is as it seems—not the case, not her lover, not even the dead. (978-1-60282-893-3)

Dirty Power by Ashley Bartlett. Cooper's been through hell and back, and she's still broke and on the run. But at least she found the twins. They'll keep her alive. Right? (978-1-60282-896-4)

The Rarest Rose by I. Beacham. After a decade of living in her beloved house, Ele disturbs its past and finds her life being haunted by the presence of a ghost who will show her that true love never dies. (978-1-60282-884-1)

Code of Honor by Radclyffe. The face of terror is hard to recognize—especially when it's homegrown. The next book in the Honor series. (978-1-60282-885-8)

Does She Love You by Rachel Spangler. When Annabelle and Davis find out they are in a relationship with the same woman, it leaves them facing life-altering questions about trust, redemption, and the possibility of finding love in the wake of betrayal. (978-1-60282-886-5)

The Road to Her by KE Payne. Sparks fly when actress Holly Croft, star of UK soap *Portobello Road*, meets her new on-screen love interest, the enigmatic and sexy Elise Manford. (978-1-60282-887-2)

Shadows of Something Real by Sophia Kell Hagin. Trying to escape flashbacks and nightmares, ex-POW Jamie Gwynmorgan stumbles into the heart of former Red Cross worker Adele Sabellius and uncovers a deadly conspiracy against everything and everyone she loves. (978-1-60282-889-6)

Date with Destiny by Mason Dixon. When sophisticated bank executive Rashida Ivey meets unemployed blue-collar worker Destiny Jackson, will her life ever be the same? (978-1-60282-878-0)

The Devil's Orchard by Ali Vali. Cain and Emma plan a wedding before the birth of their third child while Juan Luis is still lurking, and as Cain plans for his death, an unexpected visitor arrives and challenges her belief in her father, Dalton Casey. (978-1-60282-879-7)

Secrets and Shadows by L.T. Marie. A bodyguard and the woman she protects run from a madman and into each other's arms. (978-1-60282-880-3)

Change Horizon: Three Novellas by Gun Brooke. Three stories of courageous women who dare to love as they fight to claim a future in a hostile universe. (978-1-60282-881-0)

Scarlett Thirst by Crin Claxton. When hot, feisty Rani meets cool vampire Rob, one lifetime isn't enough, and the road from human to vampire is shorter than you think… (978-1-60282-856-8)

Battle Axe by Carsen Taite. How close is too close? Bounty hunter Luca Bennett will soon find out. (978-1-60282-871-1)

Improvisation by Karis Walsh. High school geometry teacher Jan Carroll thinks she's figured out the shape of her life and her future, until graphic artist and fiddle player Tina Nelson comes along and teaches her to improvise. (978-1-60282-872-8)

For Want of a Fiend by Barbara Ann Wright. Without her Fiendish power, can Princess Katya and her consort Starbride stop a magic-wielding madman from sparking an uprising in the kingdom of Farraday? (978-1-60282-873-5)

Swans & Clons by Nora Olsen. In a future world where there are no males, sixteen-year-old Rubric and her girlfriend Salmon Jo must fight to survive when everything they believed in turns out to be a lie. (978-1-60282-874-2)

Broken in Soft Places by Fiona Zedde. The instant Sara Chambers meets the seductive and sinful Merille Thompson, she falls hard, but knowing the difference between love and a dangerous, all-consuming desire is just one of the lessons Sara must learn before it's too late. (978-1-60282-876-6)

Healing Hearts by Donna K. Ford. Running from tragedy, the women of Willow Springs find that with friendship, there is hope, and with love, there is everything. (978-1-60282-877-3)

Desolation Point by Cari Hunter. When a storm strands Sarah Kent in the North Cascades, Alex Pascal is determined to find her. Neither imagines the dangers they will face when a ruthless criminal begins to hunt them down. (978-1-60282-865-0)

I Remember by Julie Cannon. What happens when you can never forget the first kiss, the first touch, the first taste of lips on skin? What happens when you know you will remember every single detail of a mysterious woman? (978-1-60282-866-7)

The Gemini Deception by Kim Baldwin and Xenia Alexiou. The truth, the whole truth, and nothing but lies. Book six in the Elite Operatives series. (978-1-60282-867-4)

Scarlet Revenge by Sheri Lewis Wohl. When faith alone isn't enough, will the love of one woman be strong enough to save a vampire from damnation? (978-1-60282-868-1)

Ghost Trio by Lillian Q. Irwin. When Lee Howe hears the voice of her dead lover singing to her, is it a hallucination, a ghost, or something more sinister? (978-1-60282-869-8)

The Princess Affair by Nell Stark. Rhodes Scholar Kerry Donovan arrives at Oxford ready to focus on her studies, but her life and her priorities are thrown into chaos when she catches the eye of Her Royal Highness Princess Sasha. (978-1-60282-858-2)

The Chase by Jesse J. Thoma. When Isabelle Rochat's life is threatened, she receives the unwelcome protection and attention of bounty hunter Holt Lasher who vows to keep Isabelle safe at all costs. (978-1-60282-859-9)

The Lone Hunt by L.L. Raand. In a world where humans and Praeterns conspire for the ultimate power, violence is a way of life…and death. A Midnight Hunters novel. (978-1-60282-860-5)

The Supernatural Detective by Crin Claxton. Tony Carson sees dead people. With a drag queen for a spirit guide and a devastatingly attractive herbalist for a client, she's about to discover the spirit world can be a very dangerous world indeed. (978-1-60282-861-2)

Beloved Gomorrah by Justine Saracen. Undersea artists creating their own City on the Plain uncover the truth about Sodom and Gomorrah, whose "one righteous man" is a murderer, rapist, and conspirator in genocide. (978-1-60282-862-9)

The Left Hand of Justice by Jess Faraday. A kidnapped heiress, a heretical cult, a corrupt police chief, and an accused witch. Paris is burning, and the only one who can put out the fire is Detective Inspector Elise Corbeau…whose boss wants her dead. (978-1-60282-863-6)

Cut to the Chase by Lisa Girolami. Careful and methodical author Paige Cornish falls for brash and wild Hollywood actress Avalon Randolph, but can these opposites find a happy middle ground in a town that never lives in the middle? (978-1-60282-783-7)

Every Second Counts by D. Jackson Leigh. Every second counts in Bridgette LeRoy's desperate mission to protect her heart and stop Marc Ryder's suicidal return to riding rodeo bulls. (978-1-60282-785-1)

More Than Friends by Erin Dutton. Evelyn Fisher thinks she has the perfect role model for a long-term relationship, until her best friends, Kendall and Melanie, split up and all three women must reevaluate their lives and their relationships. (978-1-60282-784-4)

Dirty Money by Ashley Bartlett. Vivian Cooper and Reese DiGiovanni just found out that falling in love is hard. It's even harder when you're running for your life. (978-1-60282-786-8)

Sea Glass Inn by Karis Walsh. When Melinda Andrews commissions a series of mosaics by Pamela Whitford for her new inn, she doesn't expect to be more captivated by the artist than by the paintings. (978-1-60282-771-4)

The Awakening: A Sisterhood of Spirits novel by Yvonne Heidt. Sunny Skye has interacted with spirits her entire life, but when she runs into Officer Jordan Lawson during a ghost investigation, she discovers more than just facts in a missing girl's cold case file. (978-1-60282-772-1)

Blacker Than Blue by Rebekah Weatherspoon. Threatened with losing her first love to a powerful demon, vampire Cleo Jones is willing to break the ultimate law of the undead to rebuild the family she has lost. (978-1-60282-774-5)

Murphy's Law by Yolanda Wallace. No matter how high you climb, you can't escape your past. (978-1-60282-773-8)